THE CHANGEUP

MARY BILLITER

HOT TREE PUBLISHING

For information, contact the publisher, Hot Tree Publishing.
www.hottreepublishing.com
Edited by Hot Tree Editing
Cover designed by Claire Smith
Book design by Inkstain Design Studio
ISBN: 978-1-925655-86-5

10 9 8 7 6 5 4 3 2 1

THE RESORT ROMANCE SERIES

Do Not Disturb

Escape Clause

Rule Breakers

Spirited Away

Wine Thief

The Changeup

LAKEWOOD, CA CIRCA 1953

When I was ten years old, my family moved from Louisville, Kentucky, to Huntington Beach, California. My introduction to the Golden State was made through my Irish grandparents, Howard and Norma Flanagan (pictured above beside my mom and her younger siblings). I had buck teeth, a thick Kentucky accent, and unruly curls that looked like I had been zapped by electricity. But when I awoke in my grandparents' Lakewood home, I was introduced to my first orange picked from their backyard tree. I discovered that toast tastes better with orange marmalade, and when my grandmother Flanagan took me shopping, she told me, "Every California girl should know the magic of a sundress." And it worked. When I saw myself in the mirror, I felt pretty.

The differences between Kentucky and California were vast.

But what is universal is grandparents. I didn't have nearly enough time with my California grandparents before they passed, but the influence they had on me was everlasting.

My grandfather was a baseball player and coach. I learned to love baseball because of *his* love of the game. So when I got stuck in the writing process, I turned my thoughts to my grandfather, who reminded me of my first taste of California. That memory became a turning point for Rebel.

I always knew *The Changeup* would be based in Lakewood and Long Beach, California, in homage to my grandparents, who are never more than a thought away. I hope you enjoy this slice of California through the eyes of Rebel and Ryan.

THE
CHANGEUP

CHAPTER 1
REBEL

"*Are you always so difficult?*" Special Agent Jude Fallon seemed to savor a good rhetorical question.

When I was told that my FBI handler was named Jude, I thought I'd be working with someone who looked like Jude Law. No luck. Jude was shaped like an egg with legs. Her best assets were her slender legs that seemed to get lost beneath her wide frame, short neck, and full face. Worse, Jude Fallon made Judge Judy seem like a real softy.

"For someone who was granted immunity despite the fact that you destroyed evidence *and* went directly against orders from the judge to preserve the personal email accounts"—her mousy brown hair slowly swayed from side to side—"I'd think you'd be more appreciative."

"I am." My voice rose but so did my composure. "Jude, I am extremely appreciative. But," I paused, knowing that in respect to this subject, I walked on holy ground, "I was granted immunity *in exchange* for my testimony. So it's not like I walked away scot-free. I still have to testify." When she didn't rebuke me or roll her eyes, I continued. "I just don't understand why I have to leave Napa. I did *everything* you wanted me to do. I worked in the hotel as a wine educator in a dark, damp cave."

"Yes, well, the property is drawing too much attention to itself." Her arms crossed over her dull gray blazer that seemed like the uniform standard for the FBI.

"That's it? That's all you'll give me." I was willing to beg for more info. "Jude, the Point's a five-diamond resort—that *alone* draws attention. If you didn't want me discovered, you should have had me work at some Travelodge along the highway."

"That's still an option." When Jude exhaled, her nostrils flared, which wasn't a very good look for her. "But I don't trust you being so close to a truck stop."

It felt like the air was knocked from my lungs. *Low blow.*

"That's not fair." My eyes stung, but I refused to let her see me crack. "What happened in Wyoming was different."

"You're right. In Wyoming, you just broke about a half-dozen federal and state laws."

"That was never my intention," I said, but it didn't matter how many times I pleaded my case to Jude, she'd only see me as a rule breaker. Or worse, a criminal.

Still, my fate was in her mannish hands so the faster her tirade ended, the sooner I'd discover where I was being sent.

"So, where am I headed now?" My voice sounded as deflated as I felt. Until the Wyoming case went to trial, I'd forever be hopscotching from one Point resort to another, always with the intent of staying under the radar. Jude figured the best place to hide me was out in the open. People never saw what was right in front of them. And no one in Wyoming would ever think to look for me at a five-diamond resort.

"You have two choices—New York or Long Beach."

I didn't remember a Point resort in Long Beach, but I only googled their flagship properties. And I knew from online chat groups that the New York City Point Resort did not treat their employees well. Long Beach had to be far less crowded than New York City. Plus, unless it was false advertising, it had a beach. There weren't any beaches in Wyoming. *Score.*

"Long Beach." I smiled.

"Listen, Roberts, you draw any attention to yourself, you're going to Kansas."

I didn't remember any Point resorts in the Midwest. "What's

there for me in Kansas?"

"Leavenworth."

"But that's a men's prison," I said.

"No, it's a men's penitentiary and you'll be mighty popular there," she said without a hint of a smile.

"So, the West Coast, then." I tried to bring the conversation to something happy like the sun, a sandy beach, and not seeing Jude. A break from my egg-shaped handler would be welcome.

CHAPTER 2
RYAN

"**L**isten up, the next phase** in the application process is twofold—document intake and a background investigation, which, if you take a look at the handouts in front of you, includes a personal history statement and other financial, personal, and employment forms that are required to proceed in this process. There isn't one stone we don't turn over." Deputy William Stanley's buzz cut fit his square-shaped head and boxy frame. He was one person I didn't want to piss off.

The classroom, which had triple the applicants and not enough seats when this process began six months ago, was now far less crowded.

"All these forms are provided in an electronic PDF format so they can be typed or printed. Some forms have to be handwritten, so you'll want to make sure you read all the instructions," he said.

I knew the steps in the Los Angeles County Sheriff's Department application process better than the person who wrote it.

"If you've made it this far then you've already been scheduled for an initial background investigation appointment. The document intake forms are very extensive and require that you have several documents that you may not normally have in your possession," Stanley said.

"Like what?" Milford Sims was the most annoying applicant in the process. She constantly asked questions whose answers could be found on the website. I think she just liked the attention Deputy Stanley always gave her.

She was annoying, but hot. I didn't think the drab sheriff uniform could look good on anyone, but fuck if Milford didn't make olive my new favorite color. Still, I couldn't get past her voice that sounded like she was twelve and not twentysomething like the rest of us.

"Solid question, Sims," Stanley said, and I knew his lower half was talking. "You'll need unopened high school and college transcripts," he raised his hand as if taking an oath, "*if* you attended high school or college. If not, we need an unopened copy that you passed the GED test. Tax returns for the last three years, a current passport-type photo, an unopened credit report and things of that nature. Again, it's all on the website and there's a brief overview on the bottom sheet of the handouts in front of you."

"Thank you, Deputy Stanley." Her childlike voice may work on other guys, but it was a complete turnoff for me. I didn't want some woman who sounded like puberty passed them by. It just wasn't sexy. And her laugh drew the wrong amount of attention in my book. There just wasn't a room soundproof enough to silence her squeaky voice. Nope, there wasn't anything that could ever make being with Milford right. I shuddered.

"Everything okay back there, McHenry?" Deputy Stanley didn't miss a beat.

I straightened in my seat. "Yes, sir."

"Okay, if there aren't any further questions, I'll let you get at it. Your personal statement and writing exercise is due by the end of the day, which is five o'clock, folks—not midnight." Stanley stepped away from the podium. "You're welcome to work on your application in here if that's convenient for you."

We all stood when he exited the room. I grabbed my laptop from my backpack, fired it up, and went to the file that contained my core values writing exercise.

The first two questions were standard and easy to answer— why do you want to be an employee of the Los Angeles Sheriff's Department and what will the job mean to you. That's where I dropped in my uncle's name. Blue was in my blood. All cops are blue-blooded and the color of the uniform doesn't matter. When one LEO, or law enforcement officer, died on the job, everyone in the local area put on their official uniform for the funeral procession and it was a rainbow of textiles, but blue blood was in all their veins. It's what they did when my uncle lost his life while saving a woman and her child from an armed assailant. I think it's why I wasn't so devastated when my baseball career ended abruptly. I knew serving with LA's finest was in my DNA.

It was question three, which asked what the core values of the department meant to me and whether I would be able to follow them on and off duty, that I wasn't a hundred percent on my answer.

I skimmed the PDF document to what I had written. I hit all the points about the importance of the core values; I just wasn't sure if I nailed my conclusion.

There is no off-duty for cops; you do what's right at all times and put service to others above yourself.

My finger was hovering above the Submit button when her squeaky voice was in my ear.

"That's solid, McHenry."

That was the other thing about Milford that grated on me. She mimicked Deputy Stanley like she was his little protégé.

"Thanks, Sims," I said with a nod behind me to where she stood like a creeper. Personal space was not something this woman knew.

"What else did you write?" Her breasts pressed into my shoulder when she bent over me, and I quickly closed my laptop.

"I'm going to grab a coffee," I lied as I grabbed my backpack and headed toward the door.

We were being watched. I knew from the moment I applied that my life would be public knowledge to the department. I didn't need Milford's breasts to be the cause of a sexual harassment claim. No one would ever believe that her breasts brushed against me and not the other way around. Even I found it hard to believe and I'd felt it happen.

Nope. Better to leave a bad situation than have it get worse. There was only one thought that guided my thinking—walk the straight and narrow if I wanted a career with the thin blue line.

CHAPTER 3
REBEL

"*So that's what I'm dealing* with." Phil Greenberg leaned against the black leather high-backed chair and seemed to fix me in his sights. "As soon as you can organize and streamline the operation downstairs, the sooner we'll find you an upstairs office on the seventh floor."

I wasn't sure what constituted the downstairs of this hotel, but it couldn't be worse than working 130 feet underground in a wine cave. Besides, if I worked any further down, Satan would be my officemate.

"Don't be surprised if you're met with resistance from the staff," Phil said. "But stay the course. You have the conference sales employee handbook that Lisa mailed?"

"Read it on the plane," I said.

"Excellent, excellent." Phil had a thick, dark mustache that completely covered his mouth. When the director of conference services wasn't jawing off about the lack of production from his downstairs conference service staff, he had an annoying habit of chewing on his mustache hairs. The more he ate his 'stache, the more I lost my appetite. *Trim the thing or shave it off, but stop gnawing on your facial hair. It's disgusting.*

"I should probably have you meet my assistant, Lisa Evans. She handles all our guest meet and greets for conference services." He didn't even have to lean forward to press the button on his phone. Phil's stretch was pretty impressive. He was all legs and arms. The guy's physique could not be described as anything but lanky.

By comparison, when his assistant walked into the corner office, she looked like a fly next to the nimble spider-like man, who was anything but a superhero.

"Lisa, this is Rebel Roberts, the new floor manager for conference services. She transferred from our Napa property," he said by way of introduction.

I stood and greeted the petite blonde whose wide blue eyes seemed to bug out from her face. Maybe my fly analogy wasn't too far off.

"Welcome to the Long Beach Point Resort. We're very

excited to have someone supervising the downstairs staff. They've been operating on their own, and just today, I noticed an invoice pending for office supplies and furniture." Her eyes widened to owl-like dimensions. All I could see was the whites of her eyes. It was as if Lisa's bright blue eyes had rolled completely to the back of her head. Either that or she was channeling her inner zombie. "We just can't be everywhere at all times."

Lisa's tone was so pleasing that while I knew she was slamming the downstairs staff, she did so in the politest way possible.

"If there's anything I can do to familiarize you with the property, I'm one call away." Her smile looked painted on her fair, flawless face, and that's when I knew she was one of them.

From my experience, there were two types of Point Resort employees: the ones that followed the strict, never-break-the-script employee handbook and those that didn't. I fell into the latter group.

"Are you new to Long Beach? Is this your first time to our urban waterfront playground?"

Urban waterfront playground? Yup, she's corporate all the way. Even though Lisa had insect-like eyes, she didn't possess the broad field of vision to see beyond the scope of the Point philosophy. Unfortunately, all her vision was focused on was following Point policy and practices, which meant she'd only ever see me as a subhuman staff member. *Good to know.*

"First time here," I said in as chipper a voice as I could stomach without vomiting. I needed this job. I'd have to play along with the corporate game—just not all of it.

"I thought Long Beach was known as 'The International City.'" I couldn't help myself. The happy on her perky, flawless face seemed forced. *Is there anyone real in there?*

"Long Beach *is* 'The International City,' but *locals* prefer to think of it as our waterfront playground," she said without missing a beat.

Sure, because waterfront playground might mask the fact that it wasn't Surf City, Huntington Beach, or the affluent Carlsbad just down the coast. After I chose Long Beach for my reassignment, I casually brought the city up in a conversation with Chloe Dorsey, who I worked with in Napa. Chloe had relocated from Southern California and was a straight-shooter—Long Beach was surf-poor and had poor median income. It had to settle for the motto "The International City" because, without its cargo ports for overseas trade, Long Beach would be just another town dwarfed by the shadow of the state's biggest city, Los Angeles.

"Since this is your first time to Long Beach," Lisa said with a bouncy nod toward Phil, "we'll have to take you to Naples for lunch some afternoon."

"Naples?" Despite my better judgment, I took the bait.

"It's a quaint community built on three islands in Alamitos

Bay. The islands are separated by canals that open into the bay. It's very Italian with gondola rides, bistros, and the best cannoli this side of New York." A slow grin spread across his face. "Of course, the main difference is that the people in Naples, California, don't need to be reminded to 'leave the gun—take the cannoli' like they do in *The Godfather*." It was the only time Phil showed that he wasn't some blowhard.

"Are you from New York?" I asked.

He reached behind him, and within seconds a baseball hurled toward me. By dumb luck, I caught it, which seemed to please him.

"Good reflexes," he said.

Oh, you have no idea. Thankfully it was just a stuffed toy baseball, so even if a miracle hadn't happened when I snagged it, I wouldn't be toothless had it hit me smack in the face.

"No wonder your Dodgers made it to the World Series," he said to Lisa. "The rest of the Empire State has to wait until next year."

"Empire State? So, are you a Yankees or Mets fan?" I asked, hoping those were the only two teams in New York.

"I'm from the Bronx, so of course I'm a Yankees fan. Hell, the only time I'd ever root for those Queen upstarts are when the Mets have an interleague game with an American League East opponent, like Boston or Toronto," he said.

I had no idea what he was talking about, so I went to my fail-safe mode by just nodding knowingly—even though I knew nothing.

"Our trusted leader could talk nonstop about his days in the Bronx, but," Lisa glanced at Phil, "Bernie's already waiting for you in the conference room."

"Is that today?" He chewed on one end of his moustache.

"Every Friday," she said.

"Do you have my numbers?" Phil asked, and I thought Lisa was going to vaporize him with her deadly glare. Either that or Lisa had suddenly lost the ability to blink, because the look she gave Phil clearly meant that any talk about numbers was about as appropriate as sexual innuendos. Those digits must be so controversially off-limits, because it appeared that Phil would have been much better off asking Lisa for sex than for the numbers. *So, what data is that untouchable and clearly unmentionable?*

When neither of them spoke, I did.

"What's every Friday?" I invited myself into their conversation. Ever since Wyoming, I was keenly aware that when bad things happened in the executive office, trouble trickled down to the troops.

"Every week, Phil has to sit in on the revitalization, I mean *restoration* committee," Lisa said. "Why do I always say revitalization?" She looked toward Phil for the answer.

"The shoreline went through a revitalization, I bet that's what it is," he said.

"Oh, right." Her voice dropped and her eyes suddenly looked glassy like she was about to cry.

What could be upsetting about a revitalization or restoration?

"What's being restored?" I'd rather be told to butt out than be uninformed.

"Well, that's the thing—nothing," Lisa said.

"There's a group that formed when the hotel submitted plans to the city to expand next door into the bank," Phil said.

Confusion must have shown on my face because he continued.

"The bank's lease is about to run out and we have it on good authority that they won't be able to handle the rent at the new market price," he said.

"So, what's the problem?" I said. "If the hotel purchases or leases the property, it seems like a win for the city. More employees are hired and the property doesn't sit vacant."

"I wish you were on this committee," Phil said. "The property wouldn't sit vacant because we'd gut the bank and replace it with convention space and much-needed additional parking. Unfortunately, there's the band of *concerned citizens*, basically retirees, who don't have anything better to do and aren't in favor of convention space."

"Is the bank a landmark?" I asked.

"No, it's relatively new," Phil said.

"Does the land hold some significance to the city?" I asked.

"Some could argue that," Phil said, and I instantly knew it did.

So, basically what he and Lisa weren't saying was that this

group of concerned citizens didn't want a chunk of land lost by a land grab. I didn't know the dynamics of the group, but these concerned citizens seemed to be sitting on the right side of conservation. As my friend Chloe would say, "My kind of people."

"How old is the bank? Or actually the land that the bank's on," I asked.

"Why don't I walk you through the maze of offices to the elevators so you can begin your first day?" Lisa said, and I knew the conversation had ceased.

"Excellent," I said.

It was the only time Phil stood. His black pinstripe suit, crisp white dress shirt, and silver tie would be overkill in Napa, but not Long Beach. A long, thin arm extended toward me like an arachnid leading me to its web of no return. "Rebel, welcome aboard. Like Lisa said, if there's anything you need, just give us a call."

"Thank you." His hand was bony and I felt like I would crush it if I pressed too hard. I quickly released my grip before he creeped me out any further.

I grabbed my backpack from the thick carpet and saw a man pacing the hallway. His long black jacket blew back with each step and a silver cross swayed on his gray shirt. A wreath of grayish-white hair circled his dark head. Combined with his circular glasses, he reminded me of Laurence Fishburne's character in *The Matrix*. He caught me staring from Phil's office and smiled. He didn't look like a priest, but the cross on his chest was too big to ignore.

"You ready?" Lisa asked when my focus lingered on him.

I nodded and followed her soft-footed steps from Phil's corner office and million-dollar views of the "urban waterfront playground." Long Beach may not be a surfside town like Huntington or Carlsbad, but it wasn't shabby. The coastal panorama was just as magnificent as the multimillion dollar views seen from neighboring Newport Beach and Rancho Palos Verde, only at a tenth of the price. I caught another glimpse of the Queen Mary moored in the harbor. The world-class ocean liner was once a newcomer that made Long Beach its new home, which was what I hoped would happen for me.

CHAPTER 4
RYAN

"**M**cHenry, what deliveries you got going on today?" Lenny Burnetti stood with his hands on his hips and a pencil behind his ear. A clipboard was parked beneath his arm, and I was sure it already reeked of the spicy, funky salami subs he powered down every afternoon. The guy was predictable, which I banked on working in my favor.

"I got the weekly office supply for Signal Hill Insurance, a few stops in Alamitos, and a pretty big order of paper and furniture for 12 ½ East Ocean Boulevard."

"The Point?" Lenny reached for his pencil and his comb-over shifted sideways. He glanced at the clipboard while his pencil ran the length of the paper. "Oh, right. It's for conference services."

"Yeah, but not the offices on the seventh. This is for the gals in the basement, so I don't have to deal with maintenance or the freight elevator."

"Unless your truck won't fit under the subterranean parking. You make sure you tawwk to them. They had some idear to add more spaces to their garage and made modifications. So, check with 'em first, right?"

Lenny was from Queens and at least once a day, the kid from the borough surfaced. He dropped *r*'s on a regular basis, which was hard at first until I realized "Mawning" was my boss's way of saying, "Morning." And idear was idea with an extra letter attached. When he wasn't prolonging words like talk into tawwk, he substituted *d* for *t* or *th*.

"Give me doze shipping papers from yesterday and then you can get on your route," he said.

"Sure thing. About my route. I was thinking of hitting the Point last…."

Lenny's dark eyes looked up from the clipboard. "What you got goin' on tonight, Ryan?"

Fuck. He only used my first name when I was busted. And it's the only time I tried to win him over with my smile.

"Nuh-uh." He wagged his clipboard at me. "Those pearly whites and dimple might work with the ladies, but it don't do shit for me."

Now I couldn't stop smiling. Lenny had my number. "I was going to hit happy hour downtown with the team."

"The Dirtbags?" The pencil went behind his ear and the clipboard resumed its position under his arm.

"Yeah, Sam Murphy's in town and we thought we'd get together for some beers and bullshit."

"You boys had a good team."

Lenny was one of Long Beach State's biggest baseball sponsors. I was pretty sure it was due to our team's nickname, which was so popular it was stitched on our uniforms.

"You just can't lose with the Dirtbags—it's gritty, not fancy— kind of like the city of Long Beach, you know?"

It was the same conversation anytime one of my former college teammates dropped by or I mentioned that we'd be meeting up.

"Yeah, but only Sammy was good enough for the Major Leagues," I said.

Lenny's clipboard was in his hands in a matter of seconds. He shook it at me with real conviction. "Listen, McHenry, you had your shot, and there ain't no shame that things didn't work out for yous."

I nodded. "You okay then with me parking the truck at the Point and I'll pick it up on my way to work tomorrow?"

"You walking home from the bar?"

"That was the plan," I said.

"Well, sure, okay. The Point's got security. Just lock 'er up tight. And if we get any vandals spray-painting the side, it's yous who's cleaning the thing up. Understood?"

"Yes, sir. Thanks, Lenny."

"Say hi to the fellas for me." He waved his clipboard before heading to his glass-enclosed office in the garage, and I hopped in my truck.

CHAPTER 5
REBEL

he elevator doors slowly shut and the seventh floor with its sweeping views of the shoreline disappeared. But thankfully so did Phil. I wasn't sure what to make of my new boss, but I couldn't argue with the bustle of life that stirred on the boardwalk just below the seventh floor. An office above ground would be a welcome change.

The elevator picked up speed and zipped past each floor, bypassing the lobby level in its descent. I leaned against the smooth handrail and glanced at my reflection in the textured walls of the cab. The patterned design in the slate blue and clear overlay finish gave the appearance of rain and my reflection was a washed-out version of me. The lights in the ceiling that cast shadows didn't help. The more I stared at myself, the more I looked like some wild, red-headed creature from Atlantis that not even Aquaman could save. But I'd had to change more than my address when I was relocated; I also had to change my appearance, and my new strikingly startling red hair would be the one thing people would now notice and remember about me. The only good thing that had changed since going underground was my weight. I dropped forty pounds when I stopped eating my feelings, and now I looked more like the athletically toned rodeo rider from my high school days. My ass finally looked good in a pair of jeans again. Not that I got to wear them with the Point's dress policy. And since I wasn't sure what I was supposed to wear in Long Beach, I stuck with my Napa Valley wine cave standard: khaki pants and a red polo.

I redirected my attention to the center of the glass where the Point Resort's emblem of a high arching wave, shown in five overlapping sections of a single wave, was etched in gold. Each overlapping section was a richer layer of gold because each section of wave represented the stars earned by the hotel. Five stars—five golden waves. It was a less-than-subtle reminder that, in the hotel industry, the Point Resorts set the gold standard.

A bell dinged as the elevator passed B1, B2, and B3. When it finally settled on B4, the last button on the console, the ground vibrated. I stepped from the elevator into a dimly lit entryway.

"Hello?" My stomach tightened and I tucked my arm against my camouflage backpack slung over my shoulder, as if something would suddenly pop around the corner and grab me or my bag.

"Back here," a cheerful voice said.

I practically tiptoed, not wanting to sneak up on anyone or be snuck up on. When I rounded the bend, I was met by a beautiful, warm smile.

"You must be Rebel." She pushed away from the arched reception desk that looked like a wooden punch-out of a half moon and stood. "I'm Ria Bell."

Her hands were smooth and silky like her voice, which seemed suited to the soft cadence of her name. *Ria Bell.* Her dark hair was pulled into a French twist that highlighted her velvety-looking ebony skin. Pearl stud earrings were in each lobe, contrasting against her raspberry-stained lips. Her face was otherwise minimally made up.

She reached into the bowl of candy on her desk and grabbed a root beer barrel. "Would you like one? The guests love them. They're super yummy." She unwrapped the candy and popped it in her mouth.

"No thanks," I said.

"You meet with Phil?" Her plump cheeks didn't even show signs of the candy.

"Just left." I glanced at the fake palm tree in the corner of the reception area beside two tan-colored armchairs spotted with stains.

"It's a little different down here than up on the seventh." She rapped the pencil's eraser against the black blotter that covered the desk.

"It's homey," I said.

"More like homely."

I turned to find a woman with shoulder-length twist braids entering the reception area. The floating silver heart around her neck sparkled against her red tank top in the low light. The white blazer that hugged her slender frame contrasted strikingly against her reddish-brown skin. Her natural skin tone was what I wished I had. But I was too white. Whenever I dared venture into the sun, I freckled and burnt. In slim-legged black slacks that tapered around her skinny ankles, she teetered on wedges that matched her tank top and lips. She was stunning and from her pursed lips, no-nonsense.

"The only thing this place needs is a devastating fire." She crossed her arms over her chest.

I wasn't sure if she was a hotel staff member or a guest, so I played it safe and courteously smiled.

"I don't know what you're grinning about, you're stuck down here now, too," she said, and I knew what side of the proverbial hotel fence she stood on.

Staff took care of guests' needs and guests found no need

to care about the staff, which often left a sour taste, or in this woman's case, bitter look on their face.

I breached the distance between us. "I'm Rebel Roberts."

Hand extended, she gripped mine, but not too hard, just enough to set a firm boundary.

"I'm the assistant floor manager." She announced her title and I think waited for a reaction, when I didn't give one, she offered her name. "Da Nise Price."

"Denise?" I said, and her grasp intensified.

"No. *Da* Nise—two words. Not one like Denise."

I swore on my granddaddy's grave it still sounded like Denise. But I wasn't about to second-guess her double name. Although, maybe she was originally from Chicago and her parents were sports fans. *Da Nise loved Da Bears*. I bit the inside of my mouth to keep from laughing and creating more tension between us.

"Lot of guests get it wrong," Ria said, offering the bowl of candy toward Da Nise, who waved it away. Ria reached for another piece. The large glass bowl was half-full. I sensed Ria was the peacekeeper and candy was her offering.

"Did you use to work at Target?" Ria asked.

I felt the heat rush to my cheeks. "No, this was the uniform they made us wear in Napa and I wore it so often, I guess it's just habit." I tugged on my red shirt. "But yeah, khakis and a red polo definitely get me confused with someone from Target."

"Phil's little blonde sidekick told us you left Napa Valley for Long Beach. Who in their right mind would leave Napa for Long Beach?" The sass in Da Nise's voice along with the exaggerated eye roll presented a first-day-on-the-job challenge. I could sass back, shrug, or ignore her.

"Have you ever *been* to Napa?" I never made the easy choice.

"No." The smug left and a tinge of pink spiked her umber cheeks as she drummed her long, acrylic red nails against the edge of Ria's desk. "Farthest north I've been is to Valencia when Steve and I took Jordan to Magic Mountain. Jordan's our little boy. It was crowded, hot, and pricey. Lord, was it pricey."

I laughed. "So, basically like every amusement park in California."

Her face softened and her dark brown eyes, which were almost black, glanced at me. Her red lips sealed into a smile. "Amen, sister. Amen."

Ria leaned against the back of her chair and the suspension moaned. I wasn't sure if it would handle her weight. Ria was a big woman.

Da Nise pointed toward the entryway behind Ria's desk. "Girl, don't be standing over her like some white shadow, she's got work to do. And so do we."

I followed Da Nise into the elongated office space tucked behind the reception area. A sign on the door announced Conference Services Administrative Suite.

The room didn't live up to its name. The suite was a large rectangular area with no windows, drab, putty-colored painted walls, and a brown-weave carpet that had more wear patterns than the balding tires on the used car I bought. The carpet was probably about as safe as my outdated convertible Bug, which I already regretted buying. I was a car dealer's dream—falling hard for the soft top and new butter-yellow paint job.

A large plastic mat covered the floor in front of the telephone console and computer. Two rolling chairs were pushed against the countertop that lined the wall. It wasn't that the office just didn't have ergonomic appeal, it was the fact that it was clear from the arrangement of countertops in lieu of desks that the whole space was an afterthought.

I slid into a chair beside Da Nise and her body spray filled the space between us, a blend of musk, vanilla, and something floral, which was fragrant without being repugnant.

"If you've worked at a Point Resort then you know we always answer the phone with the hotel name, our name, and then how can we help or assist them. So, I'd say, 'Good morning, Long Beach Point Resort, this is Da Nise, how may I assist you?' And you'd do the same when you pick up a call." Da Nise strummed her fingernails on the keyboard. "That's why you're down here with me, isn't it? To train, right? That's all they told me."

I nodded. "I was told to cross-train in every position in the back office," I said.

Her fingernails methodically moved to the blonde countertop. "What position *were* you hired for? Phil's twit didn't say. But she did say a lot about the desk and chair Kathy ordered."

"Conference Services Floor Manager?" It wasn't a title we had at the Napa Valley Point Resort and Winery.

"Kathy!" Da Nise pressed against the counter and wheeled herself away from the switchboard. "Kathy!" She looked at me. "That girl never hears me. Kathy!" Da Nise's voice rose to the point of deafening. Thankfully we weren't just in the back of the hotel away from guests. The PBX and conference offices were located on the ground floor of the subterranean parking structure that connected to the hotel. The only thing I had to worry about was Da Nise setting off a car alarm.

An older, tall, thin, dark-skinned woman in psychedelic-printed bell bottoms, a white top with no bra, and hair that looked like it hadn't seen a brush—ever—appeared around the corner.

"What are you yelling about now?" She rubbed the sleep from her eye and stretched. "I told you I was on my break."

"Since when you tell me you were on a break?" When Da Nise shook her head, it was like her sass continued through the gesture. "Break, my ass, you were on a break. You were in your office sleeping."

"Da Nise, what do you want?" Kathy crossed her legs, and

bony ankles protruded from her black slip-ons.

"I want you to meet the *new* conference services floor manager." Da Nise crossed her arms over her blazer, and it didn't take a genius to know she was pissed.

I stood and extended my hand. "I'm Rebel Roberts."

"Ah, someone's parents were as fond of alliteration as mine." Her hand swung into mine. "Kathy Klein. I handle any secretarial work that conference guests have."

"Why don't you just call yourself a secretary?" Da Nise said.

"I think the preferred title is administrative assistant," I said, and immediately wished I hadn't. Da Nise shot me a look that practically silenced my pulse.

"Secretary. Girl Friday. Admin Assistant. Whatever. It's all semantics." Kathy scratched her head and her locks of black hair barely moved. She had this whole dreadlock thing started and given enough time she'd own it. Combined with her hippie vibe and how she was dressed like she'd never left Woodstock, which from her age, she may have attended, I sensed we'd get along well.

"Welcome to Long Beach," Kathy said with a hint of a smile. "Finally, a token white girl."

When we all laughed, I sensed the ice was beginning to thaw.

"Yeah, we really needed some lack of color around here," Da Nise said, and I knew the ice was officially broken.

"Lucky for you I'm multilingual," Kathy said with an elbow

nudge to my ribs. "I can speak both Caucasian and Republican."

"There's a difference?" Ria said, so seriously that I thought I'd lose my breath from laughing so hard.

"Oh, my gosh, stop," I said when I finally came up for air.

"Now, wait a second, I'm black, Republican, and never voted for Obama," Da Nise said.

The other girls were suddenly quiet and it felt like our breaking the ice moment chilled.

"That's 'cause I wasn't even old enough, girl!" Da Nise kicked out her foot and hit Kathy's shin. "I didn't turn eighteen until a week after his reelection! I missed crossing party lines and voting for Barack by seven damn days!"

The laughter ensued, and my first-day on-the-job jitters melted away.

Kathy smiled, pulled a blunt from her pocket and waved it toward us. "Now, that we're all getting along, I'm going on my break."

My mouth fell open. I quickly closed it, but Da Nise didn't miss a beat. Her laughter was as deep as she was intense and as broad as her shoulders that shook. "Oh, Lord, did you see her face? That was good."

I felt the heat rise to my cheeks. "Yeah, what you do on your break is off the clock, just make sure you smoke that"—I nudged toward the tightly rolled joint—"off property."

She saluted me before she left and I wasn't sure what to make of it or her. I couldn't make sense of anything. I was stuck in a circle of hell even Dante hadn't imagined, with a pot-smoking secretary, a sassy assistant manager, and a candy-crunching PBX operator. I began to wonder why I'd left Napa for Long Beach. Despite the FBI immunity deal, this new job was proving to be a prison of its own.

CHAPTER 6
RYAN

"**H**ey, good-looking." I leaned on** the edge of her desk and poured a bag of wrapped butterscotch disks into the crystal bowl.

"Why do you keep doing that?" She crossed her arms over her ample chest and her breasts pressed together. "You know I'm trying to lose weight."

"Ria, you're beautiful." And I wasn't lying. Her eyes were like onyx and her personality was equally as strong. Ria's beauty came from her heart that seemed open to everyone. I'd never seen her be rude to anyone. She was one of the few clients I liked seeing on my delivery route.

"Thanks, Ryan, but you know after Ricky I don't date white guys," she said, and I laughed.

"So you've told me repeatedly." I grinned. "You always forget that I used to play ball with Ricky. And"—I held up my hand—"not all white guys are like him. And just for the record, I don't hit on my clients."

When Ria smiled her eyes practically disappeared. "I know that. But it's just not my thing." She drummed her pencil against the desk. "You got a delivery for us?"

"Yes, ma'am, I do." I placed the clipboard on her desk. "It's pretty big too. And Lenny mentioned some new changes to the parking. My deliveries usually aren't this big, so I park on the street and use the dolly, but that won't work with furniture." I lifted my baseball cap off my head, brushed back my hair, and put the cap on backwards. The brim got in the way during any delivery.

"Where are you parked?" She signed the top sheet of the three-carbon set, tore off the middle pink sheet for her files, and returned the packet to me. It was another thing I liked about Ria, she knew the drill. No matter how many times I went to some clients, they seemed surprised when I handed them the pink copy of the invoice. Ria wasn't a dumbass and that counted for a lot in my book.

I tucked the paperwork beneath the silver clasp on my clipboard and nodded toward the parking lot. "Right now, I'm in the loading zone. I was thinking I could pull into the bottom level and unload, but I'm not sure if my truck'll fit. I didn't realize how low the new entrance was until I saw it."

She held up her finger while her other hand punched an extension. "Let me ask Rafael. He works part-time in security and part-time in maintenance, but he'd know."

While Ria called Rafael, I ducked into the administrative office. Kathy sat in front of the backup switchboard.

"Hey, Klein, what's the word?"

"Allouche."

"Allouche?" I shook my head. "I don't think I know that one. How'd you use it in a sentence?"

"Todd Allouche is a douche."

I gripped the doorframe to keep from falling when I burst out laughing. "You got me. I didn't see that one coming."

"Yah, me neither."

"That blows. Was he the guy who took you to San Diego for the weekend?"

Her head barely registered a nod, but it was enough to know her getaway weekend didn't end well.

"He was only interested in my weed," she said.

"Well, I've got a new office chair and desk, if that'll make you happy."

She slightly grinned. "Nah, I ordered those for the new floor manager."

"Did Da Nise get the promotion?"

She curtly shook her head. "Yeah, probably don't want to say that too loudly."

"Right." There wasn't one person I'd met who wasn't a little afraid of Da Nise, even if they wouldn't admit it. I lowered my voice. "So, who got it?"

"Rebel Roberts. She transferred from the Napa Valley property."

"Rebel?" I chuckled. "That's her name?"

"Yup."

I was about to ask more about her when Ria called me.

"Ryan, Rafael said the parking structure is up to code and that van-accessible parking is on the first level, but the multilevels have a lower clearance."

I tucked my clipboard under my arm and crossed my arms over my chest. I was turning into Lenny. "If it's code, the clearance is eight feet two inches, but it doesn't look like it's high enough for my truck. It looks more like seven feet."

Ria shrugged and reached for a butterscotch. "I don't know, that's just what Rafael said."

I pursed my lips together and thought of Da Nise, who did the same thing when she seemed deep in thought. I understood as I verbally worked out my dilemma. "Basically, with the revamped parking structure, deliveries can only be made on the street level, which will require that I use the freight elevator to access the basement level."

Ria nodded. "That sounds about right."

Kathy appeared beside Ria. "The hotel's courtesy vans fit on the first level, but they can't access the basement."

"That makes no sense whatsoever. What about guests that use your conference services?" I glanced around the reception area that could benefit from a higher-watt light bulb. "Don't guests utilize this space too?"

"For administrative support, but all our conference rooms are on the first and third floors," Kathy said.

"Right." I leaned against Ria's desk. "I was supposed to leave my truck here overnight."

"Date?" Ria asked, and I shook my head.

"Pub crawl?" Kathy said, and I smiled.

"Yeah, my boss gave me the okay to park here. You're the last stop for the day." I ran my hands through my hair. "Fuck."

It wasn't something I'd normally utter on the job, but the downstairs crew were chill. When I had dented furniture that couldn't be returned, I gave it to them and they always seemed to make the mismatched pieces work.

"Park in the alley," Kathy said, "beside the hotel. No one uses it during the night. And security has cameras there. Security doesn't monitor the *whole* alley, but the cameras catch enough."

"If anyone knows where the security cameras are on this property, it's this stoner," Ria said, and Kathy didn't deny, but she did clarify.

"Ria, you know I have a prescription for my arthritis," Kathy said.

"Medical marijuana? I didn't know that," I said.

"Yeah, I have arthritis bad in my hands and since I type all day and do transcription, this helps," she said. "But it's not very strong."

Kathy was the oldest in the downstairs crew—or was, I didn't know about this Rebel gal. I glanced at her hands and it was the first time I noticed how craggy they were. Her fingers bent like claws in the claw machine at the Pike.

She tucked them behind her back and I felt like an asshole for staring.

"Sorry about that," I said, and she shook it off. "So, the alley beside the coffee shop?" I redirected the conversation.

"No, on the other side next to the bank," Kathy said.

"Oh, yeah. My truck would totally fit there." I grabbed my clipboard and tapped it on the edge of Ria's desk. "Thanks, ladies." I turned to leave and then pivoted on my sneakers. "Hey, would you mind phoning Rafael again to activate the freight elevator for me?"

Ria picked up her phone and was dialing when I hopped in the elevator and hit L for the lobby. The sooner I unloaded this haul, the faster I'd be downing the first of many IPAs.

CHAPTER 7
REBEL

"**'m guessing you applied for** the floor manager position?"

Da Nise was midbite into her BLT and nodded without making eye contact, which I already sensed from our introductory meeting was unlike her. Da Nise didn't back down from anyone or anything. This job obviously meant a lot to her.

I didn't want to settle with the pat "I'm sorry" response, so I said what I felt. "I've never understood how the Point picks who goes where. But if it's any help, this is the second time they've put me underground."

I almost got sprayed with bacon and tomato. Luckily, she caught it with a napkin as it flew from her mouth.

"Apparently, I'm not front-office material," I said, and when Da Nise smiled, the hard edge softened.

"I just don't know why they even let us apply if they already know they have someone they want for it," she said.

I paused. *Do I tell her that the top guru at Long Beach, whoever that was, probably didn't have a say in the matter? That when the Feds got involved, they pretty much had to take me? Or do I follow my egg handler's directions, shut my mouth, and stay under the radar?*

"For what it's worth, titles don't mean dick to me," I said, opting to stay in Long Beach longer than I had in Napa.

She shrugged. "Yeah, but it was almost two bucks more an hour."

"I didn't know that." I moved the crushed ice around in my cup with the straw. I wanted more soda, but I didn't want to be rude.

Da Nise nodded toward the machine. "It's free refills and it's a lot cheaper than the pop they have in those vending machines they have for us by the locker rooms."

I pushed away from the corner table she'd placed her keys on when we walked into the deli, which was a block from the hotel. I hadn't even asked where we were headed. When Da Nise announced it was lunch at three o'clock, I didn't argue. My stomach was more than willing to follow.

Pete's Sub Shop was top shelf. The corner, glass-enclosed deli was an Italian-lovers' paradise with fresh-cut salami, an olive bar, and an espresso machine. But what sold me was the Long Beach locals lunch—sub, chips, and all-you-can-drink for five bucks. Couldn't find that in Napa, *anywhere*. Da Nise introduced me to Pete, who acknowledged me with a grunt. I smiled in his direction as I filled my plastic cup with Coke and a splash of cherry flavoring. Pete slung a dish towel over his shoulder and shook his head like I was an annoyance. Or maybe the free refills were just for people he liked.

I quickly returned to my seat across from Da Nise, whom Pete did seem to favor.

"Why don't you eat at the hotel?" I lowered my voice lest he hear me. "I mean, they have an employee cafeteria, right?"

She shrugged. "Yeah, and it's free, but the food's crap. Plus, I like to get outside and see if the sun is actually shining."

"You're speaking my language," I said. "I wasn't kidding about working underground. In Napa, the wine caves were 130 feet underground, a mile and a half long, and cold as hell."

She laughed. "I don't think hell's cold."

I wagged my finger. "No, I'm convinced hell *is* cold. It's like when a steamy romance turns tepid, you're in relationship hell. Even if the relationship runs hot and cold, it's the latter half that's hellacious."

"Is that why you left?" She wiped the corners of her mouth with her napkin. "For a warmer climate? Or because a relationship turned cold?"

"No luck in the relationship department." I half laughed. "I never had time. All I did was give wine tours for rich people who didn't tip. If I'd known the hourly rate was so low, I would have stayed in Wyoming." My heart jumped to my throat and I was sure my face revealed my panic.

"You okay?"

I nodded and swallowed hard. *Shit.* I just blurted out the one thing I wasn't supposed to tell anyone—Wyoming. *Fuck. Fuck. Fuck.*

"What's Napa like?"

Da Nise either hadn't heard Wyoming or didn't care. I imagined the latter.

"Napa's beautiful." I focused on what I could share. "It seems like it has the longest growing season ever, so the sun is constant, but I thought working near the beach wouldn't be so bad," I said, which wasn't a lie. The Feds had presented two options: New York or Long Beach. I just wasn't ready to give up the West Coast for the East Coast. I'd never tell Yankee-loving Phil that, but California felt more like home.

Da Nise neatly folded the sub wrapper and tucked it into the brown paper bag, which she carefully discarded into the trash. Her tough-as-nails, in-your-face demeanor dropped and little miss manners surfaced.

"Always leave a place better than you found it," she said.

"Thoreau?"

"I don't know who that is. It's my mama. She always told me to leave a place better than I found it. If I stayed at someone's house, before I left I made sure the trash was empty and the rooms I used, including the bathroom, looked better than when I arrived."

"I like that," I said.

She grabbed her keys and headed toward the door. "It's not just about cleanliness and recycling and stuff, it's also about life. I hope that every guest I meet and work with at the hotel, that they feel like they are in a better place afterward."

For all her briskness, I sensed Da Nise was a softie.

"Even with the real difficult clients, I try to find ways to encourage them or not take it personally when they aren't appreciative of what I've done." Da Nise pushed the button for the crosswalk. The oncoming traffic began to slow as the signal changed from green, to yellow, to red. A bleeping sound and the white silhouette of a person that flashed on the crossing signal indicated it was our turn to cross Ocean Boulevard. I'd only lived in Long Beach a handful of nights, but I already knew Ocean Boulevard connected to everything downtown.

"So no matter where I'm at or what I'm doing, it's like I'm conditioned to leave it better than I found it." Even in high wedges, Da Nise's long, slender legs moved fast. I tried to keep up with her.

"My dad called it the campsite rule, but it was basically the same thing—leave the campsite better than you found it. But I never thought of it for my life," I said.

Da Nise seemed to appreciate my honesty, from the glance and subtle smile in my direction. "If you ever meet Mama, she'll tell you how it applies to everything in life. Like if you're in a relationship, no matter how hurt you get, she says it's my responsibility to leave a man better than how I found him."

"I kind of hope I never meet your mama," I said, and Da Nise actually giggled. "From past relationships, I seem to leave a man far more *bitter* than he was before we met."

Da Nise's braids swayed against her shoulders when she shook her head. "You crazy."

"My exes would agree." I chuckled.

The hotel came into view and I really hadn't taken a look at the front during the daytime. Anytime I'd driven past it was either at night or early in the morning. Now in the late afternoon sun, I could see why locals may refer to Long Beach and its surroundings as an urban waterfront playground.

The hotel was located in the heart of downtown within walking distance to everything a traveler to the West Coast would want—the beach, easy access to freeways, and expansive balconies with views of the Pacific that stretched as far as Catalina Island. The hub of activity was nonstop downtown; guests wouldn't ever have to get into their cars if they took advantage of everything Long Beach had to offer. I knew from the employee handbook that the Long Beach Point Resort was amenity-rich, business friendly, and competitively priced.

Unfortunately, from talking to Chloe Dorsey, I knew Long Beach suffered from Middle Child Syndrome. It was geographically sandwiched between the distinguished elder city of Los Angeles and the younger, and incredibly spoiled, Orange County.

Situated between the two powerhouses, Long Beach etched its own niche in the marketplace and as Da Nise and I walked toward the mirrored glass hotel, our reflections showed our physical differences. Thankfully we were in the heart of a city that drew strength from differences and made us, and Long Beach, the better for it.

CHAPTER 8
RYAN

glanced at my phone—four thirty. Record time for Friday deliveries. I double-checked the truck doors and cargo bed. When I was convinced everything was locked tight, I pocketed the keys, tied a sweatshirt around my waist, and headed toward the stop light that crossed Ocean Boulevard. My cell vibrated in my jeans pocket. I glanced at Snapchat.

"WTF McHenry. Beer's warm." A picture of the guys giving me the finger followed.

Dirtbags.

I jogged across the street and snapped a picture of the boardwalk and the leggy, bikini-clad vixen walking toward me. A towel was draped over her shoulder, and with each step, her heels slapped against her sandals. The repetitive *flip flop, flip flop* was as sassy as her walk.

"Did you just take my picture?" she said when our paths crossed.

"Snapchat. Does that count?"

She laughed. "I guess not."

"I had to give the guys a reason why I was late, and well," I shrugged, "you're a good reason to be late."

"*Ay, Dios mio.* Does that work on *anyone*, McHenry?"

"Only you, Georgina, only you." I wrapped my arm around her small waist and pulled her into me. She smelled like salt water and coconut suntan lotion. "How you been?"

"Another day in paradise." She twisted her hair into one long rope and wrung the water from her auburn mane. Water dripped down her caramel-colored skin. "You know I'm still gay." She didn't even bother making eye contact with me.

I grinned. "Yeah, yeah, yeah. How could I forget? I was the one who hooked you up on your first date in high school."

"Michelle Stewart." Her catlike green eyes practically danced. "You never forget your first."

"All right, all right. You're still Demi's little sister and there's some things I don't need to know."

"He told me the Dirtbags are having a reunion tonight." She wrapped a towel around her body and walked beside me on the boardwalk.

"Yeah, Sammy's in town."

"Don't tell LaTesha, she'll come unglued. She's still convinced they're going to end up together."

"You think?" I readjusted my baseball cap. "This is just for the team—we don't need any drama."

"Then you might want to switch hats." She flicked the brim of my cap, but it stayed on my head.

"Hey! What the hell?"

"Dodgers?" she said, walking into me.

"Yah, I bleed blue." I shrugged her off me.

"But you know the rest of the team are Angel fans."

"I can't help it if my former teammates are living in the past and ignoring the local team north of us. Sure, none of us were even alive when the Dodgers last won the World Series, but at least they've won the pennant in this decade. That's more than the Angels can claim."

Georgina's laughter caught the attention of a group of guys waiting for a table at Rick's Bistro. They stopped talking and admired her as we passed. She wrapped her arm around my waist like we were a couple, and I grinned.

"You're so bad."

"It's easier than having to deal with frat boys," she said.

"Where are you parked?" I asked when we turned right onto

Marina Drive and Sullivan's patio bar came into view.

"I came with Demi," she said.

I held up my hand. "No drama. Whatever you've got cooking, put it out."

She swatted my hand hard.

"*Pinche cabrón pendejo.* When have I ever brought drama?"

"Settle down. I just don't want to have to play referee between you and some drunken idiots who think they have a shot with you."

"Then tell Demi. He's the one who throws the first punch."

I stopped midstride and looked at her. "For real?"

Her cheeks turned crimson. "Okay, okay. I'll behave."

"McHenry!"

We both turned toward the shouts. Demi, Sammy, Mike, and Patrick raised their pints.

I untied my sweatshirt and handed it to my best friend's little sister. "If you don't want trouble, then wear this."

"Party pooper," she said, tucking her head into the sweatshirt.

It was practically a dress on her, but it was better than having her walk into the rowdiest bar on the waterfront in nothing more than a bikini and a smile. When men saw Georgie, they didn't see a woman—they saw a conquest. It pissed me off. I may not have as much luck as the other guys with women, but none of us treated them like meat. Whoever the woman was, she could be somebody's sister and at a minimum, she was someone's daughter.

No matter how drunk we got we had one rule—go home alone and lose with honor versus scoring by disgrace.

I took the lead into the bar with Georgie on my heels. I hadn't even sat down when a frosty pint of Long Beach's best IPA slid toward me.

"Friday night and the Dirtbags are in the house!" Sammy raised his glass toward the center of the table.

Our mugs collided and the hoppy, craft beer was down my throat in an instant. Friday night indeed.

CHAPTER 9
REBEL

Kathy *leaned against the boxed* desk that had been delivered while Da Nise and I were at lunch.

"You missed McCutie," she said.

Da Nise shrugged. "He'll be back."

"Who's McCutie?" I asked.

Ria's voice came from the front. "Only the cutest office delivery guy in Long Beach."

I slowly nodded. "Is he from Staples?" This prompted a good chuckle from the three of them.

"Staples would save the hotel money, but they don't have McCutie," Kathy said.

"Besides, with the income we generate down here, we should be able to get our office supplies wherever we want," Da Nise said.

"Is McCutie with an approved vendor?" I asked, knowing from Napa that we could only work with corporate approved vendors.

Da Nise nodded. "Ryan works with Burnetti & Sons Office Supply, who is an approved vendor."

I shrugged. "Then I don't see the problem with it." It was the only time Kathy and Da Nise both looked at me like I had crossed a line.

"Come on," I said. "You don't think I got an earful from Phil about operating costs?"

"I bet you did," Kathy said.

"So, if you like using this Burnetti & Sons and they're an approved vendor, then I don't see why that has to change," I said.

Da Nise's arms crossed over her body.

"I meant it when I said titles don't mean anything to me, but I'd also like to keep my job," I said. "There's got to be other ways to cut costs."

"The only way our operating overhead is going to go any lower is if there's one less body down here," Da Nise said.

Ria suddenly appeared in the doorway to the back office. "Is that what you were hired to do? Cut one of us?"

I shook my head. "No, not at all." But I could tell the trio didn't believe me. "On my granddaddy's grave, the only marching orders I got from Phil were to streamline production and lower the operating expenses, but he didn't say anything about cutting staff."

"I believe you," Kathy said, "but that doesn't mean that's not in the works. And just to be clear, we need four people just to operate the floor—Ria to man the switchboard, Da Nise to process the guests' requests and back up Ria when the switchboard is crazy, which is daily. Me to do the clerical work, and a floor manager to oversee the billing, put out any fires, and fill in when I'm out."

"I agree," I said. "From working the phones today, I don't know how you've gotten anything done."

"This was a slow day," Ria said.

"Who was the last floor manager?" I said.

"Patty Smith." Da Nise said her name like it was a curse.

"What happened to her?" I was almost afraid to ask.

Kathy and Da Nise exchanged a glance, saying nothing. It was Ria who answered.

"She decided to be a surrogate for one of the hotel guests," she said, and I about fell out of my chair.

"Are you serious?"

Ria laughed. "Yup. The daytime Emmys hosted a luncheon at the hotel and one of the soap stars needed something faxed to her agent. Patty helped her and they got talking and apparently Patty knew that this woman was trying to have a baby by surrogate but hadn't found a surrogate she felt comfortable with, and next thing we knew, Patty gave notice," she said.

"Damn. So she's going to carry that woman's baby for nine months and then just give it up?"

"Like you said, it's the woman's baby, not hers," Kathy said.

"Good point. While I'd love to make more money, I have *no* interest getting knocked up with my own kid, let alone someone else's," I said, and they laughed. And while the mood had softened, I seized the moment.

"I really meant what I said. Phil never mentioned staff cuts, and if he does, I'd argue against it. I'll have to have the numbers to back me, but from what I've experienced today, I can't imagine that'd be hard," I said. "Kathy's been processing work requests as fast as they come in, and that's income."

No one said anything.

"I know I'm new to you," I said. "But I'm not entirely new to the Point Resorts. I know how the reward system works and who's front office material and put in higher-tipped positions and who's placed underground. Or in this case the basement. If you give me the chance, I think you'll find that I don't bullshit—very well." I laughed. "I'm certainly no doctor, but I do believe in, first, do no harm. I'm not here to do any harm."

"So, will this be your first weekend in Long Beach?" Kathy said.

I tilted my head back and tried to remember when I arrived. "Uh...."

Da Nise yawned. "All I want to do this weekend is binge sleep."

"Me too," I said, still trying to deconstruct my timeline.

"So, is this your first weekend?" Ria popped her head toward the front switchboard that remained thankfully silent.

I pressed my thumb against the side of my head to stop the throbbing. "Yes, this will mark my first full week in Long Beach."

"Well, you only started today," Da Nise said.

"Not true." I wagged a finger. "I began two days ago when I had to go to the corporate office in Orange County and attend those seminars conducted by human resources on sexual harassment, workplace safety and, my personal favorite, Internet security. There's two days of my life I'll never get back. So, while it may seem like I just started on a Friday, I've had my boots on the ground since Wednesday."

"But this will be your first weekend in Long Beach?" Ria said.

"Yes, it is." I paused and looked at Ria, who wasn't sucking on any candy, which I already knew was unusual. "Why?"

She smiled at Kathy, who elbowed Da Nise. "Call Steve and tell him you'll be home late."

"Nuh-uh," Da Nise said. "I'm too whooped."

"You can sleep when you're dead," Kathy said. "It's tradition, and you don't mess with tradition."

"What are you talking about?" I glanced from Ria to Kathy, and finally it was Da Nise who answered.

"You are twenty-one, aren't you?"

"Uh, yeah. I'm almost—" I realized revealing that I was almost thirty could work against me in a supervisory role when Kathy was closer to fifty. "Yeah, I'm legal. Why?"

"Once you shut down the computer and forward the phones to the upstairs operator like I showed you, there's one more thing we have to do to complete your training," Da Nise said.

"After one day my training is complete?" I said.

Kathy laughed. "If you graduated high school, you can do this job. There's a lot to it but it's not difficult—answer phones, be polite, transcribe notes, fill coffeepots, and basically do everything they don't want to do on the seventh floor for the hotel guests."

"You caught on to the phone system fast, and the computer is all Word and Excel," Da Nise said. "Besides, what you worried about? You took enough notes to fill a binder."

"I figured there'd be more I'd have to learn," I said.

"Oh, there is," Da Nise said. "We haven't gone into billing, invoicing, and posting payments, and most likely Phil will have more crap for you that his little blonde troll doesn't want to do, but for today, you've got the basics down."

Ria clapped. "So, now it's time for the real test."

I shook my head and smiled. "I'm not so sure I like the sound of that."

"Grab your Army pack or whatever *that* thing is you slung in the corner," Da Nise said. "Your real training is about to begin."

CHAPTER 10
REBEL

City lights twinkled off the coast and the ocean looked like a dark sheet of glass I could walk across. While the water was calm, the boardwalk buzzed and a low hanging moon seemed within reach. The Ferris wheel at the Pike glowed in the distance and the boisterous echo of laughter hung in the air. For a city stuck between Orange County and Los Angeles, Long Beach belonged to no one, which made it all the more appealing to this outsider. And the International City shone on a Friday night.

"Where are we going?" I asked, again trying to keep up with Da Nise's long legs.

Ria looped her arm through mine. "Long Beach Club Roar."

"What is that?"

"Only the seediest bar on the waterfront," Kathy said.

"So, it's our kind of place," Da Nise said without looking for traffic when she jaywalked across the street. Ria moved faster than I'd seen all day to jog behind Da Nise. The deep bellow of a car's horn startled me. I nervously laughed as I darted toward Da Nise and Kathy.

"When it comes to dive bars, Long Beach has some of the best," Ria said.

"Oh-kay," I said.

"They don't have wine." Da Nise's braids swung over her shoulder when she shot me a look.

"Good. I'm sick of wine," I said.

"But if you want cheap beer, wild stories and, don't, well, um, mind the smell, or crowd, you're going to love LBCR," Ria said.

"And just so you know, there aren't any yuppies sitting around sipping a Cosmo and discussing the finer points of Paul Ryan, so if that's a problem…," Kathy said.

"Hold up." I stopped, and the trio turned toward me. "First off, yuppies have been replaced by hipsters—you're still living in the eighties. And secondly, what part of me screams yuppie or hipster, Republican or conservative, or even someone that's afraid of a dimly lit dive?" I straightened my posture and my camo backpack slid down my arm. I swung it back on my shoulder and crossed my arms over my chest.

"In case you missed it, my name's Rebel—not Rebecca, Randi, or something cute, popular, or cheerleaderish like Ricki. My mom wanted a girl that would rival any boy, so she named me Rebel Jean. So maybe you three could stop jawing off and get us to this skanky pit so you can each buy me a shot. Unless of course, you'd rather shoot the shit because God knows you guys know how to do that." I raised an eyebrow and Da Nise grinned.

"Okay, then," Kathy said. "May I offer one last piece of advice?"

I uncrossed my arms. "Go ahead."

"People will offer you pizza and such," Kathy said. "But don't *ever* eat anything at Club Roar."

I shrugged. "I'm not hungry."

"Well, in case you are, don't," Da Nise said. "The bartender has a habit of putting shrooms on everything."

"And not the good ones," Kathy said.

I nodded. "Good to know."

There are places where even an alcoholic would rather be sober than set foot into because the bar floor was so sticky that they'd probably lose a shoe before they gained a buzz, and the Long Beach Club Roar was that place. It was the classic dive bar down to the $1 Busch beer and the local favorite, Milk of Amnesia—a combo of Fireball, rum, and milk. It made my stomach curdle just thinking about it. But the bar was well stocked. I saw a few personal favorites on the shelf.

I followed the girls and I turned heads, but not in the good way. It was in the what-the-hell-are-you-doing-here way, which was when I realized I was the only white person in the place.

I tugged on Ria's blousy top. "What the fuck? Is this a black bar?"

She grinned. "We don't see color here."

"Sure, because you blend in and I stick out like a neon sign in Amish country," I said.

Old-time pictures of Long Beach hung on the wood-paneled walls and the only white thing in the black-and-white photos was the moon shining in the distance and the moonshine in the Mason jars. *I'm fucked.*

"Milo, we'll take a round of Busch in a schooner," Kathy said and placed a twenty on the bar.

I reached into my backpack for my wallet, but Da Nise gently stayed my hand. "It's tradition. You don't pay."

"Somehow, I'm thinking I'm going to pay for this later," I said, and they laughed.

"Rebel Jean, sit your ass down here and let's see what you're made of," Ria said. "Milo, we're going to need four shots of that yummy rum."

I hopped on the barstool and placed my backpack at my feet. Three heads shook at me.

"Do we have to teach you everything?" Kathy said.

"What?"

"Leave it on the floor and money's out the door." Da Nise handed me my bag. "Keep it on your lap or on your back, but don't *ever* set your purse or Army pack down."

"It's not an Army pack, it's a camo-colored backpack," I said, and realized there wasn't much of a difference.

"Whatever you call that thing," Da Nise said. "If you leave your purse on the floor, money's out the door."

"You mean people will steal your wallet?" I picked up my backpack just as the largest glass was placed toward me.

"Stop asking questions and drink," Kathy said.

I raised the glass that was large enough to float a boat, which was probably why they called it a schooner, but I was more than ready to set sail.

CHAPTER 11
RYAN

Sullivan's patio bar on the marina stayed open until 2:00 a.m. and the Dirtbags usually closed it down. For a bar, it was considered upscale, even trendy. It wasn't that way in college when they offered buck beers, but like most things in Long Beach, it got revitalized. Now it was an overpriced hipster hangout for the overindulgent.

"McHenry, how's your app going with LA Sheriff's department?" Patrick Flanagan had a knack for remembering what mattered to each of us. I didn't know how he did it when he outdrank us, only that he did. His sister, Katie, couldn't hold her alcohol as well. I went to high school with Katie, who was married and already expecting her first baby.

I smiled. "They haven't cut me."

Patrick raised his pint toward mine. "Then that's good news."

Our mugs clanked; beer spilled over the rim and down my hand. "Good thing I'm walking," I said, and the guys laughed.

"That's why they created Uber," Sam said.

"Or little sisters," Demi said with a nod toward Georgina, who was chatting up the bartender.

Since we'd arrived and the female bartender noticed Georgina, our rounds had been on the house. I wasn't crazy about what that meant for Georgina.

"She can handle herself," Demi said, as if reading my thoughts. "She's no one's fool."

I slowly nodded. "Yeah, but I'd feel better if we were paying."

"Jesus, McHenry, you're such a bleeding heart," Mike said.

"Fuck you, Murphy," I said, and his brother Sam looked at me. "What'd I do?"

"Not you, your shithead brother," I said, but Sammy still seemed confused. He never could handle his beer.

"How long you in town?" I asked him.

"The rain delay in Seattle put us back a week," he said. "But it gave us all time off the road, so can't argue that."

"I bet." I emptied my pint and pushed away the glass.

"Another round?" Patrick said.

"No." I clenched my fist and delivered a quick, sharp thumb up like an umpire calling someone out. "I'm outta here."

"What?" Sam said. "We just got here."

I glanced at my cell. "Uh, Sammy, like six hours ago. I've been here since five."

"Yeah, and in that time you've nursed three pints," Patrick said. "It's not even midnight."

I shrugged. "You know that the sheriff's office can randomly drug test me at any time during the application process. I don't want my blood alcohol content to rule me out before what could be the biggest career play of my life. I haven't gotten this far to blow it now."

"Smart thinking," Patrick said.

"Occasionally," I said, to the Dirtbags' amusement. "Besides, I still have to get my ass up tomorrow to move Lenny's truck back to the shop so I can get my car."

"One word," Mike said. "Uber."

"Two words," I said. "Fuck you."

Mike and I had been roommates in college. Sammy wasn't just two years ahead of us, he was also leagues ahead. Sammy was recruited for the minor leagues his junior year in college when the rest of us we were happy to make the college team as freshmen and be official Dirtbags.

"One more drink," Sammy said.

I was about to say yes when my cell buzzed with an incoming call. I glanced at the number. "Why would the hotel be calling me?"

CHAPTER 12
REBEL

"*It's Rafael, right?*" *I tried* to sound as sober as possible, but I wasn't sure if Rafael came out sounding like his name or if I was speaking in tongues, which sounded a lot better than slurred speech.

It was rare when I could see the top of a man's head, but Rafael wasn't very tall. Or at least, he was shorter than five foot six. I almost wanted to pat him on head to feel his shiny black hair. The thought made me chuckle, which I quickly choked down.

"Yes, it's Rafael." He was dressed in a security uniform complete with gloves, which would seem odd anywhere other than a Point Resort, where white glove service wasn't an expression but a literal part of the uniform.

"Uh, yes, well, you see, I made the mistake of parking on the lobby level in the garage and I just realized that after hours, cars are rerouted to the *back exit* of the hotel, which is fine, only I didn't know that. And instead of turning left to exit onto Broadway, I turned right and now I'm in an alley and there's a truck blocking my exit."

Rafael seemed to follow my stream-of-consciousness ramble.

"I saw it on the security feed," he said. "I don't know why you didn't back up."

"Well, that's the thing. If you saw me on the camera, you know I tried to back up, but there's a dumpster that I somehow skimmed past, but now it's *totally* in the way," I said, trying to keep a straight face when I suddenly wanted to burst out laughing. My driving skills were questionable at best when I was sober. "So, anyhoo…." I grinned. "It seems the only way to exit is to go forward—and to do that I kind of need that truck to skedaddle."

He slowly nodded. "I already called the delivery guy, Ryan McHenry, and you're lucky that he's still in the city." Rafael kept creating distance between us, which was when I realized I probably smelled like Club Roar.

"Thank you." I took a step back and lowered my chin so my breath would funnel toward the marble floor in the lobby. "I'm just going to actually park my car back in the hotel lot, if that's okay, and catch a cab home. I don't think I should be driving."

It was the only time he smiled. "That's probably a wise choice."

"Yeah, it's kind of how I messed up and got my car stuck." My voice cracked. "Please don't tell anyone, like Phil or his blonde troll." I lowered my voice and cupped my mouth with a hand as if what I was going to tell him was top secret. "That's what the girls downstairs call his assistant, Lisa—his blonde troll." I slapped my leg when I chuckled. "Troll. She's not even that short, but she is a bit statue-like. I mean really, who's *that* perfect. Am I right?"

"Lisa's my fiancée," Rafael said, and I thought he was joking so I burst out laughing. Only he didn't laugh too.

"Oh, really?" I already thought I was going to be sick, but now I was convinced I'd hurl all over the white marble. But I didn't because I vaguely remembered Ria telling me Rafael worked in security *and* maintenance. And I didn't want him left to clean up my mess or worse, step in any more of my disasters. "Lisa's *really* cute," I mumbled. "Okay, well, if you already phoned this Ryan guy, then I'll just go wait by my Bug."

"Lady, what's your problem?" A guy stood with his hands on his jeans-clad hips, his cap on backwards and an annoyed look on his face. "I could drive a semi through the space I left."

His angry tone was so unexpected that I stammered. "A… semi?"

I was met by his scoff. The guy actually scoffed at me. *Who is this asshat?*

"A semi?" I repeated, which didn't sound any better than the first time I muttered it. "Sure." I saluted him the way Kathy had when she left the bar to get high on what she explained was medical marijuana. "I'd like to see a semi squeeze through the space you left." I spun on the rubber heel of my clog and almost threw up from the sudden movement. I zigzagged toward my Bug, realizing I had no business even driving my car out of the alley.

"Ah, whatever," I said over my shoulder. "I don't need this tonight." I was walking toward my Bug to sleep it off when I heard footsteps behind me. I whipped my head around to find him closing in on me.

"What are you doing? Or do you just like to be difficult?" I knew the effects of the rum were coming to fruition when I began sounding like Jude. "Listen, asshat, I just want you to move your truck, but I guess that's too much to ask. That's gratitude, especially after I vouched for you today, too. *Jerk.*"

"What do you mean you *vouched* for me?"

If he puts his hands on his hips one more time, I'm going to loop my arm through one and do-si-do his skinny little white ass all the way to Wyoming.

"I. Vouched. For. You. Today." I bugged out my eyes. "Is that slow enough for you, Ryan, right? The delivery guy?"

"Uh, yeah."

"Or do you prefer McCutie?" I laughed or snickered, I'm not sure which.

"McCutie? It's McHenry. I don't even know you. And you don't even know me."

"Never a truer word spoken. But the women I work with in the hotel seem to like your office supply company, so despite the fact that you're probably ten times higher than Staples or Office Max, I told them they could keep their beloved McCutie with Burnetti & Sons if it made them happy." I paused. "And apparently you make them happy, which is lost on me, but *they* like you."

"They said that?" Shock was hard to fake and he wore it.

"Ah," I waved my hand, "don't let McCutie go to your head. I gave my word that they could keep you—or rather you as a vendor, and I don't go back on my word. So, there's gratitude for ya."

"Oh." His hands dropped along with his edgy tone.

"*Oh?*" I rolled my eyes. "So, now do you think you could move your truck so I could get home?"

"No." His cap moved back and forth, and I was either hallucinating or the adjustable strap on his cap changed colors from blue to white.

I exhaled. "You're annoying, you know that?" I aimed my remote key fob toward my bug, but the beep-beep that it was unlocked didn't happen. *Or is that what happens when I lock it?*

"I'm not moving my truck, because you're too drunk to drive," he said.

"*Am I?*" I took a staggering step toward him. "I'd like you to know that when the girls took me out tonight to welcome me to Long Beach, I handled three shots of rum." I raised three fingers. "Two Busch beers in a schooner large enough to launch the Queen Mary." I popped up two more fingers, "and a partridge in a pear tree, which," I raised a sixth finger, "is actually the name of a drink with vodka, peach something, grapefruit something, 7-Up, and a twist of a pear." I smiled proudly at remembering the vile drink. "But a partridge in a pear tree sounded a lot better than the Milk of Amnesia. So, I may be a little drunk, but I'm not tipsy."

His laughter was this unexpected blend of masculinity and sensuality that made my stomach stir. Or maybe it was the grapefruit juice. *That shit's nasty.*

"What are you laughing at?" I asked.

"That'd be you."

"Thanks." I saluted him again. "But I'm heading to my car for a little catnap." And then—and I'll never really know why—I meowed. But it was as if I was speaking a foreign language and he needed pantomime to explain my words and meaning. I looked at him, clawed my hand like a paw, and meowed like a cat.

His smile revealed a single dimple embedded in the side of his cheek that made my skin tingle. *Or maybe I'm allergic to pears. Why was there a pear in my drink?*

"I can't let you sleep in your car because you can be arrested for drunk driving," he said, and my stomach no longer tingled.

"Uh, no, I can't because I won't be driving, duh. I'll be sleeping. Sheesh." I aimed my key fob at my Bug, but again it didn't beep-beep.

"I think it's already unlocked," he said. "But, please, don't get inside your car. I noticed the new tags on your car and you mentioned that the girls were welcoming you to Long Beach, so I'm not sure if you're new to California, but in California, a driver can be arrested for a DUI if they are found sleeping inside their vehicle while intoxicated. There's actually a separate law that allows an officer to make an arrest for sleeping in a car, even if it's not running," he said.

"Who are you? Johnny law? Here I thought you were Burnetti or one of his worthless sons," I said.

"I'm not a deputy, but I hope to be one," he said. "I'm a candidate with the Los Angeles Sheriff's Department."

"Good for you." I walked toward him and pointed my key fob directly at him. "And when you're a sheriff you can arrest me."

"There's only one sheriff. The rest of us are deputies," he said.

"Great, well, until then," I shook my key fob, "leave. Me. Alone. I've had enough cops and Feds telling me what to do for a lifetime. You guys think you know what's best. *But you don't.* And you never will. It's like you forget what it's like to be human." I dropped my head and the same alcohol that had fueled my anger now turned on me. The sadness and regret I'd been running from since Wyoming exploded inside me. My chest felt heavy and my eyelids no longer wanted to stay open. "I want to go home," I spoke into my chest, "not an empty apartment in a new town I don't even know. I want a home. I want *my* home."

"Okay." His hand was gentle on my shoulder. "Where is that, and I'll get an Uber. I'll even go with you to make sure you get there okay."

He gently tilted my chin and I locked on to his hazel eyes.

"No. I can't have you do that. It's not allowed. If I don't maintain a respectful distance with people I meet, the system may just be done with me." I raised my fist in the air like I was warring against the man, something I knew Kathy would do, but even I knew the gesture was meaningless.

"Why? I don't understand. Is that a hotel rule?" His face looked tanned, or maybe that was just his coloring, but it made the green in his eyes look brighter and the brown darker. His teeth were super white too.

My tongue rolled across the top of my teeth.

"Are you okay?" he asked, and I realized my mouth wasn't closed when I tongued my teeth.

"Yes." My tone was a bit snappier than I intended.

"Sorry," he said. "I just thought maybe you were going to

have a seizure."

"If I was going to have a Caesar I would have had it at lunch where they served one." I slapped my leg and threw my head back laughing. "Oh, that's good."

Like Rafael, he didn't appear to appreciate my humor, but I was grateful the booze had turned the happy switch back on.

"Hey, I was going to walk home before I got the call from the hotel to move my truck. Maybe I could walk with you?" he said.

"Sure, if you want to walk me to my car, I can't stop you." My car wasn't far away, but I took off on a dart. I moved with assurance, determined to get to my Bug before he did. I'd gone about twenty feet when the motion-detecting security light from the corner of the bank popped on and reflected on something shiny. I came to an abrupt stop and walked toward the sparkling object. It twinkled in the light like a star that had fallen from the sky. Suddenly, the hair on the back of my neck began to rise as I approached the dark mound.

The closer I got, the more he came into focus. I drew in a sharp breath. His dark jacket was open and his gray dress shirt was splattered with blood. His head was tipped back and his throat was red with an angry-looking mark that wrapped around his skin. There was a gash on his head that looked like it dented his skull. My eyes welled.

I know you. You were in the hotel outside Phil's office. You're the

Matrix man. What happened?

He lay lifeless in the alleyway between the hotel and the bank. He was positioned in the only spot in the chain link fence that had a passageway, I guess for patrons to move between the bank and the hotel without using Broadway. He clutched a silver cross that had been around his neck earlier in the day. His fingertips were blue, and when I crouched beside him, I realized his dark eyes were open.

"Shit!"

Startled, I jumped back on the heels of my clogs and lost my balance. I teetered toward the dead guy, but an arm pulled me back from falling. I regained my footing and quickly stood, turning right into the arms of the delivery guy.

CHAPTER 13
RYAN

Her breath lingered with the trace of stale beer and rum, but as she shivered in my arms, my first instinct was to protect her. And it had nothing to do with my training with the Sheriff's department.

I shielded her from the man, who I was fairly sure was dead. She looked up at me.

"He's…."

I nodded. "I think so, but we won't know for sure until the police and coroner arrive. I'll notify the hotel first."

"What?" Her body tensed in my arms. "Hotel? Police?" She pulled away and glanced at the man.

"The hotel needs to know since it's on their property, and I have to call the police to report the crime," I said.

"Crime?" She shook her head, and moonlight shone through ribbons of crimson hair that lay on her quaking shoulders. She slowly approached the man, carefully knelt before him, lowered her head, and appeared to be… saying a prayer? I wasn't sure. Only when she was through, she went from kneeling into squatting over him.

"What are you doing?"

She reached beneath his arms and began to drag him. When the light from the bank activated, she turned her head away from the glare. Or the cameras? I wasn't sure.

"You can't move the body. That's tampering with a crime scene," I said.

"No, actually, it's possibly destroying evidence," she said matter-of-factly.

"I can't let you do that," I said.

Her hair swung over her shoulder. "Listen, we're aiding a person in distress. We need to move him to a more lighted area by the bank to determine just how dead he is. I mean," she cleared her throat, "just how unresponsive he might be."

"Why the bank? Why not leave him here?"

She lugged him through the passageway of the chain-link fence until his body no longer straddled the opening between the two businesses. He was now clearly on bank property.

"Listen, if an, uh, unresponsive man is found on hotel property—it's bad. It's *really, really* bad."

"And it's not bad for the bank?" I removed my baseball cap and brushed my hair back, not that I needed to. Sweat began the moment she touched the dead guy.

"Ryan, right?"

"Yeah. And you are?"

"The hotel will lose customers and money if he's discovered on their property and it will bring a whole lot of attention that the Point doesn't need. Trust me on that." Her eyes were brown and when they honed in on me, it was as if she were pleading for help. I couldn't explain it, only that while her mouth said one thing her eyes relayed something else. "We don't want the hotel to lose customers and money when the bank already has their customers' money," she said with a humorless chuckle. "They don't have anything to lose. The hotel has everything to lose."

She brushed her hands against khaki pants that hung low on her hips and tucked her red top into the back of her waistband. She looked like she worked at Target, and I would have thought she did if she hadn't already told me she'd vouched for me with the hotel girls… which was when it hit me.

"You're Rebel. You're the new conference services manager."

Her face drained of color. "I've got to go."

"Wait." I stood in her path. "What's going on? You can talk to me." My mind flashed to the Sheriff's department's core values we memorized: integrity, courage, professionalism, respect, accountability, compassion. *Compassion. She's scared.* "I thought we were making a connection."

"Sure, because nothing stirs heat like a stiff one."

My smile was a natural reaction. Rebel was quick with a comeback, and when I grinned her ashen face softened.

"You can't leave," I said.

"But I don't want to stay," she said.

"I understand."

Worry lines stretched across her forehead as she tried to blink away tears.

"Rebel, it's okay. I've never seen a dead guy either," I said.

Her hair brushed her shoulders. "I wish I never moved my car."

She turned toward her Bug. I gently reached for her arm and caught her wrist. She didn't pull away.

"Rebel, just stay with me and I'll tell the police I found the body," I said, knowing that I'd be violating the honor code, which was a critical component in the application process to become a deputy. Still, she hesitated. "I'll keep you completely out of it."

"If they take too long to show up, I'm outta here," she said.

"This is Long Beach, and if there's more than one dead body reported over the scanner, it would be an anomaly. Still, the local newspaper will call it a crime wave. Trust me, the cops will be here before you know it."

The door to the white morgue van shut. The taillights glowed in the bank's parking lot when it drove slowly away.

"Deputy Trainee McHenry."

I turned to find Deputy Stanley. The light from the bank shone on his spiky hair.

"Sir."

"Looks like you've had an interesting evening," he said.

I slowly nodded. "Yes, sir."

"Is this a good time to talk?" he said.

"Of course." I stepped from the shadows beside the chain-link fence and into the light.

"I know you've already spoken to my partner, Oscar, but I'd like to ask some additional questions," he said, and opened his hand-sized, department-issued notebook.

I knew the drill. Deputy detectives worked in pairs and Deputy Stanley and Deputy Gonzalez worked homicide. *But why are they in Long Beach?* This was not their jurisdiction.

"Did you know the man?" he asked.

"No."

Stanley tapped his pen against his notepad. "You didn't recognize him?"

I shook my head. "No, sir, should I?"

Stanley closed his notebook. "McHenry, the man you found was your uncle's partner—Bernie Thomas. He recently retired from the department."

I took a staggering step back like Stanley had punched me in the gut. "That was Bernie?" I lifted my cap, brushed my hair back, and placed it back on. Even though the county coroner had taken him, my focus strayed to where Rebel had discovered him. "I haven't seen Bernie since my uncle's funeral, and that was…."

"More than twenty years ago, I know."

"I was nine." I was instantly transported to fourth grade and the day my dad unexpectedly showed up at school. His eyes were bloodshot and his hands had trembled. *"It's Uncle Mark. He's been killed."*

Stanley gripped my shoulder. "You okay?"

"That's why you're here," I said, and he nodded.

"When the responding officer recognized Bernie, he contacted dispatch immediately. When it's one of our own, nothing else matters."

His grasp on my shoulder tightened. "You're certain nothing else happened here tonight?" He cocked his head toward Rebel.

I shook my head. "No, it's like I told Deputy Gonzalez, I was called to move my truck and when I arrived, she was already in her car waiting to exit."

His dark eyes focused on me. "The hotel provided us with her info." He released my shoulder, opened his notepad, and thumbed through a few pages. "Here it is. Rebel Roberts. She just began working at the hotel—transfer from their Napa hotel. Is there anything you can tell us about Ms. Roberts?"

There was a lot I could tell—like how she discovered my uncle's former partner and moved him off hotel property. Or how she lost her shit when I mentioned calling the cops. But instead, I steadied Deputy Stanley in my sights and honored my word to her.

"No, sir. When I found him, uh, Bernie, I asked Ms. Roberts to stay in her car." The adrenaline that had coursed through my veins turned to sludge. I still couldn't believe the man was Bernie. "He had a cross." The thought came out of my mouth. "He was holding it."

"It's been bagged," Deputy Stanley said.

"I remember my family called him the preacher," I said to Stanley's nod.

Deputy Stanley said, "Okay," but continued to stand in front of me like things weren't okay. And they weren't. My uncle's partner was dead less than a block from where my uncle lost his life twenty years ago trying to protect a woman and her child from a convenience store robbery gone wrong.

I stared at the forensics team working the "canvas," as they called the crime scene, and uttered the next thought that came into my mind. "I don't think Rebel's in any shape to drive."

"Agreed," Deputy Stanley said, and lightly whacked my shoulder with his notebook. "You handled this situation well tonight, McHenry. From contacting the local authorities and then staying with the body to preserve the crime scene, fine work."

Not really. I looked away from the fence where blue fluorescent lights highlighted the ground in search of trace evidence and stared directly at the man who oversaw my application and future, and owned the compliment I didn't deserve. "Thank you, sir."

CHAPTER 14
REBEL

McCutie drove with the windows down in my Bug and the radio off. I no longer felt drunk, but I'd probably fail a sobriety test. My hands shook as I dug through the bottom of my purse for a stray cigarette. "Fuck."

"What's wrong?" He shifted his focus from the road onto me.

I shook my head. "I'm out of my addiction."

"Alcohol?"

His candor made me laugh. "No, cigarettes. I usually don't drink—that much."

"You said the Franklin, right?"

"Correct," I said with my sights set on locating a butt somewhere in my car.

"I didn't know the hotel paid that well." Normally, his directness would rub me wrong, but after I moved a corpse and he covered for me, which could curtail his career plans, I guessed he'd earned the right to bluntly ask any question that suddenly popped to mind. The courtesy filter for questions had died like the man I moved.

Besides, I knew what he was thinking. The Franklin was marketed as cutting-edge apartments. Located in the first treasury building in Long Beach, the Franklin had been transformed into an upscale residential community. Or so the glossy brochure that Jude provided promised. She'd been the one to find the secured building and agreed to pay the first six months of rent. But after that, I was responsible for the two grand a month to live in a one-room apartment. I certainly couldn't tell McCutie that the price to live in a secured building came at much higher cost than two grand. So I told him a partial truth.

"I'm able to live at the Franklin because of an inheritance that just matured," I said.

"Huh," he said, less than convincing.

Fuck me. The guy was going to make a great cop or deputy or whatever he was applying for.

"Yup," I said. "I made money off money." I laughed, but he didn't.

His hazel eyes questioned me like a human lie detector so I

stuck to partial truths.

"I found that when you're investing an inheritance with an investment firm," I said of my inherited relationship with Jude, "you ask for all you can and settle for what terms they offer."

He remained silent.

"So I'm making the most of it by having six months of living the high life in the high rise," I said honestly.

Not surprisingly, the truth seemed to satisfy his curiosity. "You know your apartment is only a short walk to the hotel," he said.

"If I knew all the side streets and shortcuts of Long Beach, yes, but I don't. I'm also within walking distance to the beach. But after tonight, I'm not going near any alley or back street ever again." I pulled out the ashtray, and there wasn't anything in there except some spare change that wouldn't even be enough to buy a loosie from the corner liquor store.

My blonde-brick apartment building came into view. And the dead man's face suddenly flashed in my mind. I closed my eyes to shut him out, but his dead eyes stared back at me. I shuddered.

"Listen, I'll see you up to your apartment," he said, and I didn't argue.

I fumbled retrieving the card key from my wallet. My fingers didn't want to work. They kept shaking. I pulled the card out, and it flew in the air, falling by his feet. He palmed the floorboard until he found it.

"It's okay," he said.

It's what I'd say to him if it were true. But it wasn't. Jude would be all over my shit within a matter of hours. My reassigned surname was on a police report, which would wave all sorts of red flags. *Shit.*

When he handed me back my card key, I made eye contact with him. "Thank you, McCutie." I was still trying on names for him. McCutie seemed a better fit than Ryan or McHenry, which were common names for a regular guy, and he was neither. That I already knew.

Plus, it caused him to chuckle. He placed the card key into the parking lot gate and the security fence slowly opened. My Bug dipped into the subterranean parking structure that seemed like the only part of the renovation that was forgotten. The overhead fluorescent lights flickered like bad strobe lighting and hurt my eyes to navigate. But he kept his word, and after he parked my car, he got out and walked beside me. When we reached the elevator lobby, which was well-lit, I breathed a bit easier.

Still, he followed me into the chrome elevator that led to myriad levels of escapism: shopping, dining, the cultural art center and, of course, the pathway to the beach. To access my studio apartment, I had to place my parking key into the slot into the elevator, but my hands continued to shake. He gently reached for the key and inserted it for me. I pressed nine. The fourteen-story building reserved the top four floors for the two- and three-story penthouse townhomes. The monthly rent for those floors began at five thousand, which sadly really didn't seem high after leaving Napa. The rooftop, though, was available for all tenants. And right about now, a swim in the rooftop pool sounded like a sobering idea.

My hands would not stop trembling, so when we reached my corner apartment, I handed him the key.

The main room was carpeted and still carried that "new" smell that greeted me when he opened the door. I turned toward him, but I didn't know what to say.

He closed the door behind him, and having him in my empty apartment was a welcome change to being alone. It felt like I was always alone. Working at a hotel was nice because I was surrounded by people. But nights sucked. Whether I was in Napa or Long Beach, there came a point when it was just me and my mind.

"Do you have any water?" he asked.

I nodded.

The kitchen and bathroom were modern, which meant small but stylish. The polished concrete floors in each of the rooms was unwelcoming in the middle of the night when the temperature dropped and the floor was icy to the touch.

I grabbed a bottle of water from the refrigerator and handed it to him.

"All I want to do is burn my clothes and wash away this night," I said.

"Maybe a shower first?" His logic was disarming.

I softly laughed. "Yeah." But I was afraid to go into the bathroom, which was tucked in a back corner of the apartment, because it was dark.

"Don't these pricey apartments have a washer and dryer unit stacked in some closet?" He glanced past me toward the bathroom and the laundry closet. He palmed the wall until the lights burned overhead and shut out the darkness.

"Nice view," he said, stepping into the main room toward the floor-to-ceiling windows that looked out to Long Beach. The city still sparkled despite the fact that one man's light was extinguished.

I didn't want him to leave. I wasn't ready to face the rest of the night and the images that kept entering my mind. I went to the record player I'd picked up at a secondhand store in Napa and gently pulled a record from its sleeve. *Nina Simone.*

Her voice filled the space between us like a cry in the dark. Brass struck up behind her in a bold, powerful downpour of blues.

"Probably a cliché," I said, "but tonight her music seems right."

"Not a cliché," he said with a kindness in his voice that was so different than the angry tone I first encountered from him. "Jimi Hendrix once said the blues were easy to play, but hard to feel."

I slowly exhaled as Nina Simone's simple, beautiful lyrics fit the mood. A piano fluttered like my heart that gradually returned to a steady beat. I closed my eyes and let the magnitude of her voice carry me away. Her pain was relatable—at least tonight. The city buzzed outside my apartment, but for a moment everything stopped spinning out of control. When the song ended and the next one cued up, I opened my eyes and he was staring at me. He wasn't McCutie or McHenry.

"Ryan," I began. "Would you mind hanging out until I get out of the shower?"

"Of course." His inclination to protect was natural.

He stood in front of the window while I made my way to the bathroom, where I pulled off my shirt, and my necklace floated in the air like a warning. I reached for the small cross I wore under my shirt and my thumb gently slid across the polished rose gold. It shone, and so did my reflection in the bathroom mirror. My mascara was streaked and black eyeliner smeared my eyelids. Instead of a sultry, smoky look, I looked like a junkie and probably smelled worse.

I kicked off my shoes, pulled down my socks, and let my feet sink into the lush throw rug. I couldn't erase his dead face from my memory or the feel of his clammy skin when I'd moved him. I shuddered but the chill ran deep.

I inched off my khakis, practically ripped my bra trying to unhook it, and I may have torn my lace panties. I didn't care. I stuffed everything into the deep drum of the washing machine, turned the dial to hot, poured in a cupful of detergent, and hit Start.

Naked, I stood in the small hallway between the shower and Ryan. The feel of the dead man's skin clung to me like film. I stepped into the shower and let the hot water wash over me. I lowered my head and my chest shook.

"Why did I move him?" The night washed away and shame surfaced. *Have I become so concerned about my welfare that I forgot human decency?* The man deserved to be left alone. "What have I done?"

There was self-preservation and then selfishness. Big shit if a dead man was found on the hotel property; I didn't have anything to do with it. But now I did. Now, I placed myself into a crime scene. *And it had to be a crime, right?* His head had looked dented. And the blood. *There was so much blood on his shirt.*

I grabbed the loofah and scrubbed from my scalp down to my toes, but I still felt dirty. I stepped from the shower into a gray plush towel—one of the few bonuses from working at a five-star hotel. The towels were from the Napa property. When they replaced their towel supply, the purchasing department allowed employees to buy the old stock. It'd probably gross other people out, but these towels were like 1,000 percent Egyptian cotton. They were so soft, and as I stepped into my shared living and bedroom, I felt wrapped in luxury even if I didn't feel like I deserved it.

He turned and I no longer saw a cute guy in a baseball hat

and jeans, but a man who had kept me from doing more damage, like leaving a crime scene. I didn't want him to go, but asking him to stay…. It felt needy. And there was nothing worse than being needy. *I'd rather do anything than ask for help.* So, I walked toward him and let the towel drop.

RYAN

Her milky skin looked as untouched and innocent as her eyes that bored into mine. Her hourglass shape had dips and curves in all the right places. Her breasts were like forbidden fruit waiting for my reach. And the thin strip of dark hair could have been an arrow for where it directed my attention. But her eyes. *Fuck, if her eyes don't say something else.*

Her eyes spoke to me, and behind the canvas of her fair face the hollow look of fear that she wore like second skin shifted. It wasn't dramatic, but a small spark flickered with life. A life that I sensed had seen too much and was trying to get to a better place. And while I knew she was offering herself to me, I also knew sex was not the right course of action. Not now. It'd only be a temporary fix.

So, despite the fact that she stood baring herself to me, I looked past her nakedness to what spoke the loudest. A soul in need of rest. I walked toward her and slowly led her to the Murphy bed. I pulled back the comforter, and she collapsed on the mattress. Her head sank on the stack of pillows. I covered her bare skin with the white down comforter.

There was no need for lights when the skyline illuminated her apartment.

"Will you stay?" It was the softest she'd spoken all night.

"Wouldn't think of leaving." I sat on the edge of the bed.

"Who do you think hurt him? From all the blood on his shirt and the gash in his head, it looked like he had been hit—hard. Why would someone do that?"

"I don't know."

Her eyes were almost as haunting as Bernie's vacant stare.

"I'm sorry I moved him," she said, and a tear fell down her cheek. She quickly wiped it away. "I shouldn't have done that."

"Probably not," I said. "But at least you stayed until the police arrived."

She nodded and turned her head toward the record player where Nina Simone filled the room with the blues. She closed her eyes, and when she drifted off to sleep I moved to the couch, where I pulled out my phone and searched online for "Rebel Roberts, Napa Valley, California." Nothing materialized. I googled her first and last name separately, and still nothing. I searched all forms of social media to cover my bases and struck out. It was as if she didn't exist. She was either not who she said she was, or she had succeeded at being electronically invisible. *Who lives off the grid? And why?*

CHAPTER 15
REBEL

I *t felt like someone had* stepped inside my soul and shaken it awake. Startled, I woke from the nightmare to find Ryan on the couch. His head was back and his mouth was open. My apartment remained cloaked by moonbeams. I quietly got out of bed and tiptoed toward my backpack, abandoned by the front door. I grabbed my cell phone and headed to the bathroom where I reached for my robe. I wasn't nearly awake enough to deal with the fact that I'd stood naked in front of a virtual stranger, who now snored on my couch. Even for me, that was a first.

I slipped on my robe and returned to bed, where I searched on my phone for any news on the dead man. I found the Long Beach

Police Department's Facebook page.

The latest post was about a gunshot victim found in Signal Hill. I scrolled to their website, but it was after four in the morning and nothing current appeared. I returned to their Facebook page, hit refresh, and a new post surfaced.

PUBLIC'S HELP SOUGHT IN LOCATING ANY WITNESS TO POSSIBLE HOMICIDE

My heart jumped to my throat. I quickly sat up and began reading.

Dead body found in Long Beach, CA: A 68-year-old African-American man was found dead and abandoned in downtown Long Beach, CA.

"The body was discovered around midnight Friday evening by someone moving their car just south of Ocean Boulevard," said Lt. Stanley of the Los Angeles County Sheriff Department. Currently, the name of the man has not been released.

"When officers arrived, they found the body in the alley. The cause of death appears to be homicide," he said. No estimate was given for how long the body had been in the alley.

The LBPD and the Los Angeles County Sheriff's Department are asking for the public's help in locating any witnesses.

Anyone who has information regarding the circumstances of this crime is urged to contact Los Angeles County Sheriff's Homicide Detectives Oscar Gonzalez or William Stanley. Anonymous tips may be submitted through LA Crime Stoppers, calling the toll-free number or downloading the P2 Tips app to your smart phone.

Check back with LBLN for updates on this story.

My focus returned to the first quote and my breathing intensified.

"The body was discovered around midnight Friday evening by someone moving their car just south of Ocean Boulevard."

Ryan was only moving his truck because of me. I also knew he was to thank for keeping me out of the police spotlight. I skimmed to the only other part of the story that jumped out at me.

"No estimate was given for how long the body had been in the alley."

I leaned against the wall that served as the headboard for the Murphy bed. We left the hotel at five for Club Roar, and I returned just past eleven. Ryan showed up about a half hour later and after we exchanged insults—or rather I did—it was probably close to midnight.

"So, he was killed or left to die sometime between five and eleven?" I spoke louder than I intended.

"Closer between five thirty and nine thirty, or between ten thirty and eleven," Ryan said, wiping his eyes.

"I'm sorry," I said softly. "Go back to sleep."

He sat up with a stretch. His arms were long and flexed impressively beneath the sleeves of his shirt.

"Nah, I wasn't sleeping," he said.

I chuckled. "So, snoring is something you do when you're awake?"

His face was masked in shadows, but his smile wasn't.

"Thank you," I said.

He leaned forward on the couch. "For?"

"Well, uh." I slightly tugged on my robe as if that would explain my utter embarrassment for standing naked in front of him. But Ryan said nothing and I sensed he never would.

"Thanks for being one of the good guys," I said, but he remained politely quiet on the subject. "So, why do you think he was killed between those random hours?"

"They aren't random. The shifts at the hotel are six to two, eight to five, two to ten, and ten to six. Granted, employees enter through the back, but the alley is used pretty heavily for smoking before and after a shift. So he was either killed after five and before ten, or after ten thirty and before eleven, because that's when security logged your visit."

"And… you know the shifts of the hotel, why?"

"Well, I've been making deliveries there ever since I was in college, and then training with the department, we're always told to be observant. That's when I began noticing how many people smoke and I soon realized it happened before or after a shift."

"Huh. And you think the Matrix man was killed between shifts?" I said.

"The Matrix man?"

"Yeah, when I first saw him he reminded me of Laurence Fishburne in *The Matrix*," I said.

"Morpheus?"

I shrugged. "If that's his name in the movie, yeah."

"When you saw him tonight, he reminded you of Morpheus?"

I shook my head. "I saw him earlier today."

This caught Ryan's attention. He practically popped off the couch and moved to the edge of the bed, where he sat and pulled out his phone. "Go back to the beginning and tell me everything you remember." His finger remained poised above the screen.

I slowly exhaled. "After I met with Phil—"

"Phil?" He stopped texting himself or typing a note—I wasn't sure which.

"Greenberg. He's the director of conference services at the Point," I said, adding, "and my boss."

"Greenberg." Once he noted it in his phone he glanced up, "Okay, go on."

"Anyway, I was leaving his office because he had a restoration committee meeting," I said.

"Restoration?"

I nodded. "Yeah, because Lisa—that's his admin assistant – first called it a revitalization meeting and then corrected herself. And that's when Lisa told Phil that—" I hit the mattress with my hand. "*Bernie!* That's his name. The dead guy. His name is Bernie." I smiled, but my revelation didn't seem to impress Ryan. "Anyway, Lisa called him 'Bernie' and I turned toward the hallway and saw him pacing."

"And why was he there?"

"Uh, Lisa said that every week, Phil had to meet with the restoration committee and that's why Lisa was reminding Phil because Bernie was waiting. He paced the hallway outside Phil's office and with long, black jacket and circular glasses, I dunno, he had this well-polished look that caught my attention like Morpheus in that movie."

Ryan seemed to absorb everything. "Wait," he tilted his head, "did you say he had on glasses?"

My eyes widened. "Yes! He did. He had on these circular-shaped glasses just like Laurence Fishburne. But he didn't have any glasses on tonight."

"No, he didn't."

"And his cross. That's the other thing. It was in his hands, but earlier today, it was on this chain that hung on his chest and when he paced, it swayed. It was almost hypnotic."

"Interesting."

"I know, right? Why would someone want to kill some old guy on a restoration committee?" I said.

"Because before he was an old guy, he was a deputy," Ryan said, and I was pretty sure my mouth fell open.

"Wow. Did that cop tell you that?" I thought back to how much time Ryan had spent speaking to the cops.

"Deputy Stanley mentioned it," he said.

"Why?" Something didn't add up. "Why would he tell you that Bernie was a cop? I mean, I know you're applying for the department, but that seems like inside information? They didn't even release his name in their Facebook post or on their website."

Ryan sat for a moment without responding. He seemed to be weighing his options. *That's cool.* If he was expecting me to change the subject because of his silence, he had another thing coming. Silence may be golden, but gold melts, especially when I applied the heat. Hell, a statue in a library would be told to "Sssh" if I grilled it for answers. I raised an eyebrow and made direct eye contact to indicate I wasn't about to let this go.

"And…."

"Bernie Thomas was my uncle Mark's former partner," he said.

I sat forward with the weight of his reveal. "Oh." *Not what I expected.* "I'm sorry. Your uncle must be pretty upset."

A weary frown tugged at his lips. "My uncle died twenty years ago in the line of duty."

"Fuck."

"Yeah, which is probably why Bernie's name wasn't mentioned in the article. I'm sure they want legit tips called in and not a bunch of whack jobs keying off about something Bernie did to their second cousin once removed."

I gently smiled. "So… your uncle." I paused and glanced at Ryan's face. If there was any indication that this wasn't a topic he wanted to talk about, I'd back off. But I was met with compassionate hazel eyes that seemed to want to talk. "What happened?"

"He was off duty and went to buy a can of chew at the convenience store on the shore when a guy entered with a gun. My uncle tried to break up the robbery, gunfire ensued, and he was killed, but so was the shooter. But," Ryan cleared his throat, "a mother and her little girl who were in the store weren't injured. My uncle saved their lives and lost his in the process."

"God, I can't imagine." I'd never taken a bullet for anyone. The only thing I could relate to was sacrificing the life I knew trying to protect someone. I had to leave my family, friends, and my life in Wyoming and assume a new last name. They let me keep my first name because apparently it was a thing with the FBI, which Jude reminded me was a good thing. If I was with the Witness Security Program or WITSEC, my new last name would be a forever thing. But since I didn't need 24/7 protection, my false identity was only a temporary thing until I testified. So until then, I was Rebel Roberts. The only Roberts I knew were the Robertson brothers from Robertson Trucking Company in Wyoming. My new surname was either Jude's attempt at humor or payback—it was hard to tell with her. Still, I was above ground and breathing. Ryan's uncle and now his uncle's former partner weren't as lucky.

"What convenience store?" I asked. "I haven't been in Long Beach long but I've only spotted like three in the downtown area and only two of them sell single cigarettes."

"It used to be on the boardwalk until the city revitalized the shore. It was a mom and pop place less than a block from your hotel."

"It's not my hotel," I said, a bit too defensively for someone who had dragged a dead guy off the hotel's property. I swiped the air with my hand as way of an apology. "Sorry. When I think of *my* hotel, I think of Napa." It was the truth, but the way Ryan steadied me in his sights, something again didn't feel right.

"Napa, huh?"

I slowly nodded. "Yup. I worked in the wine caves."

"And before that?"

I answered per the script Jude had written for Rebel Roberts.

"College," I said with complete conviction. It was also the truth. I went from high school into college. Four years later, I jumped into the corporate world. Or as corporate as Wyoming possessed. Still, to land a position as CFO for a regional trucking company like Robertson wasn't shabby for a rural kid like me. Who knew I'd discover that the truckers were transporting more than what was listed on their loading manifests. *Fuck me and my forensic accounting skills.* But it was why I liked math. Math was perfection; math was universal. It was never subjective and never changed. So when something didn't add up, then north must be south because erroneous accounting called correct turned my world upside down. And when that happened, I had two choices—either accept the inconceivable or put on my miner's helmet and be prepared to dig through a shit ton of accounting figures to figure out what was really going on. Yet, after all that math mining, I was the one who got the shaft. Now I had a name not even a stripper would claim.

"I went to Long Beach State," he said by way of a less-than-subtle inquiry.

"Chadron State College," I said and watched his face as he tried to make a state connection. "Nebraska. Small college football and agricultural—the best of everything."

"Agricultural?"

I grinned. "Yeah, before the hotel life grabbed me, I envisioned life as an ag reporter—covering farms across the western United States."

"Huh."

I nodded. "I know, thrilling, which is why when the Point hosted a table and interviews at our college recruitment day, I checked them out."

That part was true. The Point had arrived at Chadron, but they weren't interested in my undergraduate degree in finance. They wanted someone with a background in hospitality. Jude had kept my new life similar to my own, I guess so I could sell it.

"Rebel Roberts, that's a memorable byline," he said, throwing in some journalism lingo. The guy was good.

"I suppose," I said. "But any editor worth their salt would probably want me to change it to R. Roberts—you know, like E.B. White or C.S. Lewis—to keep it gender neutral." Fuck if I knew what editors wanted or why two of my favorite childhood authors used their initials, but it sounded legit.

"Sure," he said to another lie I peddled his way. "And your parents?"

"Dead." Another Jude spin.

"Both of them? *Both* your parents are dead?"

I slowly nodded. "Killed in a car accident when I was younger. I was raised by my aunt." *Fuck, did Jude take my story from Spider-Man? The backstory she created has all the misery and woe of a superhero and, likewise, none of the believability. While the truth may be stranger than fiction, nothing is quite as unbelievable as a science fiction-worthy backstory.*

When Ryan didn't say anything, I found myself biting my lip.

"It sounds worse than it is," I said. "I mean, I was so young, I barely remember my parents. And my aunt Bea was really great."

Bea? Why not Auntie Em and we could throw *The Wizard of Oz* into this shit show.

Lying was exhausting. I leaned against the wall and fatigue sank into me with the weight and burden of a hangover—my body ached, my head hurt, my eyes burned, and I was pretty sure alcohol seeped out of my pores from the actual hangover I had. Exhaustion simply added a new layer to the fog. I wanted to tuck back into bed and sleep away the last twenty-four hours. I didn't want to lie anymore to anyone but what choice did I have? Until the Robertson brothers were securely behind bars and not out on bail awaiting trial, I was stuck.

"Thank you for covering for me tonight." It was one of the few truths of the evening.

"I gave you my word and I don't break my word."

I tugged on the comforter to pull it toward me and cover the chill that seemed present in my bones, but his ass weighed the blanket down. I cleared my throat and nodded toward his well-defined butt. "Help a girl out?"

"And here I thought I already had."

I faintly smiled. No matter how kind, charming, or considerate Ryan McHenry was, there wasn't any space in my life for him.

"Hey, you know… I'm okay now." I swung my feet off the bed and headed toward the door like we hadn't shared the once-in-a-lifetime experience of finding a dead guy. "Thanks for staying, but it's almost light out and…."

"Of course." He opened his wallet and placed a card on the counter that extended from my kitchen and served as my dining room table. "Back in college, we had to have business cards made for a class—so while it's a bit old-school, all the relevant info is the same." He shrugged. "You know, if you need anything."

I glanced at the black card with gold lettering. "Dirtbags?"

"It's the baseball team for Long Beach State."

I chewed on my lip because I didn't know what to say or do.

"Anyway, if you need anything, text or email—whatever." He lifted his cap, brushed back his dark hair, and put it back on.

I wanted to wrap my arms around him and hug him. Kiss his cheek. Something. Anything. As sorry as I was to send him off, and as much as I wanted such a gorgeous distraction from the ugliness I'd escaped from, I needed to stay focused.

I'm walking a tightrope and I can't let my mind or eyes wander, regardless of how wonderful he seems. When this nightmare was finally over then maybe I could dream about a future. *And I hope he's still around then, but if I keep letting my guard down by keeping him close, there may not be a future for me.*

So, I did what I had to do. I opened the door and let my midnight hero walk away.

CHAPTER 16
RYAN

ebel. If that was really her name. But who would come up with a name like Rebel? I laughed. *Rebel.* It didn't take the academy's course in profiling for me to read that her personality—while guarded now—probably wasn't always that way. Her energy was electric and like electricity, she was someone who couldn't be contained. Nor should she be. So why was she holed up on the ninth floor in one of the priciest, snobbiest apartment rentals in Long Beach?

The only thing that remotely looked personal in her corner studio was the tattered record player. Everything else looked sterile—like a model apartment shown to prospective tenants, not someone's home. It lacked her imprint. I sensed from her red, almost maroon hair, her older convertible Bug, and acknowledged cigarette addiction that Rebel was not colorless. She was wildly free and bohemian-like. There were contradictions and then there were complete inconsistencies. *Rebel Roberts, who are you?*

I rode the elevator to the lobby level and nodded toward the security guard, who had either woken up from his overnight shift or was just arriving. It was hard to tell. Yet it was another thing I wouldn't have noticed before beginning the application process for the sheriff's department.

Now, the sheriff's department drilled those of us that remained in the process as if we had passed and were deputies-in-training. Observation skills were always stressed. But so was something else—coincidence. I pulled up the note section on my phone and read the summary from one of Deputy Stanley's lectures about crime and coincidence.

You're better off believing in Santa Claus than in coincidences. The former means you're ignorant and the latter means you're incompetent. And while there's no shortage of dumb cops, we'll never tolerate incompetence. Two crimes committed similarly or with similar traits isn't a coincidence—or random—it's the MO, the modus operandi, of the criminal.

My uncle died by an armed robber less than a block away from where his partner was killed. *That can't be a coincidence, could it?* Twenty years later and his partner was tragically murdered. *What ties them together?* I closed the training notes and opened a new tab in my phone, hit the microphone button, and spoke as I walked. My cell phone transcribed my thoughts.

"Okay, technically they were both off duty—even retired cops remain cops. They were both killed in downtown Long Beach." I paused and let the screen fill with my notes before I resumed talking. I was the only person walking east on East Broadway. When it connected with Atlantic Avenue, I turned right. I walked through that period between night and day where the sky shifted in shades of dark to light. And as the sidewalk crested over East First Street the ocean materialized in the distance.

The shore looked like a one giant parking lot for boats that were docked in the harbor. Long Beach was a boater's haven. Boats were protected from waves by the massive breakwaters. Surfers hated Long Beach. Before the seawalls were built, Long Beach was a long board surfing paradise. Now it was more of a boater's beach. Still, to be within walking distance to the Pacific was pretty sweet. I lived inland, but I always made sure one of my routes took me past the beach.

I watched a few early risers park along Ocean Boulevard and head toward the sand. It was quiet for a Saturday. I hit the record button and resumed talking.

"There weren't any witnesses in both crimes—or no known

witnesses at this time." I paused, remembering the mother and daughter who took cover behind the ice-cream freezer and closed their eyes when my uncle was killed. The mother claimed in the report I read that they didn't see anything, which made sense. *Why would she lie?* I turned the phone's recorder back on. "Two cops dead—one by an armed robber and the identity of the other assailant remains unknown."

What's the MO? I glanced at my notes—nothing popped out. Cops. No witnesses. Long Beach. I didn't have anything more than when I started. *Shit.*

I reached Ocean Boulevard and headed toward Lenny's truck that was still parked in the hotel's alley. It had been dusted for prints, which Lenny would not let me forget. Yellow crime scene tape, strung across the chain link fence, cordoned off the area between the hotel and the bank.

What are the odds of Rebel seeing Bernie earlier that day and then finding him dead later that night?

I knew from her reaction when she found him that Rebel wasn't responsible for his death; still, there was something unresolved about her. I didn't know what it was, but I intended to find out. Besides, it would give me another opportunity to see her.

CHAPTER 17
REBEL

"*The conference rooms get booked* probably more than the hotel rooms," Da Nise said as soon as I sat beside her with a cup of stale coffee from the employee cafeteria. I hated Mondays, but after my lost weekend, I was actually grateful for the routine.

"So, the key here is to upsell them. If someone calls looking for conference room space for their event, our job is to upsell them on a hotel room package." She stopped, crossed her ebony legs that shone beneath her cream-colored skirt, and took a sip of the oversized energy drink on the built-in counter we shared.

Her jacket matched her skirt, and a shimmery silver blouse that draped at her neck with a single strand of pink pearls was just one of the reasons she should have gotten the promotion. Da Nise dressed for success.

Still, sitting beside her admiring her attire, it was as if Bernie's death had never occurred. Da Nise was in full swing and neither she nor Ria had asked me about the dead guy. And better yet, Jude hadn't darkened my door. *Did it really happen?*

Kathy sauntered into the back administrative office in a pair of blue wide-legged pants that were covered in a white Hawaiian floral print and swished every time the crinkly fabric brushed against her skinny legs. Combined with her leather sandals that wrapped around her bony ankles and tangerine tie-dyed tee, she was sporting a beachy vibe that made me want to close the office and play hooky.

"Are those gauchos?" Da Nise leaned against her chair and studied Kathy's cropped pants.

"Dunno what you call 'em. I call 'em comfortable." She scratched her hair that still looked like it hadn't ever been brushed.

"Where'd you find them—Goodwill?" I now knew from hanging out with Da Nise at the bar that she just had a tone. From the way she eyed Kathy's pants she genuinely wanted to know where our resident hippie had scored her vintage clothes.

I was curious too. Despite barely sleeping all weekend and

never leaving my apartment, I'd managed to pull something together that didn't look like I worked at Target. Still, my green paisley printed dress that had a rounded neckline and white collar and hung past my knees looked absolutely Victorian, and made me feel old compared to Kathy's beach-inspired attire and Da Nise's chic suit.

"Goodwill? Nah." Kathy's head shook, but her locks stood still. "That place is overpriced. I found these at CC's Closet."

Da Nise snapped her fingers. "I always forget about CC's."

"Where's CC's?" I said.

"It's just a few blocks away. It's a used clothing store," Da Nise said.

I grabbed my phone and was about to text myself a note when I thought about Ryan and set down my phone. *Where is he and what is he doing?*

"You okay?" Kathy cocked her head toward me.

I nodded.

"Kind of a crazy weekend," she said.

When I didn't comment, she went on.

"Bernie didn't deserve what happened to him."

"Bernie? What that fool do now?" Da Nise said.

Kathy's dark eyes widened. "Bernie was killed and left by the bank."

Da Nise almost shot out of her chair. "No!"

Kathy frowned. "Afraid so."

"Gang related?" Ria popped her head around the door.

"Don't think so. A gun wasn't involved, which," she looked at me, "is pretty standard with gangs."

How'd she know he wasn't shot? That wasn't online, unless the police updated their feed. Bernie's vacant eyes burned in my memory and I shuddered.

"I hear you were there," Kathy said.

Da Nise switched her attention to me and Ria held up a finger. "Don't say anything until I answer that call."

While I waited for Ria to return, the awful weight of discovering Bernie's lifeless body pressed on my chest until it hurt to breathe. *Why did I have to find him?*

Ria reappeared and popped a root beer barrel into her mouth. She rubbed her ruby-stained lips together like she was savoring every taste.

Da Nise's pointy elbow struck out like a bird's wing. "Okay, spill."

I slowly exhaled, trying to temper my breathing. "Well, I left Club Roar before you guys and walked back to the hotel, got to my car, and…." I took a breath and tucked my hair behind my ear. "I didn't know how the parking garage exited—I mean whether I was supposed to turn left onto Broadway or right. I turned right and ended in the alley where Ryan's truck was parked."

"Ryan?" Ria said with an arched eyebrow.

I shrugged. "Yeah, he was there. He came after I asked Rafael to have the truck moved because I *may* have driven a bit haphazardly into the alley and then when his truck blocked my way, the dumpster blocked my ability to back up. I was pretty fucked-up," I said, and the girls laughed.

"Little bit," Kathy said.

I grimaced. "Anyway, Rafael got a hold of Ryan, who moved his truck and in the process, he found Bernie…." I twisted the silver thumb ring on my left hand until it practically severed my thumb. "And… well, I waited in my Bug until the cops arrived."

No one spoke. They seemed to be absorbing the alibi Ryan created for me. *Shit, between Ryan and Jude I'm not just living a double life, it's more like a triple and possibly heading for more. At this rate, I'll have more lives than a cat.*

"That must have been tough," Ria said, and without warning my eyes brimmed with tears and my bottom lip trembled.

"Oh, Reb." Da Nise rolled her chair into mine and wrapped her slender arm around me. "I'm sorry you had to experience the darker side of Long Beach."

She was the last of the three I'd expect empathy from, which made me more emotional.

"And to find *Bernie*. He drove me crazy with his work orders, but he was such a good man. I'm so sorry," she said.

Da Nise extracted emotions from me like a tool drew samples

of wine from a barrel. From my days in the vineyard, I knew the latter was known as a "wine thief." And Da Nise was a tear thief, because her compassion continued to make me cry.

"I can't even imagine," she said.

"It was awful. His eyes were open." I buried my head on her shoulder. "And his head...."

"You saw him?" Kathy said, and my body flushed.

Fuck.

Da Nise gently squeezed my shoulder before she released me. I tried to collect myself, but it was pointless. I was a mess. "You can't tell anyone. Ryan covered for me with the cops. I didn't want to have my first week at the hotel noted for finding a dead guy."

"I get you," Ria said. "Ryan's a good guy, but he wouldn't do that for just anyone. You must have been real spooked for him to lie."

I nodded.

"It must have freaked you out," Da Nise said.

"It did. I've never seen a dead guy—you know, unless it's at a funeral," I said.

"It's pretty fucked-up." Kathy crossed her arms over her chest and I wasn't sure if her comment was aimed at me for lying to them or finding Bernie. My ability to stay centered was off. When she didn't offer any clue on where her comment was directed, it felt like the weight of lying and keeping a secret identity would sink me.

"I'm sorry I lied." I rolled my head, but the tension in my neck and shoulders was permanent. "It really messed with me so when Ryan offered to have my six, I took it."

"Have your six?" Ria said.

I exhaled. *Great.* Another slip of the tongue. Having someone's six was pure Wyoming. "It's an expression I once heard," I said. "It means having your back."

Ria's eyebrows furrowed with confusion.

"You know, like the hands on a clock. If you picture yourself at twelve on the face of a clock, then six is behind you. So, if someone is 'at your six' they are behind you. Or if they have your six, they have your back," I said.

"Sure," she said. "McCutie's the kind of guy to have your six."

It was my first smile since Friday night.

"Why was Bernie killed?" Da Nise asked, and I shrugged.

"It sounds like you guys knew him better than I did. I only saw him once outside Phil's office," I said.

Kathy uncrossed her arms. "Phil's office? Are you sure?"

I nodded. "Yeah, he was pacing outside Phil's office in a long black jacket, gray shirt, and his cross swung from his chest."

Kathy laughed. "Preacher man."

I questioned her with my face.

"That's what he was called on the street," Kathy said.

"When he was a deputy?" I asked, and from the Kathy's raised eyebrows I think I actually impressed her.

"He was with *LA* county—he didn't work Long Beach," she said. "But he went to Long Beach Wilson—that's one of the high schools. Bernie was a local boy."

"So, why preacher? Because of his cross?" I asked and reached for my cold coffee.

She shook her head. "At one time Bernie wanted to be a preacher."

"For real?" Ria said. "I never knew that."

"That's why he was always leaving those little bible cards," Da Nise said. "I don't know how many scriptures we laminated for him." She gave a nod toward Kathy. "Once you blabbed and told him we had a laminating machine I never thought we'd see the end of him." The words barely left her mouth when her cheeks tinged red. "I didn't mean that."

"We know," Kathy said. "It's messed up what happened to Bernie."

Either I'd appeased Kathy or her comment was never directed at me. I really didn't know anymore. And I hated how insecure I had become. Living a lie was not easy. I couldn't do it anymore. Hell, I didn't want to do it anymore.

I grabbed my phone and looked at the three women who had huddled around me.

"I've got to make a personal call," I said without apology.

"We've got your six," Ria said, and I smiled.

"Listen, if the Robertson brothers found me and tried to prevent me from testifying, would it be so bad?"

"Calvin and Jim Robertson wouldn't *try* to prevent you from testifying, they'd *silence* you so that you'd *never* testify," Jude said.

"A quick death would be preferable than living multiple lives and remembering the even greater number of lies." I was numb, and in that cold, deadened state I didn't care.

"Rebel, I *really* don't think you understand," Jude said, and her voice seemed to even out and lose the edge. "Living with these lies is nothing compared to the agony the Robertson brothers would inflict on you. A quick death would be a luxury, and the Robertsons are a family of stingy, sadistic bastards."

It was the first time it felt like Jude was on my side and not just simply following orders. Tears pulled at the corners of my eyes. I didn't want to cry—again—but it felt like my only response to everything happening.

"I surrender," I said. "Just put me in jail."

Her laughter was so unexpected it stopped the crying and replaced it with a smile.

"Rebel, if I could have thrown you into jail when this happened and let the local authorities deal with you, I would have gladly. But it seems someone's forensic accounting skills uncovered that the local authorities were well compensated for turning a blind eye to the unjust working practices and truck routes of the Robertson brothers."

"Swell. Me and my accounting skills," I said.

"Despite your methods, you uncovered years of illegal shipments across state lines," she said. "And we uncovered their uglier side. Trust me, you don't want to cross them any further than you did through your forensic accounting."

"So, for my efforts, you stuck me in a hotel under an alias surname that's eerily close to theirs?" I said.

"The Point Resort isn't a downgrade. If anything, it's a five-star upgrade from the federal penitentiary. So, do we need to change your reservations or are you going to continue to play ball?"

I shook my head and smiled. If Jude hadn't locked me up by now, it wasn't going to happen—even after I asked for it. And the fact that she made no mention of Bernie meant my name may be on a police report, but it must be buried so far that it hadn't raised any flags. *Should I tell her about Bernie? Or will that place another target on me?* My stomach tightened and my jaw clenched. Indecision was worse than lying. So, while lying was exhausting, it was better than ending up like Bernie. "Thank you," I finally said.

"For?" Jude said.

"Grounding me," I said.

"Eh, it's what I do when you're not being difficult."

I rolled my eyes. Having Jude leave things on a high note

would be like a mob boss forgiving a debt and wanting nothing in return. Both were too good to be true and I'd likely regret believing it. Nope, Jude's pragmatism brought me back to center. And I knew exactly who I needed to talk to next.

I'd turned from the parking garage into the barely lit conference services lobby when Da Nise walked out of the shadows and grabbed my elbow.

"Jesus!"

She chuckled. "Sorry, did I scare you?"

"Ya think?"

"I wanted to get you before you went into the reception area because we've got some hotel guests talking to Ria," she said.

"What's wrong?" I knew from her hurried breath and widened eyes that Da Nise wasn't just out to give me a jump scare.

"Phil's little troll called a few minutes ago and they want to see you on the seventh," she said.

My stomach turned. "Am I in trouble?"

She shook her head. "No, I don't think so. I'm sure they know about Bernie since you said Phil was working with him, but it sounded like they just wanted to touch base with you—that's all."

"How long ago did they call?"

She grimaced. "About ten minutes. I told them you were showing guests the secretarial services we offer and introducing them to Kathy."

"Smart move," I said.

"Listen, if they ask just tell them it took longer than you anticipated. Phil's big on instant gratification. When he beckons for someone, he expects them to materialize out of thin air."

"Good to know."

The elevator finally dinged, announcing its arrival to our dungeon level. The doors opened, and I stepped inside.

The elevator no sooner opened on the seventh floor than I found myself front and center with Lisa. She was all bright, blue-eyed, and blonde ponytail swinging behind her as she smiled. In her pink suit with pink pumps and pink clipboard, she reminded me of Elle Woods from *Legally Blonde*. The only thing she was missing was her Chihuahua.

"Rebel, it's *so good* to see you again," she said a bit too enthusiastically, which signaled my bullshit detector. *No one, not even little miss smarty pants, is that chipper.*

But I played along and acted like the robotic model Point staff member, which meant I had to be more plastic and fake than a mannequin.

"Hi! Oh, my gosh, thanks for meeting me." I grinned like a mindless garden troll. "I didn't make a mental map last time I was on the floor so I wasn't sure if I'd be able to find my way to Phil's office again." I smiled until my cheeks hurt. As if locating a corner office in a square-shaped high-rise hotel was beyond my skill set.

But in my drab green dress with a starched white collar, I could really sell stupid. Lisa didn't know I had a degree in accounting and a double minor in business and finance. I was sure she already checked my fake personnel file in Phil's office and thought I was some dumb hayseed Aggie graduate.

The only person who may have an inkling that I wasn't who I said I was, was Phil. But I doubted he knew. I wasn't sure who Jude had told—if she did. I didn't think the FBI was allowed to break my cover to anyone. All I did know was that they put me into the Point Resort properties, which made moving me around easier. Shit, a pawn on a chessboard had more value and moved less than I did.

I happily walked beside Lisa as if I didn't have a care in the world—as if I hadn't uncovered a dead Bernie on Friday night.

The seventh floor wasn't difficult to navigate, but there was a long hallway that led to Phil's office. I used the time to make small talk with Lisa.

"So, is Long Beach your home?"

She turned toward me with a smile. "Born and raised."

I returned her smile because it was the first real reaction she showed. "Represent," I said.

"You know it."

"So, you must have gone to high school here. Kathy mentioned Long Beach Wilson?" I less-than-casually threw Bernie's high school alma mater into the mix. They were decades apart, but at this point, I was aiming for any connection.

Her face wrinkled. *"God no.* Long Beach Wilson? *Loathsome.* I went to St. Anthony's."

From the disdain in her voice, it was clear Lisa and Bernie weren't alumni of the same high school. Their paths probably wouldn't have crossed if it weren't for the hotel. Lisa was just way too white girl for that.

"I'm not familiar with St. Anthony's. Is it an all-girls school?" I said.

"No," her chipper tone returned. "It's one of the oldest high schools in Long Beach that's rich with history."

Duh.

"My parents are graduates. It's where they met."

"That's cool," I lied. "So, your parents decided to stay in Long Beach?"

Her chin seemed to rise. "They only owned one of the best shops on the shorefront."

My parents owned a trailer in Wyoming and considered themselves pretty fucking lucky.

"I didn't know that," I said, and wanted to wipe the smug off her face. "What's it called? Maybe I'll pop in after work."

She tucked the clipboard against her chest and directed her sights on Phil's office. Her voice lost its enthusiasm, returning to its usual biting tone. "It lived up to its reputation, it was *undeniably the best*, but it's closed now."

"I'm sorry." And I was. There was nothing worse than when young couples started a business that didn't quite take off. Usually poor financial planning was the cause—but I wasn't about to mention that to Lisa.

"It's a thing of the past," she said and her chin jutted forward again. "They moved on to something bigger and better." Lisa extended her arm toward Phil's corner office, which was lit by the warm Southern California sun, which again made me want to skip work and head to the beach. My feet practically felt the grains of sand slip beneath my toes. *After work*, I promised myself. *After work.*

Phil's chair was turned to face the windows so all I saw was the black backside of the high back. When Lisa left his office and closed the door behind her, his chair slowly turned toward me.

"*Someone* had an interesting weekend," he said with his long spindly fingers interwoven. The guy was too spider-like for my taste.

But as with Kathy, I waited to see where he was headed. If I had learned anything since the FBI placed me into protective custody, it was to let the empty space be quiet. I discovered more when I didn't fill the space with noise.

"Bernie Thomas." Phil slowly rocked his chair back and forth like an old man in a recliner.

Still, I remained mute. Besides, all I knew about Bernie Thomas was that he went to Long Beach Wilson—not the more preferred St. Anthony's. He was known as "the Preacher" on the street because at one time he wanted to become a preacher, which would have made more sense if he had attended St. Anthony's. But I was thinking private school was probably too rich for his blood— on many counts. *Nope, my knowledge of Bernie Thomas is limited at best.* Still, I couldn't get his vacant stare from my memory. Or the cross that he'd held in his clammy hands. I shifted in the chair opposite Phil's mammoth desk and waited.

"Did you ever meet Bernie?" he asked. "Of course, I mean before his death."

I opted for the truth. "I didn't meet him, but I did see him outside your office."

Phil continued to rock, but his eyebrows rose in the question he apparently wasn't going to ask.

"Friday," I said, "when I was in your office and you had that meeting." I knew exactly what meeting it was, but I chose to omit that detail. "Bernie was in the hallway."

Phil rocked. "Of course, of course. The revitalization meeting."

"Revitalization? I thought it was called restoration." And again, I realized the value of keeping my damn mouth shut. Loose lips sink ships, and from the spark in Phil's eyes, I could tell I'd sunk myself.

"It *is* called the restoration meeting," he said. "Lisa tends to call it revitalization and I tend to refer to it as the redevelopment, but you're right, Bernie was part of the restoration committee."

I shrugged. "I just remember Lisa correcting herself, which," I widened my eyes to really sell it, "I'm sure doesn't happen often because she's so on top of things. It was really nice of her to meet me at the elevator. I'm still learning my way around the hotel." I paused long enough to let Phil catch up. "It's why I ended up in the alley on Friday night. My sense of direction is *so* poor that instead of turning left onto Broadway at the exit to the parking structure, I turned right and then really got myself into a pickle."

I could keep going it if meant Phil only thought I was clueless and not culpable. Besides, if I bored to death any suspicion he had about me, it'd be worth assuming a mantle of boring stupidity.

"I wondered why you were in the alley," he said.

I rolled my eyes. "If I didn't have GPS on my phone I wouldn't know how to get back to my apartment."

He rocked and steadied me in his sights. I almost laughed. If Phil thought I'd break and confess to finding Bernie, he was sorely mistaken. After Jude, no one intimidated me.

"What was it like stumbling across a dead guy?"

I shrugged. "I don't know. I stayed in my car. Ryan McHenry from Bernetti & Sons found him and then directed me to stay where I was, and I wasn't about to challenge him." I slowly exhaled. "Nor did I want to." The shudder that followed was real, but my next statement wasn't. "I can't imagine."

Phil rocked. "I'm sure you saw him when you got out of your car to answer the questions the police had for you."

Keep fishing.

"I glanced toward the fence, but by that time, it was blocked off and there was a ton of people everywhere," I said.

Phil's chair swayed while he looked to be contemplating his next question.

"I thought maybe you asked to see me to get my initial impression of the staffing and conference service operations." I tried to redirect the conversation.

"You've only had a day in the trenches, it would be premature," he said.

"Of course, I just thought you'd be interested in the forecast of conference room bookings." Usually once I dropped finances into a conversation, it shifted the direction. "Over the weekend, I plugged last year's numbers into a new spreadsheet to analyze traffic to see if there was a certain quarter that did better than another. Or perhaps a day and time." It was true. When TV couldn't hold my attention, I turned to the one vice that worked: math. Da Nise and Kathy had stuffed the year-end reports in my backpack along with their service sales for the last quarter before we left the hotel to walk to the bar. They thought it was a punishment when in reality it was a treat. Math got me out of my head.

"Did you discover anything?" Phil's stern and stony countenance was so unwavering, the presidents on Mount Rushmore would blink first.

I leaned forward and threw the bait. "I did."

His rocking slowed. "And…."

I was about to toss out actual numbers when the door to his office swung open abruptly and Phil's expression crumbled. A woman in her late forties, probably my mom's age, thrust through the door in a creamy tulle blouse and gray skirt with a frayed, raw hemline that would have made anyone else look homeless. But from her expertly styled white-blonde hair down to her sandals that had these amazing zigzag straps that hugged her petite, perfectly pedicured feet, she crushed it. A silver chain-strap across her body led to a Prada handbag that hung at her waist. The purse alone was more than two grand. Prada wasn't cheap; something I learned digging into the Robertson brothers' financials and the women they bought trinkets for.

"Sheila…." Phil's face went from granite to putty before she even spoke.

"Are you happy now?" She was as bold and scene-stealing as her entrance. "I'm sure Bernie's death was the highlight of your weekend."

"I… uh… I had nothing to do with it." He stopped rocking and sat upright.

She didn't ask if he had anything to do with it—so why would Phil rush to defend himself?

Her French-tipped manicured hands gripped the edge of his desk and her blue eyes sparked with anger. I was afraid to move.

"You had nothing to do with it? I find that very hard to believe," she said, clearly oblivious to or not interested in the fact that I was still in the room.

Phil's stoic demeanor dissolved. "It's the truth."

Her blonde hair swayed. "Darling, you don't know the meaning of the word."

He cleared his throat. "Perhaps we can discuss this later."

She leaned closer toward him. "*Later* is now."

"If you have any questions about Bernie, you should probably ask Rebel." He nodded toward me, but her attention never left him. "I was just asking her about it. I want to know what happened to him as much as you do."

Her position never wavered. "I have no interest in talking to your latest dalliance."

Dalliance, what? Me and Phil? Ew. Gross.

"I want to know why I had to learn of Bernie's death from the newspaper," she said, and when Phil didn't respond, a slow smile spread across her mauve lips. "Of all the announcements, I thought *this* would be one you'd want to break to me."

"Sheila, it's not like that."

When she laughed, the corners of her mouth turned into a smirk directed at Phil. "You hated Bernie from the moment he set foot into your office."

"No." Phil stood. "I hated Bernie when he began sleeping with my wife."

Oh, shit.

"I haven't been your wife for years," she said.

"The state of California may argue differently on that point," he said.

"We'll soon find out. Miles filed the paperwork for our divorce this morning."

"Let the asset shuffling commence," Phil said.

Sheila's smile now looked sinister. Angry spouses were the worst.

"Darling, there's no need to shuffle assets," she said. "As two of the main stakeholders in Greenberg-Mendel, if either of us fudges any numbers, Sarbanes-Oxley will have us both behind bars before either of us can cry foul."

Damn! Sheila knew her shit—to an extent. The Sarbanes-Oxley Act was passed by congress to protect investors from the possibility of fraudulent accounting practices by corporations. It's one of the many laws I learned in corporate finance. However, assets that were legally shifted, such as through a divorce, did not violate SOX, as Sarbanes-Oxley was abbreviated in financial reporting. So, while I hated to side with Phil, asset shuffling would legally commence. If Sheila was the money source for whatever Greenberg-Mendel was, she could doctor her other assets in a divorce and nothing much would happen—except what was already likely, a bitter lawsuit. I wasn't sure whose money they were fighting over. I suspected Sheila was the Mendel in Greenberg-Mendel. But unless they had a prenuptial agreement, their assets were joined.

A standoff ensued between Phil and Sheila and I wasn't sure who would move first. If this had been a western, then the fastest draw would win the day. However, these days, the fastest draw was who had the best legal team. Since I wasn't in the movie theatre watching a western, that meant I could leave my seat, which was what I did. I slowly inched off the chair and walked as quietly as I could out of Phil's office.

Phil's wife was sleeping with Bernie? Oh. My. God.

On the way to the elevator, I texted Da Nise, who had programmed her number into my phone at the bar in case I got lost walking back to the hotel.

Me: Ordr office supplies – don't care what – ask 4 McCutie 2 dlvr by end of day. Hav 2 get something frm apt. BRB.

Before I entered the elevator, I hit send on the message.

I exited the elevator on the lobby level and bypassed the

security cameras I knew the Point Resorts positioned in certain corners of the lobby. As an employee, I wasn't allowed to exit the property from the front drive, but I did.

It was more preferable than having my car captured on the security feed leaving the garage before noon. Besides, my apartment was within walking distance and despite wanting to avoid alleys for the rest of my life, ducking between buildings was again more desirable than being spotted off property when it wasn't even lunch. If I'd learned anything since switching careers from accounting to hospitality, it was that hotel workers were plentiful and loyal. If someone saw me ditching out early, their concern wouldn't be about shorting the hotel my time, but what it meant to Kathy, Da Nise, and Ria.

So, even though the sun shone in a cloudless sky, I tucked my head and focused on the asphalt that led from the hotel's alley to the next back street in downtown Long Beach.

Bernie was having an affair with the wife of the director of conference services. And Bernie was also found dead at the hotel. *So, not only are Phil and Sheila suspects number one and number two, but the hotel may not be the safest place for me.*

When my cell phone's GPS announced, "Arrived at your location," I glanced up and the Franklin appeared like a mirage in the desert of my thoughts. My total walking time was only fifteen minutes, but it was fourteen minutes too long in my head.

My overactive mind and walking had wreaked havoc on my stomach. I feared I was about to do a number one and number two in my pants if I didn't get to my apartment. Still, while I approached the apartment building, the questions remained constant.

Did Phil have something to do with Bernie's death? How long was his wife sleeping with him? Who else knew Sheila and Bernie were knocking boots?

If this had been Wyoming, the entire town would know before the unsuspecting spouse. Small towns were good for two things: spreading rumors and blowing them out of proportion.

I entered the building through the underground parking garage. The elevator bypassed the lobby level and the security guard. After Sheila's big reveal, I suddenly didn't know who to trust.

My apartment was located closer to the stairwell than the elevator, but I hadn't quite mustered the enthusiasm to climb nine flights or descend them. Besides, the elevator always smelled nice. My apartment card key was tucked in the purple pocket stuck to the back of my smartphone. The smart pocket was a graduation gift from one of my professors at Chadron State who knew I was forever misplacing my wallet. The sleeve on the back of my phone—albeit bright—functioned as a wallet for my key cards, credit cards, ID, and cash. It was a girl's best friend.

I'd paused outside the elevator to fish my card key from my phone when his deep, smoker-like laugh drew my attention.

No one was in the main hallway, but when he laughed again, the wheezing seemed to originate from the alcove outside my apartment. I glanced down the hall and broad shoulders came into view. *Who is that?*

Jude favored the ninth floor because each alcove contained a private entrance to individual apartments. There wasn't any other apartment in that particular alcove but mine. *What the hell? Who's the guy?*

I ran toward the nearest alcove and was about to spy on the wheezing guy when the elevator dinged. *Crap.* My stomach tightened, my shoulders pulled in like an injured bird's, and sweat beaded on my forehead. Adrenaline shot through my body and the rush kicked in my fight-or-flight instinct. For all I knew the person on the elevator was a maintenance worker. But the man in the alcove of my apartment wasn't in uniform and whatever he was doing there didn't feel right. While my brain was still trying to sort through everything, my body had already responded. My adrenal glands had shifted into overdrive and within seconds my hair clung to my head like it had been badly painted onto my scalp or I had somehow stepped back in time and was coated in hair gel. Either way, it was gross.

What do I do?

I did the only thing that made sense. I turned toward the door with my back to the hallway, pretended like I was entering the apartment, and prayed that whoever exited the elevator didn't live here.

Heavy footsteps echoed in the hallway. With each step, my heart beat faster and faster, and echoed louder and louder in my mind until I could no longer hear the footfalls. Because of my deafening heartbeat, I had no clue if I was in the clear or still in imminent danger.

When the weighty walking seemed to stop in front of the alcove, I was pretty sure I was either going to puke or have a heart attack. Possibly both.

"Excuse me, ma'am, but I think you're in the wrong corridor."

Even though my ears rang with his voice, my words seemed trapped in my throat. It was like I was frozen.

"Ma'am?"

When his hand gripped my shoulder, my need to scream was silenced by my fear of the unknown. *Maybe this is his apartment. Maybe he saw me shaking and sweating and he's concerned. Maybe... I'm screwed.*

"Ma'am? Are you lost?"

Crap. I slowly turned toward the voice to find McHenry standing with a shit-eating grin on his face. I grabbed his hand off my shoulder and yanked him further into the alcove, where I placed my hand over his mouth.

"Shut it," I hissed. "And don't ever do that to me again!" I swatted his shoulder. "You scared the *shit* out of me."

Astonishment and I think excitement sparked in his hazel eyes. His mouth moved, so I pressed my hand more firmly over his lips and leaned in toward him.

"There's some guy in the alcove of my apartment and he's not wearing a building uniform," I whispered. "I don't know what he's doing there, but it doesn't feel right."

Ryan's face instantly relaxed. Calm instantly settled over him like armor. He quietly removed my hand and walked me to the corner of the alcove. It was the second time I'd noticed that when things were the craziest, Ryan was the calmest.

"Stay here," he said.

"Where are you going?" Panic gripped me.

"Rebel, please—stay here."

"Well… since you asked so nicely."

His million-dollar smile broke the serene composure he wore so well.

"Actually." He gently reached for my phone and asked for my passcode, which I provided. "Okay," he said with his attention on my smartphone. "I want you to use the stairs and call one of the girls at the hotel to drive you to my house." He finished typing something into my phone and handed it to me. "I pinged my address in your maps, so all you have to do is follow it to my house."

"What?" I shook my head. "I don't understand."

"Rebel, I don't think you should be here."

"Okay, so I'll go back to work."

A curt shake of his head and I knew that idea was scrapped. "I was just there and the girls said that after your meeting with Phil you left for the day."

"I didn't *leave* for the day." My voice threatened to reveal us. I leaned toward him. "I just wanted to get something from my apartment."

"What?"

"What do you mean, what? I'm confused," I said, hoping to redirect the conversation.

"What did you want to get?"

"Oh." I exhaled. *It didn't work.* "Well, now it seems stupid, but I have this spiral notebook that I keep notes in and I wanted to get it for work."

I wasn't as good a liar as I thought.

"What did you *really* want to get from your apartment?" Ryan planted his hands on his hips.

"My gun."

His baseball cap pointed toward the ceiling when he leaned his head back, and his cool composure all but left. "Why would you need a gun?" He returned his attention to me.

"I don't feel safe."

"Guns don't keep people safe," he said.

"Sell that bullshit to someone who'll buy it. I'm not from

California. I'm from rural America, where help is at least an hour away and a .22 or a .45 is your only 911."

"Where's your gun?"

Clearly, this wasn't the time for a conversation on Second Amendment rights.

"In the bottom of the record player." When my answer didn't seem to register with him, I explained. "I created a false bottom. If you flip the turntable over, there's a small hole in the plywood that a pen or pencil will fit perfectly into that'll remove it. My gun is taped to the other side of the plywood."

Ryan pinned his focus on me, I was sure imagining my makeshift gun safe.

"Impressive," he said. "Give me your card key and if I can get into your apartment, I'll get your gun." Flecks of green in his hazel eyes intensified. "*To hold.* I'm not sure if it's registered, but it's better if I keep your gun in my safe."

"Lot of good it'll do me in your safe," I said, but handed him my card key.

"Hey, how 'bout you get on board with the idea that I'm trying to help." He pocketed my card key, lowered his baseball cap, and steadied me in his sights. "Okay, why don't you leave and take the stairs."

"The stairwell is next to my apartment. Whoever that guy is, he'll see me," I said.

Ryan no sooner uttered the word, "Elevator," than the ding of the elevator made me flinch.

"Shit." There wasn't anywhere for us to go. We were already tucked in the corner of the alcove closest to the elevator. "If that guy has a friend, we're screwed."

Ryan wrapped his arm around my waist so quickly I didn't have a chance to react. He pulled me into him and practically covered my face with the brim of his cap when he swooped in and his lips pressed against mine hard. The more his mouth lingered on mine, the softer his kissing became. And the more I liked it. The scent of the ocean clung to him like sea spray and he tasted faintly salty. The echo of footsteps grew closer, but instead of tensing, my body surrendered to Ryan's touch. His arm held me against him in a protective embrace and his mouth opened, inviting me in. With my eyes closed, the world and all its worries drifted away. I no longer felt lost. Warmth replaced the chill that ran down my back, and as I abandoned myself to his touch, our connection was effortless. His tongue glided in my mouth, alternating with his teeth that gently nibbled my lower lip. The more he kissed me, the more I forgot where I was. Whoever exited the elevator faded to white noise and all I heard was my heart beating against his chest. There was no denying that McCutie could kiss—and well.

When our lips parted, I felt dizzy, giddy, and light. *Damn.*

"Elevator." His mouth remained close to mine. "Take the

elevator directly to the parking garage and walk down East Broadway until it intersects with Atlantic."

"Broadway and Atlantic," I said, staring up at him like some lost puppy I hoped he'd rescue.

He smiled. "There's a Vons grocery store on East Broadway. Phone one of the girls at the hotel to meet you there."

"Vons. Got it." I didn't want to leave. "Clothes," I said, and he slightly shook his head. "If you get inside my apartment, will you grab me a change of clothes? They're in my closet."

His crooked smile went straight to my heart.

"Clothes and a gun—got it. Now go to Vons and call the girls."

I spun out of his arms when I wanted to remain blanketed by his warmth. But there was still some strange guy by my apartment, Bernie was in the morgue, and my hotel boss's wife had been sleeping with him—all the markings of a bad situation for someone trying to maintain a low profile. Despite what my body wanted, my mind reminded me that getting involved with someone vying for a career in law enforcement was bad news for both of us, no matter how well he kissed. *And damn did he kiss well.*

CHAPTER 18
RYAN

When *I heard the elevator* ding, which thankfully wasn't loud, I glanced to make sure Rebel disappeared inside. I pulled the Glock from the back of my jeans and checked the safety. It was a registered weapon and my concealed carry license was in my wallet. Still, regardless of being legally allowed to own and operate a gun in California, retrieving my firearm carried weight. I tucked it back into the waistband of my jeans. There was no need to bring a gun to what could amount to nothing at all.

Shit, if I pointed a gun every time I didn't know what was going on, I'd be a fatal accident waiting to happen. Besides, officers followed the same rules for gun use whether they were on duty or off. I wasn't a deputy yet, but I wasn't about to violate the department's policies. And one of the oldest policies was for a deputy to de-escalate a confrontation prior to brandishing or using a weapon. I knew the policies and procedures verbatim. So while I didn't know who or what I was walking into, the whole idea of trying to settle a confrontation peacefully suited me just fine. And from the frightened look on Rebel's face when I found her and the fact that she thought she needed a gun to protect herself, the less chaos the better.

Guns. The topic of gun control in California was a heated one. As a future deputy sheriff, I believed that gun control was a necessary safety measure. But I knew I was a rarity in law enforcement circles. I'd already heard future deputies argue that gun control violated the Second Amendment.

Nope, what violates the spirit of the Second Amendment are the soulless douchebags whose sole purpose for carrying guns is to engage in violent premeditated crimes.

Background checks and other California gun laws saved lives. If I could get Rebel to truly understand the danger, maybe she wouldn't rely on a weapon for her safety.

I lowered my baseball cap and walked toward Rebel's apartment, which was at the end of the hallway. Before I reached her alcove, the man turned around and blocked the entrance to her apartment.

"Deputy Trainee McHenry."

I quickly shifted gears from high alert to covering my ass. I nodded toward Deputy Stanley.

"Sir."

"What brings you to the Franklin?"

I could ask you the same question.

"Honestly," I said, scratching my neck while making eye contact with him, "I wanted to check on Ms. Roberts." It wasn't hard to sell that I was attracted to Rebel. I just wasn't sure if it was smart to tell Stanley. "I walked her to her apartment Friday night, or rather Saturday morning, and I just wanted to make sure she was okay."

"Very thoughtful of you," he said with about as much conviction as the spur of the moment reveal I had just delivered. But now I was trapped in my own web of attraction and I was sure my training officer was there to see if I could work my way out or hang myself out to dry.

"How'd you access the ninth floor without a card key?" he asked.

The advantage to being Irish was that when I was embarrassed, it showed on my face.

"I hopped on the elevator in the garage with a tenant." It was the truth and I knew my reddened face proved it. It wasn't my best moment but it sold my story to Stanley, who had no jurisdiction in Long Beach, fallen officer or not. Nor did I imagine he possessed the necessary search warrant to comb through Rebel's apartment, which was what I was pretty sure was happening. Stanley was clearly the lookout man and from his broad stance, he was there to make sure no one saw what he didn't want them to see. The questions were, who was he covering for? And what did they hope to find in Rebel's apartment?

"Well, it looks like you've got her safety covered," I said, by way of exiting.

"That we do," he said and then quickly added, "LA's finest is on the scene."

Sure, try to cover your slip. As if the "we" he mentioned was referring to the collective Sheriff's department. *Not a chance.* Stanley was there with someone else, and by his lack of uniform, I highly doubted his visit was sanctioned by the department. *What the fuck is going on?*

I nodded with a convincing smile. "LA's finest."

"See you at tomorrow's training briefing," he said.

Stanley's less than subtle reminder that my employment with the department remained tentative wasn't lost on me.

"Yes, sir." I headed toward the stairwell without looking back. Hopefully whoever was searching her apartment wouldn't find her gun.

CHAPTER 19
REBEL

Kathy's *camo-colored Jeep wasn't what* I expected to pull into the grocery store parking lot. But when the back window rolled down and Da Nise waved me over, it felt like I had found my tribe.

"You rang," Kathy said when I hopped into the front seat.

"Thank you." I buckled in and glanced from Da Nise to Kathy. "Please tell me Ria is still at the hotel answering the switchboard."

They collectively laughed.

"Yeah, Ria's got us covered," Kathy said. "If Phil or his troll call or come looking for us, we are with guests working on a project."

"Is there a project that supports this?" Creating a cover was one thing, actually having it work was another.

"Yup. Mr. Lockerbee."

"And he is…?"

"Only the yummiest man that uses our secretarial services—all the time," Da Nise said.

I chuckled. "Well, I've met McCutie and you weren't wrong there, but yummiest?"

Kathy glanced away from the road to make eye contact with me. "The man is fine."

"Good to know. And this fine man… why does he use our secretarial services? Is he a returning hotel guest?"

Da Nise shook her head. "No, he has an office off Broadway, but he doesn't have a secretary so when he needs something to look professional, he gives it to Kathy."

I slowly nodded. "What does he have you do?"

Kathy volleyed her thick locks from one side to another. "Spreadsheets, PowerPoints, stuff like that."

"Gotcha." I did a quick mental inventory of the services listed on the spreadsheets I'd studied over the weekend. There was one customer who continually surfaced on the reports. "Is he BT Inc.?"

Even with traffic flowing past us, the Jeep grew quiet.

"What?" I asked.

"BT Inc. was Bernie Thomas," Kathy said.

"Oh." My stomach tightened. "I'm sorry, I didn't know. It was a name I regularly saw on the sales reports."

"Bernie was always having scripture cards made and laminated," Kathy said.

"I remember Da Nise saying that," I said. "But when you guys said he used your services, I didn't realize Bernie was a weekly client—or at least according to the sales figures you gave me."

Kathy shrugged. "Sometimes, Phil had us do something for the restoration committee and charge it to Bernie's account."

"What?" I practically hit the dashboard when I leaned forward. "Phil used a client's account for the work you did for him?"

"Yup," Kathy said.

"Did he charge Bernie for this work?" I was afraid to ask but I had to know. There was creative accounting practices and then downright accounting fraud.

"Nah, his blonde troll always came down with cash to settle the account," Da Nise said. "Which, if you ask me, is stupid because then we have to make a bank deposit and it's a whole lot of extra work on our end when it seems like they could just transfer money from their hotel account into our hotel account."

I slowly nodded, recalling the financial spreadsheets. *Why hide income under Bernie's account?* The obvious reason was that it inflated Bernie's expenses and in turn falsified how much he actually spent on hotel services. "You wouldn't have kept a copy of Bernie's actual work?" I volleyed my attention from Kathy to

Da Nise.

"Yeah, we have copies of each month's billing statements," Da Nise said.

"Not the billing statements but the actual work orders?" I said.

"Every month I keep the work orders in my file drawer and at the end of the month, I rubber band them together and put them in storage with all the others," Kathy said, and I wanted to kiss her. Instead, I pumped my fist in the air.

"Excellent! And these work orders are the ones that guests get from Ria to fill out, right?"

"Yeah," Da Nise said.

"So they'll show Bernie's work and then Phil's?" I asked.

"Phil always had his troll call with a work order that one of us would take over the phone," Kathy said.

"But, it's not in Bernie's penmanship, right? It'd be in yours or Da Nise's or Ria's?" I said.

"Correct," Kathy said.

"Perfect!" I hit the dash with my hand, startling them. "Sorry, but numbers make sense to me. And after reviewing the spreadsheets this weekend, it looks like BT Inc. used the services a lot. So, I know it's going to take some time, but I'd really like to go into storage and pull all of Bernie's actual invoices and compare costs to the conference services that Phil requested. I had actually planned to return to the hotel, but then shit just started unraveling."

"Yeah, what happened?" Da Nise leaned forward in her seat and sandwiched her head between Kathy and me.

I released the anxiety that seemed lodged in my chest.

"I went to my apartment to get something when I heard this guy laugh. I don't know all the tenants on the floor, but this guy's laugh was hard to miss. And when I looked down the hallway, he was in the alcove that led to my apartment. I can't explain it, but something felt off and my gut kept me from approaching my apartment. That's when Ryan showed up, scared the shit out of me, and then came up with the idea that he'd check the guy out while I walked to the grocery store and had you guys pick me up."

"Damn," Kathy said. "Trouble seems to follow you."

The tightness in my chest returned and I glanced out the side window.

"Ah, Reb, don't get like that," Da Nise said. "Kathy's always saying shit like that."

I shrugged. "She's probably right. I seem to gravitate toward shitty situations."

"Ain't no thing," Kathy said. "We all got baggage."

"Amen," Da Nise said.

"In case you ever need to get to McCutie's house on your own, you can take the 710 freeway, but at this time of the day it's already filling up, that's why I'm staying on Atlantic until I hit Del Amo Boulevard." Kathy glanced over her shoulder as she switched lanes.

I was about to counter that there wouldn't be a reason for me to go to Ryan's house, when Kathy interrupted the mental protest I was mounting.

"What happened in Phil's office?" she said.

"What *didn't* happen. His wife busted into his office and went off on him about Bernie's death and how she had to read about it in the newspaper," I said.

"Why would she care where she read it?" Da Nise said.

I raised my eyebrows. "Apparently Sheila, that's Phil's wife, was having an affair with Bernie."

Kathy's palm slapped the steering wheel. "Hell, no!"

"Hundred percent," I said.

"Damn, that's cold," Da Nise said.

"For who?" I said, and they laughed. "Would you willingly want to sleep with Phil?" I winced. "Yuck. At least Bernie had style and that whole swagger when he walked. The man may have been older than Phil, but if I had my choice, Bernie would have been it."

"Good point," Kathy said. "Phil's too selfish to be a good lover."

"Ew." I couldn't stop shuddering. "He's so hairy it'd be like having sex with a tarantula."

When Da Nise didn't chime in, I glanced in her direction.

"What? I think Phil's kind of cute," she said. "For a white guy."

"Oh, no." I waved my hands in front of me like I was trying to erase the image her comment evoked. "No. No. No."

My reaction simply made Da Nise and Kathy laugh.

"So, McCutie's house?" Kathy waggled her thick eyebrows.

"It was his idea," I said. "I wanted to return to the hotel and finish my shift."

"*Uh…* no," Da Nise said. "If Phil's wife was hitting it with Bernie and you were there when she unloaded on Phil, do you really think Phil's going to have any love for you right now? The man's going to be embarrassed and in that embarrassment, he's likely to take it out on you."

"And here I thought you were a Phil fan," I said.

"I am, but when men get publicly shamed like that, it comes out sideways, and since you were there to witness it all, you'll be the likely target for his anger," Da Nise said.

"You're probably right, but that's bullshit. I didn't want to be in his office to begin with, and then to have his wife come all unhinged on him, it wasn't fun for me either. But to now worry that Phil's going to take his shit out on me, or worse on my staff, it's not right." I thumbed my cell phone awake and was about to phone the hotel when Da Nise grabbed the phone out of my hand.

"No, you don't," she said.

"Da Nise, I want to head this off before it becomes a thing," I said.

Kathy shook her head. "That'd be great if Phil was rational. But let's think about it, his wife's lover just ended up dead by the hotel—

and by now the entire seventh floor knows his wife was screwing Bernie. Don't you think Phil's going to be the prime suspect? Let him hang himself. Don't hand him the rope to hang you."

I exhaled. "This all sucks. Why did I have to find him?"

"But you didn't," Kathy said. "Remember, Ryan did."

I nodded. "Yeah, and that's exactly how I answered when Phil asked about Bernie's dead body."

"Good. Keep to the script you and Ryan created. There's no reason to get him in trouble," Da Nise said.

"I'd never do that," I said.

"Not intentionally," Kathy said. "But somehow I think you may actually live up to your name."

I chuckled. "Rebel does fit." I thought of my mom, and it was a good thing that Da Nise had my phone because I'd probably have broken the rules and called her.

"How'd you get a name like Rebel anyway?" Da Nise asked.

I watched the side streets stream by in a haze of concrete and flashing street lights. "When my mom was little, she told her mom, my grandma, that when she was older she was going to name her daughter Rebel. Of course, my grandma freaked out and forbade her from doing it. But when my mom got pregnant and found out she was having a girl, she told my dad my name. She said she wanted a girl that would rival any boy, so she named me Rebel Jean."

"Well, Rebel Jean Roberts, your mama knew what she was

doing," Da Nise said.

Brandt. My name is Rebel Jean Brandt. But I stayed the course and silenced the urge to spit out the truth since 90 percent of what I'd said was true.

"Yeah, my name was like a big fuck you to my grandma, who I have no love for. That woman made my mom's life miserable." Again the truth. I didn't like living in the gray area between the truth and a lie, but I had to if I wanted to survive and keep those around me safe. "So I'm sure you're spot-on about Phil and his reaction to me, but I don't do well having to watch my step because of someone's ego."

They laughed.

But it was Kathy who leveled the playing field.

"It ain't no thing to me if you want to be a rebel, Rebel," Kathy said. "But right now, Phil's too raw and so are you. It's not a good combination."

I leaned into the passenger seat with the weight of what Kathy said. She was right. It wasn't just Phil's ego that was getting in the way of things. Mine was too.

"Thank you," I said. "I've been known to act before I think, which rarely yields a favorable outcome."

Kathy's shrug was like her demeanor—she was easygoing until she wasn't. And that was when I tended to listen.

Da Nise tossed my phone on my lap. "Sometimes not responding is the best response."

"Agreed," I said.

When Kathy flipped on the turn signal, I glanced through the windshield to the street sign: Del Amo Boulevard. Once she made the turn, the difference between traveling on the busy, often congested Atlantic Avenue and Del Amo Boulevard was considerable. The city seemed to fade and suburbia appeared. Tall, leafy trees planted in long concrete dividers that separated the main street from the neighborhoods brightened the landscape.

Lakewood reminded me of Alpine, Wyoming, forty miles south of Jackson Hole. Tourists recognized Jackson the way they knew Long Beach—as a focal point for travel. And even though Lakewood was probably only twenty miles from downtown Long Beach, the afternoon traffic made it about a forty-minute drive, similar to the driving time between Alpine to Jackson.

Both Lakewood and Alpine had the proximity to a bigger city and 80 percent less population, which usually meant fewer problems. Still, from what I saw from the car window, the energy and volume of tourists that were vibrant in downtown Long Beach seemed to disappear and grow thinner the closer we got to Lakewood.

"Lakewood has a mall and a lot of restaurants. The smaller, post-World War II homes are being snapped up by young families that want to flip a flop," Da Nise said.

"Oh, they aren't flops," I said of the older homes. "They have character."

Da Nise laughed. "That's like saying a girl has a good personality—it's basically calling her a dog."

"But this time it's true," I said, chuckling. "These older homes *do* have character."

"I've got to side with Rebel on this one. Lakewood is really finding its own little vibe," Kathy said, and I had to agree.

The further she drove into Lakewood, the more I experienced something a bigger city usually didn't have—a sense of community. The neighborhoods overflowed with generational families, from grandparents who sat on the porch to grandkids who played on the lawn. The vibe, as Kathy referred to it, was close-knit, protective, and homey. I liked Lakewood.

As soon as Kathy drove past a street sign that announced Downey Boulevard, she glanced at Da Nise.

"Minturn is up ahead. Isn't the house number in the four-hundred block?"

"That's right." Da Nise began calling out the house numbers when Kathy turned onto Minturn Avenue and let her Jeep slow to a crawl until she stopped in front of a modest home with super cute curb appeal. Rich green grass and three mature trees shaded the home without blocking the views.

"What kind of trees are those?" I asked.

"Olive trees," Kathy and Da Nise said in tandem.

"Like black olives?" I said, and they chuckled.

"No, green olives that stain the sidewalk. They're a real pain in the ass," Kathy said.

"Oh, but they're so pretty." I missed the open green expanses of Wyoming.

A two-car garage on a sloped driveway made me cringe. "That's got to be a bitch in the winter."

"What?" Da Nise leaned into me. "Why?"

I suddenly burst out laughing. "California doesn't get snow, does it?"

"Not Southern California," Kathy said.

"Where are you from?" Da Nise said.

I shrugged. "Not sunny, warm So Cal."

The screen door opened and a thin man with grayish-white hair and a matching moustache dressed in black slacks and a white polo-style shirt stepped onto the porch. When he waved toward us, I spoke through a forced smile.

"That's not Ryan," I said.

"Duh, he's probably either at your apartment or finishing work." Da Nise opened her car door. "Hello!" She waved toward the man on the porch. "Is this Ryan McHenry's house?"

I cracked my door so I could hear his answer.

"This is where he lives," the man said with a smile. "Are you Rebel?"

Da Nise laughed. "Nah, I'm the cute one."

"Yes, ma'am," he said, and I shook my head. *Only Da Nise.*

I stepped out of the car. "I'm Rebel."

"Wonderful. I've been expecting you." He fanned his hand. "Come on now, girls, I've got dinner in the oven."

I grabbed my cell phone and checked the time. It was close to four. As I shut the car door, I whispered to Da Nise, "Do people eat dinner this early in California?"

"Rebel, the man's probably retired. Don't ask me to explain old people. They do crazy shit like eat dinner at four and wake up at six when they could sleep till noon."

I nodded and fell in line behind Kathy, who clearly didn't care what time it was if it meant food.

CHAPTER 20
RYAN

"**L**isten, *Georgie, you can do* this." I handed Demi's little sister the card key to Rebel's apartment. We stood next to the stairwell in the parking garage.

"Ryan, of course I can do it." She shook her head, and her silky auburn hair swayed on her bony cocoa-colored shoulders. "I just don't know why I'm doing it and you aren't."

"Okay, like I told you on the phone, the deputy in charge of my training, Stanley, may still be standing guard by Rebel's apartment. He already saw me, so I can't go back now. But he doesn't know you so, I thought—"

"I could act gay?" Her catlike green eyes honed in on me. If I didn't know Georgina, her resting bitch face would be enough for me to steer clear. But I did know Georgina and I knew her tough exterior was her protection against haters. Georgina preferred women to men and that didn't always sit well with some men who saw a beautiful woman and didn't understand why she wasn't interested.

"Well first, acting gay wouldn't be an act." I opted to make her smile, which she did. "And secondly, I don't think it would be hard for Stanley or whoever he's with to think that Rebel was gay."

"Why?" Georgie's green eyes flashed in my direction. "Is this Rebel chick really butch? You know that's a stereotype, right?"

I chuckled when I probably shouldn't. "Yes, I know it's a stereotype and no, Rebel isn't butch, but she does have an edge to her that makes her appear harder than she is. Rebel's not like Katie, who's so klutzy she's cute. She's a bit more like Carmen."

Katie was Patrick Flanagan's older sister and our former high school classmate. To coin a phrase, Katie was a "hot mess." And Georgie knew it. But Carmen Gonzalez and Georgie practically grew up in the same house—and I knew comparing Rebel to someone Georgie knew would help. Carmen was a sweetheart, but after her mom died she became more guarded—like Rebel. I didn't know what Rebel was guarded about, only that she was.

"Oh." Georgie's defenses began to soften when a grin lit her face. "And how would you know"—she jabbed her finger into my chest—"that this Rebel isn't as hard as she appears? Huh, *chico*?"

If I thought telling Georgie that I'd seen Rebel naked and there weren't hard edges to her would shock her, I would. But Georgie used shock as a tactic. Yet another defense mechanism.

"It's one of those things you learn about someone after you discover a dead body together," I said.

"Si." Georgie nodded. "So, you want me to go to her apartment, grab her gun—if it's still in the bottom of her record player—and get her a change of clothes?"

"That's right. And remember to keep your back to everything. I don't know if they installed listening devices or cameras. And before you say I'm getting all white-boy paranoid, my uncle's partner, Bernie, was killed about a block from where my uncle was killed. Then suddenly Deputy Stanley and who knows who else shows up at Rebel's apartment—I'm sure without a warrant—and I'm supposed to think everything's *bueno*? No. Right now, Stanley's acting like a *pinche gringo*."

Now I was literally talking Georgie's language.

"Actually, sounds like this Stanley's a real *pinche cabrón*."

"Yeah, asshole fits right now," I said, and rubbed the back of my neck.

"Uh-oh, what's wrong?" She elbowed me. "That's the thing you do when you're stressed."

I shrugged and released the back of my neck. "I don't usually jump to conclusions, especially when it comes to someone I thought

I knew, like Stanley. But when he popped up today at Rebel's apartment, my gut knew something wasn't right and that's...."

"Disappointing," Georgie said, and I nodded.

"Yeah, it sucks. And on the flipside, I want to know what that asshat was doing in Rebel's apartment."

"Asshat?"

I grinned. "It's something Rebel called me when she first met me and I guess it stuck."

"Oh, I like this girl already." Georgie waved the key card. "I'll take the stairs to the ninth floor and if this Stanley guy is there, I have a key to Rebel's apartment and in this strapless black number," she rolled her bare shoulders, "when I don't give him the time of day, I'll have him so shaken he'll question his own sexuality."

I shook my head. "No. Don't mess with him. I would have asked Demi to do this, but he's a horrible liar. Besides it's more plausible that Rebel would have given her apartment key to another woman. So if Stanley or anyone questions why you have a key to Rebel's apartment, who just moved there—then you can charm the pants off them."

The look of disgust on Georgie's face was priceless. "*Ay Dios mio*. Men? Pants? That's wrong on so many levels."

I laughed and kissed her cheek. "Thank you, *chica. Vaya con Dios.*"

Georgie smiled. She was the one who had taught me the phrase.

I kept a careful watch from the garage for familiar cars or cops while Georgie headed toward the stairwell.

CHAPTER 21
REBEL

entered the house and immediately felt at home. Hardwood floors and calming sage-colored walls offset the front room that was centered on the oversized picture window that showcased the front yard. A couch in brown tweed was positioned against the wall across from the window, and a grandfather clock stood by itself on the opposite wall. An older television on a TV cart was parked in the corner next to the window. The volume was low, and when I glanced at the screen, baseball players in white uniforms with blue caps were huddled on the pitcher's mound.

"Dodger fan," Kathy said, following Ryan's father into the living room.

"Afraid so," he said. "They break my heart every year, but I'm convinced they'll win another world series before I die."

Da Nise laughed. "Ah, they've got plenty of time."

He turned and stood with his hands on his hips—something I'd seen his son do. "Where are my manners." He extended his hand toward Kathy. "I'm Howard McHenry, attorney at law."

Kathy introduced herself as "Your typical Girl Friday."

Da Nise added her own spin, "I'm overworked, underpaid, and looking to move on—but that's on the down low."

I wanted to shout, "No. No. No. Da Nise, you can't leave!" But I sensed she had been screwed by the hotel one time too many.

Howard worked his way toward me. "And you are Rebel," he said when he stood in front of me.

I grinned. "Rebel Roberts." I gave him a firm handshake like my mom taught me. *Never give a man a fish.* My mom was big on raising a strong daughter. "My title is *way* more impressive than my skill set. Besides, our department only functions at the hotel because of these two." I gave a nod toward Kathy and Da Nise.

Howard smiled.

"You have a beautiful home," I said when he released my hand.

"It's hard to imagine that five people lived in 875 square feet, but we did. My older brother Mark and I got the convertible couch in the living room," he said with a nod toward the sofa. "And my sister Marie, who we called Mimi, had the front bedroom, on the right side behind the porch." Again a nod toward the room opposite the couch. "Mom and Dad had the back bedroom. And it only has one bathroom."

"Damn," Da Nise said. "And I thought my condo in Long Beach was small."

Howard again stood with his hands on his narrow hips. "My parents bought this home when it was first build in 1952 with the GI Bill. It allowed vets, like my dad, to get a home loan without any down payment and a thirty-year mortgage with only 4 percent interest."

"Oh, my God," I said. "You can't even get a decent credit card with a 4 percent interest rate."

He laughed.

"How much did the house cost?" Kathy asked, and Howard didn't seem offended by her candor.

"In the mid-fifties, houses ranged from seven to nine thousand dollars. My folks got this two-bedroom home for eight grand. A house just like ours, down the street, sold about a month ago for half a million," he said.

"Wow," Da Nise said. "In Lakewood?"

Again, Howard chuckled. "I remember my dad saying that when the plan for the new community was presented to the Long Beach City Council in the late forties, the developer was almost laughed out of the room."

"Why?" I asked.

"Back then, there was no appeal for a community built so far from anything else. Lakewood didn't have the ocean or a downtown area. It didn't have ties to anything. The joke was that only jackrabbits would buy the houses. Lakewood was so far on the outskirts of town, I doubt there were even jackrabbits interested in it," he said. "But my parents were convinced Lakewood just needed time to form into a community of neighbors, so they bought this house. I was born three years later and grew up here."

"And now you own it?" Kathy said.

"The house was left to my brother, sister, and me in my parent's trust…." His voice drifted off and he rubbed the back of his neck.

Another mannerism his son shared. I knew Ryan's uncle had died while he was off-duty, but I didn't know about his aunt.

"So you share it with them?" Da Nise asked.

Ryan had his father's hazel eyes, which softened when he answered Da Nise's question. "I'm the only one left. So I suppose it's mine by default."

"I'm sorry," Da Nise said, and Howard gently smiled.

"Thank you. A few years have passed since Mimi's death. She lived here until she passed. And my older brother." He held his neck. "Well, it's been nearly two decades since Mark was killed."

"Killed?" Da Nise said.

Howard released his hold on his neck and pointed toward the

folded military flag enclosed in a triangular-shaped glass frame that hung on the back wall opposite the TV and front window. "He was a deputy sheriff and tried to stop an armed robbery."

"I'm so sorry." It was all I knew to say. *What else is there to say?* Howard nodded toward me.

"And Ryan lives with you?" Kathy said.

"After my wife passed two years ago, I sold our home and moved back here. Not too soon afterward Ryan showed up one day with all his belongings." A sideways smile slid across Howard's face and again I saw his son. "He told me it was to save on rent while he worked on his Master's degree in criminal justice while he continued at the office supply company that gave him flexible hours. But then he applied for the sheriff's department, and"—Howard wagged his finger—"I knew better. He finished his Master's degree and continued living here because he was worried about his old man."

"That's sweet." Da Nise verbalized the sentiment that tugged at my heart. Ryan was one of the good guys.

"That's Ryan," Kathy said, and Howard smiled.

"Yes, it is." Howard waved his hand toward us. "Now, you ladies didn't come all the way to Lakewood to hear an old man ramble about the past. And if my wife, Norma, were here she'd scold me for talking off your ears. Besides, I want you to try my latest drink. My youngest son has informed me I have to get into the twenty-first century, so I tried my hand with Tequila Sunrises, if you'd like to join me in the kitchen."

"Ah, yah. Tequila Sunrises," Kathy said, following him.

A rectangular table with shiny grooved chrome legs and a white laminate top was tucked beside the bay window. A turquoise-colored refrigerator with a slide-out bottom freezer was the same color as the oven, which had black burners and reminded me of the chef's grill at the Napa Point Resort. The difference was that the Napa property was going for a retro look and the appliances in Howard's kitchen were the real deal. The chrome trim and handles on the refrigerator and oven had an iconic fifties vibe and I was sure dated back to when Howard's parents bought the house.

Howard reached into the turquoise refrigerator, pulled out a tray with four tall glasses, which looked like they each held a bleeding sun. As far as drinks went, a Tequila Sunrise made right, was beautiful.

"Ryan thought there might be three joining us." Howard carefully placed the tray on the counter. "Shoot," he said, shaking his head. "I forgot the orange slice." He glanced at me over his shoulder. "Rebel, would you mind getting us an orange?"

"Uh, sure." I looked at Kathy. "May I borrow your car?"

My request made Howard chuckle. "No need to go any further than the backyard."

I must have looked as confused as I felt because he nodded toward the side door next to the kitchen. "Norma always liked visiting the orange groves in Orange County, so I brought the grove to her. Or to my parents' backyard, which needed a wind block. Besides, Norma and I didn't live far from my parents, so Norma made it part of her daily walk to tend the orange trees. Just step outside and you'll find an orange on one of the back trees."

"Orange trees?" I practically ran to the door, where I pushed open the screen that led to an oversized covered patio. I walked beneath a canopy of butter-colored roses that crisscrossed the cedar beams and provided an airy, natural shade. The honey perfume from the blooms wafted in the air and like everything I had discovered about his house, it felt like home. And it was beautiful.

Beyond the patio was a fenced yard. A mature eucalyptus tree took center stage, and a small orange grove almost covered the cinder blocks of the back wall.

I carefully walked across the lush green grass toward the row of trees that edged the yard. The limbs fanned out, creating their own shade. When I stepped beneath the leafy green umbrella, a sweeter scent surrounded me. The branches drooped with ripe fruit that looked like golden globes. *Oh, my gosh.* I'd never seen anything like it.

Wyoming didn't have orange trees. Or if it did, I never saw one. The oranges in Howard's backyard were as large as softballs and practically fell into my hand. I wanted to pick the whole tree, but I didn't. I held one, brought it to my nose, and inhaled the delicious fragrance. It was like being in Willy Wonka's chocolate factory—for fruit. I was one reach away from as many succulent oranges as my heart's desire.

Napa had wine caves, hearty grape vines, and plentiful wine. But Lakewood had fruit I could taste and touch without fear of intellectual property violations, which was the wine industry's business end of a shotgun. Howard's backyard oranges were all the sweeter because they were within reach.

I would have liked to have met Howard's wife and Ryan's mom. I began to understand why Norma tended the orange trees. There was a peaceful tranquility beneath the shade. I could sit below the branches and let the citrus scent alone carry me away. But Howard was waiting.

I made my way to the house and handed him the orange.

"Norma used to get lost in her little orange grove," he said, and I grinned.

"It'd be so easy to do," I said.

"Would you like to do the honors?" He offered me the paring knife. As I cut into the fruit, fragrant, tangy juice sprayed that I could have bathed in. I wanted to dig my teeth into the orange, but instead I cut thick slices that Howard stuck on the rim of each glass.

When we all had a Tequila Sunrise complete with an orange

garnish, Howard lifted his glass and we followed suit.

"Here's to new friends," he began, "and, in the words of Oscar Wilde, 'I always like to know everything about my new friends, and nothing about my old ones.' So, ladies, tell me a little about yourselves, and when we've reached the bottom of our Tequila Sunrises you'll be old friends and I'll never ask anything about you ever again."

"Where do I begin?" Kathy chuckled as her glass brushed against the center of our glasses. "Let's just say, my journey began by following the Dead in San Fran and concluded decades ago in Long Beach when I ran out of money."

"Fare thee well, Dead Head," Howard said to Kathy's delight, and we all took a sip.

Da Nise spoke next. "I was born at Long Beach Memorial where my son, Jordan was also born. Steve and I bought a condo in Long Beach—but not downtown. I guess I'm an uptown Long Beach girl and not a downtown sister."

This made Howard chuckle. "To a fellow Long Beach local," he said, and again we all drank.

"Rebel, I'm quite interested in hearing your story, but first"—Howard waggled his eyebrows—"there's one last housekeeping item I have to finish for our dinner." He set his Tequila Sunrise on the kitchen table, opened the refrigerator, and retrieved an aluminum baking sheet lined with strips of bacon.

"Oh, damn!" Da Nise said. "That's some thick bacon."

"Yes, ma'am. The recipe called for, and this is a direct quote, 'meaty deliciousness,' so I had the butcher cut it for me directly." He held the tray in one hand and opened the oven door with the other. He carefully slid the tray of bacon into the oven.

"What recipe called for 'meaty deliciousness'?" Kathy asked, and then added, "Not that I'm complaining. I don't trust anyone who doesn't like bacon."

A hearty chuckle rose from Howard's throat while he turned the oven temperature to two hundred and set the rooster-shaped timer perched on the ledge of the oven controls to twenty minutes.

"Kathy, as much as I'd like to tell you what I'm serving for dinner, I can't." He turned and crossed his arms over his body. "My youngest and I have this, well, routine—and when Ryan arrives home from work, I'm sure it'll make more sense."

Kathy shrugged. "Works for me."

I was intrigued by whatever routine Ryan and his father shared. And it made me homesick. I missed my mom and the hit of garlic that greeted me anytime I opened the front door to the house. My mom insisted garlic cured anything so it was in everything she cooked.

Howard led us to the kitchen table, where I sank into one of the padded yellow linoleum chairs in the breakfast nook. My back was to the door, which was considered bad form in Wyoming.

But I wasn't in Wyoming. So when Kathy and Da Nise sat beside me and Howard took the seat across from me, I settled into the Southern California groove, which seemed less concerned about who was behind me than who was in front of me.

A black-and-white photo of Ryan on the pitcher's mound hung on the back of the cabinets. I leaned into the table and studied Ryan's face, which was intense and reminded me of the delivery guy I met in the alley, who was all business—until I stumbled across Bernie.

"Ryan was quite a talented pitcher," Howard said.

"What made him so good?" Kathy asked.

"In pitching, if you can't throw hard or fast, the batters will tee off on you like it's batting practice. But if you have a pitch that starts out like a fastball down the heart of the plate, but changes up and drops clean to the bottom of the plate as the batter swings, it's called the changeup. And a pitcher who can throw a changeup can have a successful career in college and sometimes in the pros, especially if they're a lefty. My right-handed Ryan had an above average changeup that was good enough for college, but according to the scouts was minor league material at best in the pros." He shrugged. "Doesn't matter to me. His changeup remains legendary in *this* family."

I thought of Ryan's kiss in the alcove and how it was as unexpected as the pitching his father spoke of. I felt my cheeks burn with the memory. I reached for my glass, but Da Nise shook her head.

"Nun-uh, not until you introduce yourself to Howard," she said.

"Okay, well," I cleared my throat, "if I could be described in just a single baseball term, I guess it would be 'the changeup.' Because just like that pitch confuses batters into believing that it's something else, I have that same way around people. I'm not always what I seem and if you don't keep your eye on the ball with me, you're sure to strike out." I grinned and was about to take a much-needed drink when his voice startled me.

"I'll drink to that."

I turned to find Ryan leaning against the kitchen's doorframe with a camo-colored backpack that looked like mine slung over his shoulder. The single dimple in the side of his face made my stomach flip-flop. I swallowed hard, but the taste of him remained seared in my memory. As much as the Tequila Sunrise was brightening my otherwise dreary day, the sight of Ryan made it shine. And I knew that if his lips were back on mine, it would make my day even better.

CHAPTER 22
RYAN

Her brown eyes practically danced when she smiled in my direction.

I quickly surveyed my surroundings. Dad. Da Nise. Kathy and Rebel. From the breakfast nook window, I saw our neighbors, the Aguas family, barbequing in their backyard. The other kitchen window revealed flattened grass in a straight path toward Mom's favorite orange trees.

"Hey," Rebel said, as if we were alone and her staff and my father weren't sitting there.

I followed her cue, which wasn't hard. Anytime Rebel was around, it felt like the world stopped and time stood still. It was hard to explain. It wasn't just the way she approached an alley like she owned it, which she did. Or withdrew into the mood of Nina Simone's music when she didn't know what to say or how to act. All those were snapshots I had experienced of her. But what got me was her energy. Rebel possessed a drive that was palpable. I didn't know if she was running to or from something—only that she was driven to get wherever she was headed. It didn't take a profiling course to tell me Rebel was competitive. She played to win, and God help the man or woman who got in her way.

Yet, for all her drive, she was this amazing contradiction. When I kissed her, I felt a softer, gentler side that succumbed to the tenderness between us, like she had been waiting for someone to take the lead. I could be completely off base, but that was what my gut told me, and when I let my head get in the way I tended to screw things up. So, I let my heart be my guide and as she sat at the breakfast table, the hard edges faded to show a happy-go-lucky fellow millennial. And I liked what I saw.

Her backpack gently slid off my shoulder and I carefully leaned it against the doorframe.

"Is that my bag?" she asked.

I smiled. "Yes, yes, it is. My friend Georgie helped me out. It has a change of clothes and that *notebook* you were looking for."

"Uh...."

I waited for her to make the connection with her gun.

"Oh! My notebook? You found it?"

"Let's just say I've got it." I nudged her with my hip to share her seat. She practically squealed when I planted myself beside her.

"How was work?" my dad asked with a grin that lit his face.

I shrugged. "Not many deliveries. I think Lenny's still sore that his truck was dusted for fingerprints. You know how he feels about his stuff."

My father chuckled. "Lenny's a good man, he'll come around."

Rebel, Kathy, and Da Nise seemed absorbed in the crosstalk between my dad and me. I looked like my mom, but I was told often enough that I acted like my dad. We shared the same hazel eyes and when I looked across at the old man, all I saw was green.

"What's in the oven?" I asked.

I knew from the way my dad tilted his head that he wasn't about to answer. So I did what we'd done since I was a kid; I closed my eyes and let my other senses take over. The aroma in the air was salty and meaty, but it was the crack and sizzle that gave it away. *Bacon.* So what would the old man be making for dinner with bacon?

There weren't any skillets on the oven when I walked into the kitchen—so not breakfast for dinner. But the cheese grater and colander were stacked on the drying rack and remnants of orange peel or tomatoes were in the sink. The old man only used the colander to rinse lettuce. I deeply inhaled—the enticing scent of sizzling bacon was strong, but there was a trace of something else. I slowed my breathing until the smell of chicken wafted into my nose. I knew the Aquas family only barbequed hamburger.

Chicken. Bacon. Cheese. Tomato. Lettuce. I smiled and opened my eyes. Everyone was staring at me, but the only person I directed my answer to was my old man.

"Chicken cobb salad."

His grin revealed the truth before he did. "And what's for dessert?"

I shook my head. "Nuh-uh. I deduced dinner—let's keep it at that."

My father playfully rolled his eyes. "Okay, if you don't want to make detective…."

Now, I mirrored his mannerism and shook my head. "Good try, old man. But figuring out dinner won't be a factor toward making detective, *which* is a bit premature since I haven't officially made the applicant cut."

"Better to be prepared," he said.

"So you repeatedly tell me," I said.

Rebel's laughter made me smile.

"Don't encourage him," I said. "It doesn't take much these days."

My dad fanned away my comment.

"Son, come help me finish dinner."

As much as I didn't want to leave my spot beside Rebel, I followed my old man, who looked happier than I'd seen in a long time.

After dinner, Da Nise pushed her chair away from the patio table and her plate that only had a few remnants of lettuce left. "So, I'm confused," she said. "The affair that Phil's wife had prevented Phil from losing his money because it voids the prenuptial agreement?" She raised her shoulders. "Wouldn't that make Phil actually *grateful* for the affair and give him no motive for killing Bernie?"

My father's hands were steepled together, which I knew was his thinking stance.

"No, I don't think that's what Rebel meant," Kathy said with a glance toward Rebel. "Is it?"

Rebel's red hair swayed back and forth against her slender shoulders. It was the first time I'd seen her in a stress-free environment and she wore relaxed well. Still, I couldn't stop imagining her naked. *Naked was good.*

"*If* Phil and his wife, Sheila, had a prenuptial agreement because Phil was the money source, then Bernie's death could mean that Phil keeps his money and his soon-to-be ex-wife wouldn't because the affair would void the prenuptial agreement. Because if Phil had the money and the prenuptial agreement stated Sheila got nothing if he divorced her for *cause*, like infidelity, the affair would benefit Phil." Rebel paused as if she was letting everyone filter the information. "And if Sheila had the money and there was a prenuptial agreement that stated Phil would get nothing in the divorce *unless* he left her for cause, like infidelity, then either way the affair benefits Phil."

"Do we know if Phil has a prenup?" Kathy asked.

Rebel's hair swung. The setting sun made it seem like there was a halo around her head, which almost made me laugh because the girl was less than angelic. Nope, there was a fiery side to Rebel that I liked.

"Only the lawyers and signers of the prenup would be aware of the prenup and the presence of any infidelity clause," Rebel said.

"So, it really doesn't lead us anywhere new," Kathy said.

"Hold up," Da Nise said. "Let's just follow this thought through. What would happen if there wasn't a prenup?"

Before my father could put on his attorney hat, Rebel jumped in.

"If there's no prenup, Sheila automatically gets half of the assets—including half of Phil's shares of the Point's publicly owned hotel that vested managers earn. And Phil's been there long enough to be vested." Rebel glanced around the patio table and she must have read the confusion on our faces.

"Anyway, since we know a divorce is imminent and we don't know whether there *was or wasn't* a prenup, whoever the money source is for Greenberg-Mendel, they could doctor other assets in the divorce with nothing much more happening than what we expect already—a bitter lawsuit."

Rebel seemed in her element talking with ease about legalities and finances, which seemed odd for a conference services manager.

"So, while everyone else—including the cops"—she avoided making eye contact with me—"will automatically think Phil killed Bernie in a jealous rage, Phil has *zero* motive. Hell, he could have paid Bernie or anyone else to cheat with his wife just so he could escape that nightmare marriage and keep his money. Again," she clarified, "if a prenup is in place."

"Husbands are suspect number one automatically when the wife's lover is murdered—that's homicide one-oh-one," I said.

"I bet, and I'm sure by now the cops know Sheila was having an affair with Bernie. Or that info will now be told to them by someone on the seventh floor, who was privy to Sheila's ass reaming of Phil," Rebel said. "However, the big *but* here is that until they can prove that a prenup did or did not exist, then pointing a finger at Phil is simply convenient and quite honestly, sloppy."

I wasn't sure if it was the second Tequila Sunrise talking, but Rebel was pretty defensive of some guy she just started working for.

I was about to counter her "sloppy cop" comment when my dad spoke.

"I knew the Point's reputation for hiring the best was legendary, but your knowledge of the intricacies of corporate finance and the law is quite impressive," he said, and Rebel's cheeks almost turned as bright as her hair.

"Google." Rebel tried to shrug off the compliment, but like mine, her fair face gave her away. "I googled Phil Greenberg, and his wife, Sheila Mendel, appeared beside him in a bunch of posts at philanthropic events. It appears that Greenberg-Mendel is a publicly traded corporation that developed software for smart cards. Then I googled the different types of divorces and things like marital asset division—it's all online."

As Rebel polished off the last of her Tequila Sunrise, my father's gaze never left her. He wasn't buying the whole Google thing any more than I was. How did she know so much about finances and the law? And why would she lie about knowing it?

"Did your online search tell you who represented Phil Greenberg or Sheila Mendel?" my dad asked.

"No." Rebel's cheery voice seemed forced. "But I can't imagine their attorneys are as dirty as these dishes."

Her comment elicited a laugh from her staff as Rebel stood from the table and reached for the plates. The girl was great at the redirect. Whether she dropped her towel or began clearing a table, she knew how to get the focus off the conversation and onto something else.

I stood, grabbed Da Nise's and Kathy's plates, and was about to follow her into the kitchen when my dad intercepted my path.

"Enjoy your guests," he said to me with a nod toward Da Nise and Kathy. "Rebel can help me with the dishes tonight."

Rebel disappeared into the house with a faint smile, my dad trailing behind her.

REBEL

I capped the sink drain, flipped on the faucet to the hottest setting, and squirted dish soap into the cavity. A mountain of bubbles formed. I didn't care about my recent manicure. If I could dive into the hot sudsy peaks and disappear, I would. *Google?* My skill at lying was diminishing by the second. I was lost in my thoughts when Howard gently cut the water.

"Have you seen the neighborhood?" he asked.

I shook my head.

"Then I have to show you," he said with a wave toward the pile of dirty dishes. "Those can wait. It's a beautiful evening— perfect for a walk."

I didn't know what it was about Howard, but even when I knew he wasn't buying my story, he didn't put me on the defensive. I followed him into the living room and the coatrack behind the front door, where he handed me a Dirtbags jacket and grabbed one for himself. I slipped into the oversized windbreaker. It smelled sweet like jasmine.

"It was my wife's," he said by way of explanation.

"Oh, I don't have to wear it." I began to peel it off but he wagged his finger.

"She'd want you to wear it." He opened the door and we stepped onto the porch. "She'd also like to know the truth about the young woman her youngest son is so enamored with."

I smiled as if he wasn't implying I hadn't been truthful.

The sidewalks were littered with olives, which I could now see would be a pain in the ass to keep clean. Smashed olives stained the sidewalk and looked like flattened bugs. It kind of grossed me out. Still, it provided a visual distraction as I walked beside Howard in silence, which I wasn't about to break. When a muffled melody filtered through the air, I paused and listened. There was only one harmony I knew that always sounded like it was piped out of broken speakers. I turned to see an ice-cream truck inching toward us.

"Oh my gosh!" Despite myself, the little kid in me emerged. "An ice-cream truck! That's so cool."

"Do you have any money?" Howard asked, and I reached for my bag, but realized it was still in the kitchen.

"No," I said and frowned.

"I'm pretty sure Norma kept a few dollars in her pocket," he said, and I wanted to die of embarrassment.

"Oh, that's okay. I just think it's neat that there's an ice-cream truck," I said, trying to pick up the pace.

"I'd like one." Howard stopped. "And I'd like you to buy it for me."

What? "Uh, okay. I can run back to the house."

"Possession is nine-tenths of the law, so the jacket you are currently wearing is presumed to be yours unless someone can prove that it is not," he said. "Of course, that adage is not literally true. However, the person in possession is presumed to have a nine times stronger claim than anyone else and places *you* in a stronger legal stance since you currently maintain possession of the jacket and any monies in the pocket."

"Okay?" *How much tequila was in that drink?*

"I'd like an orange pushup," Howard said, and waved the ice-cream truck over. When it pulled curbside, he nudged me toward the window.

I reached into the pocket and was pretty, impressed when I withdrew a five-dollar bill, which I handed to the ice-cream man. "Orange pushup, please."

The window attendant handed me two dollars in change, and when he realized sooner than I did that five bucks only bought one ice cream, he checked the large, rectangular side windows on his truck before resuming his route.

I extended the orange pushup toward Howard. "Thank you." He peeled off the top wrapper and held the orange sherbet on a stick like a seasoned pro. "That'll be a dollar," he said with his hand outstretched.

"I'm sorry?"

"Rebel, my fee for talking with you on this walk is a dollar."

I scratched my head, but the seriousness on Howard's face was legit. I didn't know what the fuck was happening, only that Howard wanted a buck. I reached into the jacket and handed him a dollar, which he folded and placed in the back pocket of his slacks.

"Since you just enlisted my legal services, through the rules of professional conduct any conversation we have is protected. What that means is that anything you disclose to me is privileged and in the context of any legal advice I provide, I'm bound by the California rules of professional conduct to protect that information."

The last time I was this shocked was when Jude arrived at the truck yard and whisked me into protective custody, warning me that as soon as the Robertson brothers discovered I had been the source of their downfall, it would be mine as well.

"So," he continued to walk and when my brain caught up to my body, I hurried to keep pace beside him, "why don't we begin by you telling me who you really are and what you're doing in Long Beach."

CHAPTER 23
RYAN

When I spotted my dad and Rebel on the sidewalk leading to our house, they were followed by Herb Elder. Two attorneys and Rebel—not a good combination. Kathy and Da Nise had left, leaving me in charge of getting Rebel home. Or not. I wasn't ready for her to leave. And now that Herb accompanied her, I wasn't sure she should leave.

As soon as my father walked into the house, he placed a folded dollar into the small cider box that he kept on the bottom shelf of the TV cart next to the remote controls. The box was filled with folded dollars that were off-limits, and I knew why.

I placed my hands on my hips. "The dollar trick, Dad? Really?"

My father turned toward his friend, Herb, who extended his hand. "Ryan, the price for this conversation is a dollar."

I glanced at Rebel, who arched an eyebrow as if challenging me. I grabbed my wallet and handed Herb a crisp buck that he folded and placed into his pocket. "Now, since you just enlisted my legal services, through the rules of professional conduct any conversation we have is protected. What that means—"

"Yes. Herb, I know." I politely cut him off. "Anything I disclose to you is privileged and anything Rebel disclosed to my father, who I'm assuming is now her attorney, is also privileged."

Rebel smiled. "And since Howard represents me and Herb represents you, we now both have attorneys, and in the presence of our attorneys, I'd like to share with you what I shared with my attorney," she said, and the expression on her face was what I'd felt when I'd struck out the last batter in a game—relieved.

"Uh, sure, what's up?" I sat on the couch and she sat beside me.

She slowly exhaled and glanced at my dad, who gave her a nod.

"What I say here has to stay here," she said.

"Of course," I said.

"You can't tell your deputy friends or *any* of your friends," she said. "And no one at the hotel can know. Not my staff. Or Phil. Or Lenny, your boss. *No one.*"

"Got it. I won't utter a word." And I meant it. The only person I fully confided in was my dad, and he already knew my suspicions about Rebel. There's living off the grid and being completely erased; my inability to find any mention of a Rebel Roberts fit into the latter.

"Five years ago, I was hired by the Robertson Brothers Trucking Company to straighten out their books. I handled accounts payable and receivable and basic accounting duties. When their CFO suddenly resigned, the Robertson Brothers promoted me, which was when I realized why the CFO left. He hadn't kept the books straight because it would have revealed his creative accounting, which included skimming from the top. And I'm sure when he discovered what the Robertson Brothers were really up to, that was enough to rid him of sticky fingers." She folded her hands in her lap, I thought to keep them from shaking. "I've never told anyone other than my parents and the prosecuting attorney this. So bear with me," she said.

"Take your time," I said, even though curiosity was killing me.

"Okay, so what I learned after stepping into that role was that the Robertson Brothers Trucking Company was violating federal safety regulations by having their drivers drive more than sixteen hours, sleep in their cabs, and cut their take home pay to offset the repairs the trucks required that they blamed on the drivers. The drivers weren't very educated so when they signed their contracts, they didn't realize that they were leasing the truck and personally responsible for the cost of any repairs to their truck.

They thought they were buying into the truck. I mean, in all fairness, there was a buyout option in the contract, but the drivers could never get financially ahead to buy the truck outright, so it was kind of a moot point. Anyway, whenever a truck broke down, the Robertson Brothers fixed it and then had me deduct the cost from the employee's pay, which reduced their take home pay to nearly nothing. *I mean nothing.*"

"In Napa? This happened in Napa Valley?" I rubbed the back of my neck and Rebel placed her hand on my knee. A small gesture that spoke volumes. Georgie and I had been friends since high school so it was a no-brainer that she knew my tells. *But Rebel?* Rebel and I had really just met, even though it felt like a month since we found Bernie. Still, she already sensed when I was stressed.

The warmth of her hand on my knee was an assurance all its own. "Hey, this is a lot to absorb. But after talking to your dad, he assured me that I wouldn't be putting you in harm's way. In fact, he thought it was in your best interest to know so you wouldn't be blindsided if Deputy Stanley found out and told you."

"What would Stanley find out?"

"That I'm from Wyoming, which isn't that big a deal. But being in the Witness Protection program is."

"Huh." *Wyoming? Witness protection?* "The weight you've carried...." I took off my baseball cap, brushed my hair back, and slipped it back on. "I can't imagine."

Her eyes brimmed with tears. "It's been a lot."

"Reb…." I placed my hand on hers. "You're not alone anymore."

She lowered her head and tears fell down her cheeks.

My father knelt before her and Rebel looked at him. "You have been incredibly brave to right this injustice," he said. "But my son's right, you're not alone. You no longer have to fight this battle by yourself. Like I said on our walk, I'll accompany you to Wyoming when you're called to testify so you won't face this bunch alone."

Rebel seemed to soak in my dad's presence. My dad just had a quiet way of letting you know that everything was going to be okay.

"Thank you," she said.

"It might cost you another orange pushup," he said before he cupped his knees and stood.

Rebel's sudden giggle was adorable.

My dad was also the only man I knew who could make the direst situation seem bearable.

Rebel took a slow, steady breath. "So," she tucked her hair behind her ear, "where was I?"

"You were telling Ryan about the culture the Robertson brothers created," Herb said.

"Right," she said. "So while I worked for the Robertson brothers, I started to see a pattern develop that by forcing drivers to finance all their repairs, they basically treated the drivers like modern-day indentured servants. By leveraging any repairs as debt against the drivers, the drivers were stuck. If the driver quit, the company kept everything the driver had paid toward owning the truck. That's when I began collecting the contracts, shipping manifests, and repair bills to submit as evidence in a labor complaint that a few drivers were willing to have me file on their behalf. But then those men went missing. Like they accepted to haul a load and were never seen again. Their trucks were discovered broken down on the highway, but the drivers vanished."

"Shit."

She glanced from my dad to Herb, who again prodded her forward.

"The Robertson brothers basically created a culture of fear in the drivers and me. There were many nights when the drivers and I were barred from going home. The drivers would return to the yard with their trucks, get in their cars to go home, and the gate to the parking lot would be locked. It happened to me and…." She shuddered. "We were literally forced to either stay overnight in the yard in our cars, go back to work, or risk being fired. And for the drivers, they'd also lose what they had managed to pay into their truck lease. It was a lose-lose situation—for everyone. The Robertson brothers didn't care. They're awful, horrible humans."

"No," my father said. "What they did was inhuman."

Rebel nodded. "You're right. They preyed on the poor. They

hired uneducated drivers who needed a job and thought they were getting this great livelihood. But their take-home pay kept decreasing, which was my first indication that something wasn't right. I couldn't believe it. The more I dug, the more I discovered. The Robertson brothers created a host of expenses, like insurance, diesel fuel, parking fees in the company lot. The drivers had no choice but to break federal safety laws that limit truckers to eleven hours on the road just to maintain any take home pay. It was awful. As more and more drivers disappeared, I got scared but determined. They were beginning to delete files so I began copying files." She let go of my hand and wiped her eyes on the sleeve of my mom's jacket, which I knew my mom wouldn't have minded.

"Ryan, this wasn't just one trucking company mistreating workers. I uncovered spreadsheets and financial reporting documents for trucking companies all over the western United States that they operated under shell corporations. They were hurting *hundreds* of men and their families," she said.

"Weren't they part of a union?" I looked at my dad. "Wouldn't a union protect them?"

"A union could be a good avenue for these drivers, but Wyoming is the least populated state in our nation. I doubt that area of Wyoming even had the number of drivers for a union to form," he said.

"I thought the same thing," she said. "I thought if I could get a union to represent these drivers then all would be fine. But that only caused more problems for the drivers. It's like the more I tried to help them, the worse it got for them." She paused and lowered her head.

"Rebel, because of what you did, you saved many," my dad said.

"I hope so. But I really don't know. Until I testify I can't return to Wyoming to know for sure," she said.

"How'd you stop them?" I asked.

She laughed. "I didn't. But the FBI did. Once I began copying files and collected enough physical evidence, I contacted the FBI. I didn't put anything on a flash drive because I was pretty sure they had corrupted their computer system and I didn't want to risk not having what I needed and looking like a crazy person." She chuckled again. "Anyway, the FBI has an office in Jackson, which is about forty miles from Star Valley."

She paused and glanced at my dad. "Their office is built behind Wendy's—like there is a staircase from the back of the fast food restaurant that leads to the FBI's second-story office. I didn't think things could get weirder until I called the Wyoming field office and they told me to meet them there. At Wendy's."

She shrugged. "Anyway, it took a while but they presented what I'd compiled to a federal judge because the Robertson brothers didn't just break state laws, they broke federal transportation laws. And the federal judge gave me orders to preserve personal email accounts, but I knew the accounts had been tampered with to make the employees look like they had targeted the Robertson brothers, so despite the judge's order, I deleted them."

The shame she carried on her face was awful to see. "Rebel, you were trying to help these men," I said.

Her drooped shoulders and frown told me she wasn't as convinced of her bravery.

"I don't know if I ended up helping or hurting the drivers in the long run," she said.

"So that's why you're in Long Beach." My focus was on Rebel, who was probably one of the strongest women I'd met.

"Until I can testify at their trial, I'm wherever Jude, my FBI handler, places me," she said. "I'm told that the judge will most likely side with the drivers in this case, but without my testimony, the evidence I gave to the FBI isn't as solid. Numbers don't lie, but Jude swears that putting a face to this case will mean everything."

"Is that why you left Napa? Did they find you?" I asked.

"No." She shook her head. "Jude said the Napa Valley Point Resort and Winery was drawing too much attention to itself, so they pulled me from working as a wine educator and gave me the choice of New York or Long Beach, and the thought of the beach after spending so much time in a wine cave sounded *really* appealing."

We all got a good chuckle out of that. And like my dad, only this beautiful redhead would make light of what could only be described as a nightmare.

"So as soon as I testify that drivers were forced to work beyond the number of allowed hours, carried overweight loads, and drove with tires and brakes that weren't properly maintained despite the supposed maintenance, then I won't have to hide anymore," she said.

"And you can return to Wyoming," I said.

She squeezed my hand. "I'm not going to lie. I miss my parents."

"They're not dead," I said.

She cringed. "I'm so sorry, that was Jude's backstory for me. I still can't have the girls at the hotel know because the fewer people that know, the better. But your dad, or rather, my attorney urged me to tell you because since we found Bernie, that could be another case we'd have to testify at...."

"That's why you moved him," I said.

"That's why I moved Bernie. It was incredibly wrong, but all I was thinking of was that I couldn't have any attention drawn to the hotel or me. I didn't want to be relocated again to another Point property with another hair color and start this process all over again. Until the Robertson brothers are securely in custody, they still have reach. They owned a lot of trucking companies in the western United States," she said. "I didn't need my name to pop up on some police report or worse, news report. Jude said the FBI usually keeps a person's first name and only changes their surname, which was what they did with me. Still, if my name surfaced in the news, it wouldn't have been good. There aren't many Rebels in this world."

"No," I said, and wanted to pull this courageous woman into my arms and kiss her again. "There aren't."

CHAPTER 24
REBEL

It *seemed like once Ryan* understood why I was really in Long Beach, what had happened in Wyoming, and my subsequent motives for moving Bernie, we became a united front. I definitely liked working with him and not on my own. Plus, the chance to show him who Rebel was—not Rebel Roberts—was liberating.

"It feels like this pressure that's weighed on me for months has lessened," I said to the welcoming smiles of Howard, Herb, and Ryan.

"I bet," Howard said. "It also explains why your first approach when you discovered Phil and Sheila's affair was to look at it from a financial angle, which isn't usually someone's initial response."

I raised my shoulders to my ears. "I'm hardwired toward numbers. Numbers don't lie. Everyone will automatically think Phil killed Bernie in a jealous rage. But depending on the presence or absence of a prenup, Phil could be eternally grateful that Bernie cheated with his wife. Of course," I grinned, "A Bronx-born kid like Phil would never say that aloud, even to the police, because he still has his pride. Plus, I just don't think Phil killed Bernie. Call it gut instinct, but I don't think he did."

"I've only met Phil at events and the symphony gala," Howard said. "So I can't really weigh in on it."

"I know Greenberg from my days serving on the Long Beach Chamber with him," Herb said, "and while there's no love lost between us, it's hard to peg him for murder."

"What rubbed you the wrong way about him?" Ryan asked Herb.

"Like Rebel said, he's from the Bronx and has this East Coast thing going on that doesn't always work on the West Coast. He's pretty abrasive. However, to echo Rebel, his pride would prevent him from disclosing more than he needs to. The most you guys will get out of him," Herb said directly to Ryan, "is for him to admit to a prenup. And even then I don't think he'd offer that up unless he was arrested and charged with murder. Otherwise, the way Greenberg operates, or at least did during our tenure on the Chamber, was that his personal life is no one's business but his own and if the hotel underlings think he's a killer, all the better for his reputation and reign."

"Damn," I said. "You do know Phil. But…" I held up my hand like a stop sign. "I will say that the Bronx boy was humbled—and hard—by Sheila. Phil was somewhat apologetic, but even then, it wasn't guilt talking, but remorse. But not like remorse from killing someone, remorse that his marriage was over. Plus the fact that he backpedaled so fast into appeasing her makes me think she was the money source in that marriage."

"Steve Mendel, her father, did well in real estate and Sheila followed in his footsteps, taking over the firm when he retired," Howard said.

"Real estate?" It didn't make sense until I realized that this was California—not Wyoming. In California, a postage-sized lot with a crappy, run-down rental house could fetch thousands in rent and sell for even more. "Got it. I'm used to the oil and gas industry, where billionaires are made from striking it rich on the oil patch."

"In California, real estate is never a gamble because it's a guaranteed jackpot," Ryan said. "But with oil and gas, it's a gamble that doesn't always pay off if you're drilling in the wrong area or the well runs dry sooner than anticipated. With real estate, your fortune is right before your eyes and like they say, 'Buy land because they're not making any more of it.'"

Ryan seemed to have the knack for making me laugh. "Good point," I said.

"So until we find out the money part between Phil and Sheila, which I give my word, I won't be one of those lazy, and I think you called them 'sloppy' cops," Ryan said with a cheeky wink, "I won't only focus on the evidence that supports the preconceived notion that all husbands kill their wives' lovers."

His determination, grit, and that sexy sideways smile made me weak and utterly defenseless to his charm.

"Who knows," I said with my own wink, "you could actually be the one to clear Phil and find the real murderer by doing the legwork the homicide detectives will most likely ignore."

CHAPTER 25
RYAN

When my dad and Herb decided to end the night with a walk to Lucky's tavern, I thought it was the old man's less than subtle way of giving Rebel and me time alone. But when he texted a half hour later to tell me he was crashing at my brother Mike's house and Rebel shouldn't go back to her apartment, I knew for sure he was matchmaking.

"Is everything okay?" Rebel asked while I stared at my phone.

I slid my thumb across the screen and closed my text messages. "Just my dad being my dad. He doesn't want you to go home tonight. He offered that you stay here."

Rebel seemed lost in thought. "Your dad's a great guy." The melancholy in her voice caused me to imagine not being able to contact my dad to let him know I was okay. *Brutal.*

"When do they think the trial will begin?" I asked.

She shrugged. "It's the million-dollar question. I'm not sure." Rebel was curled up in the corner of the couch. My mom's jacket was back on the coat rack. The longer summer day had finally yielded to night and the accompanying chill in the air caused goose pimples on her bare arms. I jumped off the couch and grabbed the afghan off my bed.

"My aunt crocheted it for me when I was like six and decided to be a Denver Broncos fan. So it's ugly, but super soft." I placed the orange and blue horizontal-striped blanket over her legs.

"Ah, yeah, a Broncos fan. This is a classic." Rebel pulled the blanket toward her like a prized possession. "The closest NFL team we have in Wyoming are the Denver Broncos. So this is perfect. Thank you."

I wanted to lean over, kiss her, and crawl beneath the blanket with her. I wanted to bite her neck, smell the honeysuckle scent that was so faint on her skin it was powerful, and lose myself in her warmth.

She reached behind her, and the unmistakable sound of a zipper sent my body into hyperdrive. *Is she taking off her dress?*

I knew my dad wasn't going to come home; still I glanced at

the front door to make sure it was locked. *Yup.*

"Uh, everything okay?" I said, and sounded like an asshat. *Is everything okay?*

She responded with a smile that went right to my cock. I nodded, trying to get a handle on the situation, trying to be the good guy, the respectful guy, but when she pulled her dress over her head and tossed it to the floor, I knew I was being outplayed.

"Oh, hey." I cleared my throat and tried to make eye contact with her when her breasts clothed in black lace were screaming for my attention and touch. "Why don't I get that change of clothes Georgie picked up." I rose off the couch, and she grabbed my wrist.

"Don't leave."

The last time she'd asked me to stay she dropped her towel. And instead of being a dog, I did the right thing. I still wanted to do the right thing, but when she knelt on the couch before me, the right thing got harder and harder to do. And so did I.

Her hold on my wrist wasn't helping either.

"Rebel…."

"Ryan…."

I slowly shook my head. "Maybe you'd like to take a bath. My dad has these really great bath bombs." No sooner had the words escaped my mouth when I realized she was either going to get the wrong impression of either my dad or my intentions, and neither of those impressions was bound to be good. *Bath bombs?*

"Bath bombs, huh?" Rebel's brown eyes twinkled. "That's your best line to get me naked? Lucky for you"—she arched her eyebrow—"it just might work."

My entire body burned. Her dark eyes sparked with desire and cranked the level of want to high. I quickly flipped my wrist in her hand until I seized hold of her and then tightened my grasp. She gasped and I raised an eyebrow.

"I just thought you might want a bath before I dive into dessert." *Dive into dessert? Fuck, McHenry, get in the game, man.*

Her hair swayed on her shoulders like a temptress and a naughty smile crossed her lips. "Why waste time in the tub when you can give me a tongue bath?"

Damn. This girl was straight-up bringing her A game and I wasn't. Rebel was swinging for the fence and I was throwing balls out of the strike zone like I was deliberately trying to walk her and not score. Things were about to change.

I dropped her wrist and wrapped my arm around her waist. Her arms instinctively draped around my neck. As she leaned into me, I cupped the back of her knees and scooped her into my arms. Her breathlessness was worth every muscle I probably tweaked in my sudden romantic gesture. *Fuck it. Totally worth it.*

I carried her into my bedroom and kicked the door shut with the back of my foot. Her startled expression was everything.

That's right, you're not the only one who's got game.

But when I laid her on my bed, my kickass, take-no-prisoners demeanor changed. Her wavy, messy red hair fanned across my pillow and her creamy skin was so smooth it looked untouched. Her gaze took me in, waiting, anticipating, watching, and I didn't want to disappoint her. But I also didn't want to be just another man in her life. I wanted to be *the only* man in her life.

I sat beside her outstretched body, leaned over her, and gently, sweetly pressed my lips on hers. No open mouth. No tongue. But if a kiss could convey my intentions, I hoped mine did. Rebel deserved an all-star and not a has-been Dirtbag who peaked in college.

I'd had my share of hookups, but Rebel was different. I'd known that from when she didn't back down when my truck blocked her way and I wasn't in the mood for sass—she'd held her ground. When she found Bernie, even though she wanted to flee, she stayed. And now I knew what that could have cost her. Rebel was different, and I wanted her to know that I was too. When our lips parted, I stared into her dark eyes.

"It could be the ninth inning, the scoreboard looks hopeless, and most of the fans have gone home. But that's when I bring my best," I said.

"McCutie, don't you think I know that? When you covered for me with the cops and then slept on my couch so I wouldn't be alone, *I knew*. When things are crazy and chaotic, that's when you're the calmest." A smile lit her face. "And let me tell you that's a good thing with someone like me who seems to stumble across crimes. It doesn't seem to matter if I'm in the Cowboy State or the Golden State, crime finds me."

I brushed a wavy strand of hair off her face. "Crime may have found you, but I think Cupid did too." I grinned. "And like the great Yogi Berra said, 'It ain't over till it's over' and *I'm the one who's going to say it's over and no one else.*"

REBEL

My hair fell forward and Ryan tucked it behind my ear. He cupped my face with his hands and all sense of time and place ceased as I lost myself in his touch.

His lips consumed mine as his hands reached behind me to unclasp my bra. His generous mouth pressed against my breast and tugged on my nipple with his teeth moving it back and forth. My back arched toward him. Ryan smelled like gasoline and grease—probably from hanging out in my apartment's parking garage, which made him even sexier. His dark hair was thick and his hands were large as they caressed my body.

My feet pressed against the edge of the bed frame, my thighs tightened, and my heart raced as this hazel-eyed, sexy deputy-in-training pierced me with his finger. The release I'd searched for found me at last. My body contracted and a surge of heat broke through me. So many things were happening at once—his mouth on my breast, his finger inside me, and his cock rubbing against my thigh—that spiked my senses into overdrive.

Yet for all the sensory overload, I felt like I was floating through a dreamy state with Ryan driving the desire and filling my body with what I knew a man like him could bring—total surrender.

His hands continued to swim across my body in a tantalizing touch that drove me wild. I squirmed beneath him and he opened his eyes.

"Please," I pleaded.

He smiled, knowing in that moment he owned me. He slid my black panties down my legs while he caressed the contours of my body. The faintness of his touch was electrifying, sending tiny jolts of pleasure to every area he discovered. My hips instinctively rose to meet the desire he sparked. His mouth covered my clit with strong, powerful strokes as he pushed his tongue inside me.

I gasped as a rush and surge erupted. His tongue bathed me in long, upward strokes that quickly brought me to the brink once more.

I wrapped my legs around his neck and practically buried his head in me until the sweet release was mine. *Holy hell.* I closed my eyes and let the orgasm wash over me, flooding my body with heat and release simultaneously. There was nothing like a man who knew how to make my body quiver and my legs shake, and

Ryan did both.

He knelt before me and peeled off the black T-shirt that hugged his toned body. He stripped off his belt and used it to tie my hands together above my head as he whispered in my ear.

"You're mine."

The desire filled my head and created hunger. But instead of devouring me, Ryan slowly teased me as he kicked off his shoes and jeans and tossed his baseball cap to the floor. He stood before me with a throbbing erection that made my mouth water.

I enveloped him, tasting his tanginess and knowing he would fill me to the point of explosion. When he pulled himself out of my mouth, I looked up at him.

"Please," I begged, craving to feel him inside me.

He reached into the nightstand beside his bed, tore open a condom, and placed it over his throbbing cock. When he finally parted my legs with his body, I felt myself get even wetter with anticipation.

His cock consumed me. His intensity and passion excited me. But when he began dipping in and out of me with the tip of his cock, I thought I'd lose my mind. With each dip, his head touched my clit and created a frenzy inside me that was unreal.

"Do. Not. Stop." I lost track of the many small orgasms that oozed over him as his cock worked overtime moving in and out of me—unearthing more pleasure, greater sensation, and heightened anticipation for the one big orgasm that I knew he'd unleash.

With his head buried in my neck and the new beard growth on his face that brushed against me, his voice was low, sexy and all male when he spoke in my ear.

"God, you feel good."

Yet, when he slowed the pace to play, the more I wanted him. He slowly pulled in and out of me, taunting us both. And the more he played with the head of his cock, the more I moaned.

"Rebel, you drive me wild."

His words fed me as much as his cock.

He gripped my loosely tied wrists and rode me repeatedly before he slowed his rhythm and looked down at me. His eyes asked the question he was too gentlemanly to ask. *Can I come?* I nodded with a smile.

Ryan synced our rhythm together until we exploded in unison. If I wasn't already lying down, I would have passed out. The orgasm shot through me down to my toes, rendering my body completely, utterly, wonderfully numb. Before he collapsed on the bed beside me, he untied my hands, gently kissed me, and placed his head next to mine.

It wasn't Wyoming, but Lakewood felt like home. And tucked in Ryan's embrace, I felt safe, protected, and cared for. There wasn't any sound between us, but the buzz of cars traveling on the street outside his bedroom window echoed in the distance, lulling us to sleep.

CHAPTER 26
REBEL

"*What are you doing?*" *Ryan* opened the shower door, covered in steam, and almost erased my math.

"Whoa, wait up," I said as he stepped sideways into the shower beside me.

"Is that…?"

"If you're thinking basic math, you'd be right." I grinned while the water cascaded across my shoulders and down my back. "The water pressure here is no joke. I practically have to run around the shower in my studio just to get wet."

Ryan chuckled as he shut the door and my math reappeared.

"Yeah, for an older house, it's got a lot to give." He grabbed the loofah, squirted a dollop of vanilla body wash on it, and gently began scrubbing my back. "So... *why* are you doing math on the shower door?"

"Okay, we know numbers don't lie and from my experience, I've also discovered that if you follow the money trail, it usually leads to the culprit."

I expected Ryan to laugh, but instead, he stopped rubbing my back and leaned against me. "I've learned from our weekly lectures at the sheriff's department that mathematics is one of the most important techniques in crime detection," he said.

"Uh... hold that thought." I leaned against him while I studied the math calculated in steam. "Basic addition and subtraction can be just as valuable as a spreadsheet, especially when you're in the shower." I chuckled. "And the figure I keep locking onto is five sixty. Each month, BT Inc., which I now know was Bernie Thomas Incorporated, was billed five hundred and sixty dollars in secretarial services."

"Is that a lot?" Ryan asked.

I slowly swayed my head. "It's not that much considering the hourly rate for Kathy's secretarial services is thirty-three dollars. And things like PowerPoint services are forty an hour. Still, a monthly tab of five sixty is roughly sixteen hours of secretarial services. What gets me is that the monthly fee was *consistently* five hundred and sixty bucks." I studied the sums. "What I know is that Bernie was retired and he had the girls laminate scripture cards, which couldn't have been more than a hundred a month in services. The other four hundred and change is the issue."

Ryan set the loofah aside and began massaging my shoulders.

"The other piece is that Phil and his sidekick, Lisa, were using Bernie's account for their services. At month's end, Lisa settled the account with Da Nise with cash."

"So what do your numbers tell you?" Ryan asked.

"Well, it may just be nothing, another thread that doesn't lead anywhere. But I've wondered if Phil has a fake vendor account where he submits phony invoices to the hotel and funnels the money through conference services, which would be credited with the funds that are under Phil's department." I stared at the calculations. "Ultimately, Phil would code the expense for double the amount to the fake vendor and pocket the difference."

"That seems like a lot of work," Ryan said, and I had to agree.

"You're right. Fake vendor accounts aren't the easiest way to skim money, but they work because the department head who verifies the invoices and authorizes the payments is often the one who knows how to use the hotel's accounting system."

"So, basically you think Phil would recycle the five sixty to pay the monthly invoice for services Kathy does, that he then doubles on an invoice to a fake vendor?" Ryan asked.

"I hadn't thought that he's using the same five sixty a month, but you're probably right."

"The only thing you're forgetting is you don't know what amount Bernie paid for his actual services," Ryan said.

I bit my lip. "I won't know anything until I pull the files. But the probability that Bernie's secretarial services were exactly five sixty each month is really low and extremely unlikely. I'm not sure what a retired cop earns, but even a hundred bucks a month for laminated scripture cards seems like he was spending too much. It's the fact that Phil was using Bernie's account to bill his secretarial services that rings bells for me."

"Sure, but weren't you the one who didn't think Phil had anything to do with Bernie's murder?"

"Yes." I exhaled, and on the inhale the steam cleared my sinuses. "Okay, McCutie, it's your turn. What do the numbers tell you about a crime?"

"I thought you'd never ask," he said with his breath on my neck. "But the days of Sherlock Holmes and his magnifying glass are long gone."

"Bummer, that's kind of sexy," I said.

He gently massaged my left shoulder, the one that wasn't pressed into him. "Then you're definitely not going to like that a magnifying glass is about as useful as gut instinct, which you claimed was your rationale for not thinking Phil was the murderer," he said.

"Well, sure, I know it's not scientific," I said, "but Phil just seems too obvious and he's too scared of his wife to have offed her lover. But this money thing may prove to be a red flag I can't ignore."

"Understood. But you of all people probably know that a jury's not going to conclude that Phil didn't do it simply based on your gut instinct and lack of financial documentation. But," he squeezed my shoulder, "forensic evidence, fingerprints, and DNA will provide juries with substantive proof that Phil *or* whoever killed Bernie."

"Which is why mathematics is used in identifying DNA," I said, thinking about the forensic math department at Chadron State, which was comprised of the smartest mathematicians. I rolled my neck and let the water and Ryan's hands massage out the kinks.

"Exactly," Ryan said. "But the kicker is that forensic biologists rarely have good samples to work with. You saw where Bernie was left—in the middle of a fence where the sample was most likely degraded and tainted to the point that it can make identification a real bitch, which is why they turn to probability."

I cringed and my shoulders tightened. "And the fact that I moved Bernie wouldn't have helped with the sample."

"True. But that's why the forensics team narrows the field with the physical factors they *can* collect. Then if they're called to testify they can testify to the probability of someone's innocence," he said.

"So, really, what Phil did or didn't pay for secretarial services isn't as convincing as hard evidence." I began to erase my math with my hand, but Ryan gently held it.

"Rebel, not all threads lead to a loose end. Sometimes, an assumption that presents the possible killer-and-motive combo pan out, other times they don't. But if your only assumption about the crime is the correct one, it would render my job useless," he said.

This guy. Math is unambiguous and completely objective. And that's the kind of perfection that I never thought I'd find in someone, until I met Ryan. He brought every positive emotion to the surface and it seemed like my heart would burst from all the feels.

He leaned his chin on my shoulder. "Don't rule out Phil—or your gut. You like math because it's exact, and as a future deputy, I know DNA evidence is as close to exact as we can get."

"Sure, because it all hinges on rigorous calculations being made." I glanced at Ryan, whose dimple was being sprayed by the shower head.

"I stopped listening after you said rigorous." He pressed into me with his hard cock.

The air was steamy, the shower doors were foggy, and as I turned to Ryan, my body gravitated toward the radiant heat of his cock. My early morning was slipping away; I could waste no time. I raised my soapy leg, wrapped it around his waist, and invited him in.

RYAN

I opened the shower door with one hand and palmed my way toward the vanity where I'd left a condom on top of the foil wrapper. It was presumptuous of me, but deputy training had taught me to always prepare for the expected and unexpected. I pulled away from Rebel long enough to roll the condom down my cock before sliding into her. She was warm, welcoming, and fit like a glove. My hands dug into her round ass while I moved in and out of her swiftly and with intensity.

"I could fuck you all day and still want more." The dirty thought flew out of my mouth and my pace practically came to a halt.

"Stop now and you'll never fuck me again," she said in my ear, and I grinned.

All right, then.

Rebel ground against me purposefully. As we pressed against the glass wall, her math disappeared and the silhouette of us took its place. Her nipples rubbed against my chest and my balls brushed against her ass. Everything was in place for a quick orgasm, but I wasn't about to lose my load until she lost hers, which I hoped was imminent.

When her nails dug into my shoulders and her moans turned to a deep groan, she tightened herself around me and even though the water was warm, her orgasm was like a heat wave that flooded over me. In that moment, I thrust into her and let myself ride the swell.

CHAPTER 27
REBEL

carefully opened my camo backpack to find my gun lying on top. I pointed the gun at the floor, kept my finger off the trigger, and made sure the safety was on before I removed the magazine, which was empty. Still, when I handed my gun to Ryan, he repeated the process. My dad raised me to always assume all firearms were loaded, and it didn't surprise me that Ryan seemed to follow that protocol.

"I'll keep this in our gun safe," he said, and while I didn't like it, I knew it was better than having it end up in the wrong hands.

I glanced in my backpack and bright yellow winked back. "Ah, my sundress!" I pulled it out of my bag and held the dress against the bath towel wrapped around my body. "I can't believe you found this."

"Georgie. Georgie found it," he said.

"Well, I can't wait to meet her. I thought I left this in Napa and I love *this* dress." If a dress could make me feel something, the vintage, vibrant flowers on this dress made me feel like I could conquer the world. Or at least the hotel's billing system.

"It's cute. Where'd you get it?" Ryan asked, and he actually seemed interested.

"My grandmother found it on one of her many adventures and mailed it to me when I was still in Wyoming. Her note said, 'Every girl should know the magic of a sundress.' It's one of the few things I grabbed when I had, like, an hour to pack." I dropped my towel and slipped the dress over my head. The slim spaghetti straps, flowy neckline, and fluttery fabric slid over my body like a second skin. I dug through my bag for a pair of pink panties that I stepped into. Ryan shook his head.

"Uh, yeah, you don't need those," he said with a sideways smile.

"Uh, yeah, I do. Underwear is *kind of* a requirement working at the Point or pretty much anywhere that doesn't involve pole dancing," I said with my own sly smile and playful swirl of my dress.

I rummaged through my backpack for sandals and was surprised to find my white leather boots with a pair of socks stuffed inside. "I like this Georgie gal and I've never met her. I never thought of wearing my lucky boots with this dress, but how cute."

"Lucky boots?"

I good-humoredly tossed my hair over my shoulder. "I may have won a few rodeo titles with these boots. I'm convinced the pointed toe, which fit perfectly into my stirrups, and the silver buckle, which my mom said shone while I rode, helped my score."

"So much about you, Rebel Roberts, that I don't know."

My hand frantically karate chopped the air. "Brandt. It's Rebel Brandt."

"Well, for the sake of keeping your cover intact. *Ms. Roberts*, why don't you call in sick to work today? I already have the day off from deliveries, so I can attend my deputy training classes and afterward I can show you more of Long Beach."

My hand instantly went to my chest, which radiated with warmth. "There's nothing I'd like more than to skip work and go to that beach that has been calling my name since I arrived, but…" I purposefully batted my eyes at him. "…and here's my big butt." I twirled until my back faced him. When I looked over my shoulder, Ryan's single dimple was in full force with a broad smile. "I don't want to leave the girls at the hotel with Phil; his wife, Sheila; his Stepford-like assistant, Lisa; and God knows who else who will show up to stake some claim or comment about Bernie. So, how about *after* your training session you meet me at the hotel and we sleuth together."

"Uh… no sleuthing without me."

I grinned. "Wouldn't think of it." But of course, we both knew that was exactly what I would do as soon as I got to the hotel and could sort through past secretarial service invoices.

It really didn't matter what happened today. My carefree sundress and off-the-charts night and morning with Ryan matched my mood. And when McCutie drove me to my car that was still parked at the hotel, it felt like together we were unstoppable.

CHAPTER 28
REBEL

"*Folks, our agency is squarely* charged with three components: public safety, school security, and finding effective ways toward improving community relations." Deputy Stanley stood with his hands behind his back at parade rest.

I quickly jotted the three areas in the notes section on my phone. As soon as my thoughts drifted to Rebel, our evening, the morning together, or how she looked in that dress, which spiked my desire to take it off her, Stanley spoke again.

"I just had breakfast with the sheriff, who had to cut the budget and implement new policies and procedures. Now"—Stanley's buzz cut and boxy frame were perfectly suited for his job. He briefly held his hand out like he was forewarning us—"I know how these things are when more new things are added to a deputy's plate each year. I also realize that sometimes we just read the morning headlines where it often seems like public policy is lost to all those folks out there who aren't working the streets...." His voice lost its momentum and his hand disappeared behind his back.

"Bottom line—we're going to see a lot of changes in the department and the best way to measure change is to measure the change," he said.

Stanley was big on bottom lining things. Hell, the bottom line was his holy grail. But he rarely spoke in riddles. *Best way to measure change is to measure the change?* Still, it was effective.

"The work and dedication of our department remains strong. We have great deputies in this state." Strength returned to his voice. "The biggest challenge is to remember what got you here to begin with. *Why did you want to be a deputy?* Our department pays well, but, at times, it may not seem that way. But don't lose sight of what drew you to law enforcement."

If I didn't know better, I'd think Stanley was actually giving us a pep talk—or dissuading us from the profession.

"Getting back to what our department is charged with, you'll discover that the outcome of public safety and school security often depends on the overall effectiveness of how well we, as deputies, improve community relations." Stanley shifted his focus to the stack of papers on the podium beside him, which was unusual. Stanley's lectures were infamous. He thrived on lengthy lectures that lasted hours just to see which applicant would break first for the restroom.

"As long as I'm in charge of training, we'll keep our eye on improving community relations," he said.

As long as he's in charge of training?

"Our biggest challenge on that front is piss-poor parenting. If we could get out in front of that issue, I think we'd have a fighting chance with drugs, gangs, and guns."

Parenting? I knew absentee parenting was an issue, but was it really the end-all culprit?

"The sheriff has set some high and rigorous standards toward making changes in our approach toward community relations." He slowly nodded as if he was still absorbing the new standards himself.

"Our department is now charged with some long- and short-term goals that aren't static, but neither should our approach with the community be. Since these kids aren't getting the necessary parenting, our presence in the community will become the new normal. I realize these are lofty goals, but the sheriff believes they're realistic. So as candidate trainees we will set goals that we can achieve and adjust. The primary objective is to close the gap between the department and the community. Folks," he clasped his hands together and the sudden smack jolted anyone who had even thought of dozing off awake, "it's all part of a bigger picture," he said. "We're going to stop looking at individual crimes and focus on the larger problem. By making safety the first priority in our state, our push for clean streets, safe schools, and how to close the gap between the community and law enforcement will be our primary focus, not because they're mandated to us but because they're achievable."

Stanley seemed like he was regurgitating what the sheriff had fed him at breakfast.

"I also know that with certain criteria and goals, at times it can seem like the task in front of us is greater than our limited resources. *Those* are the times when taking shortcuts or easier routes present themselves," he said.

"Shortcuts, sir?" Collin asked. Collin Lake was tough competition because he came from a long line of deputies, he was a skilled marksman, and if there was anyone who knew the rules and regulations better than me, it was Collin.

"*Rewards* for looking the other way." Stanley placed his hands on his hips and his legs remained outstretched. "When our department is charged with more mandates, that's when enticements pour in. And folks, it always starts off innocuously—a free meal, a promotional jacket, an extra discount to an amusement park for your family. But each of those is an example of what?"

I raised my hand along with the majority of the class.

"McHenry."

"A breach in ethics, sir. Bribes, rewards, loans, gifts, or favors are a violation of the public trust." I knew the Code of Ethics for the city of Los Angeles verbatim. When Stanley didn't comment, but gave a quick nod my way, I continued. "Basically, a member of the department is not allowed to accept a bribe, solicit or accept any reward, fee, loan, or gratuity in relation with services rendered in the performance of their duties." I sat tall in my seat. "In short, a deputy should not use their position for any favor or gratuities that would not ordinarily be accorded to a private citizen."

"McHenry, is that rule only applicable to on-duty deputies?" Stanley asked.

"No, sir. A deputy is never off duty," I said.

"And, McHenry, what's the penalty if a member of the department accepts a gift, loan, favor, or reward?"

"Expulsion from the department," I said.

"Correct. Corruption is specifically addressed separately in a training segment, however, alluding to or beating around the bush is not my style," he said, and glanced at a raised hand. "Sims."

Milford Sims had been unusually quiet during class, which was nice.

"Sir, on that note, every department has had at least one crooked cop, which is why every department also has Internal

Affairs," she said.

It was hard to gauge his reaction. Stanley wore neutrality like a mannequin in a beige suit, but with less warmth and personality.

"Circling back to Deputy Trainee McHenry, who cited that deputies are never off duty…. So then, McHenry," he pivoted his attention toward me, "by that logic, if an off-duty deputy was charged with driving home a private citizen, who, let's say, discovered a crime. And then that private citizen provided the off-duty deputy access to their apartment and a non-alcoholic drink for driving them home." He paused long enough to study my reaction, which I was sure was pretty visible. *Fucker*. While he was probably taking a stab at how that first night between Rebel and me ended, unless he was a soothsayer he didn't have definitive proof of anything other than the fact that I drove her home.

"McHenry, help me out. From your logic, if an off-duty deputy accepted a drink, like a soda, they'd be expelled from the department?" Stanley's icy stare was as unexpected as him using my situation with Rebel as an example of unethical behavior. Now, if I had slept with her that first night, he'd clearly have me on questionable behavior, but I didn't. I accepted a bottled water and then waited a few days to sleep with her. Even though I wanted to grin and flip him off, I steadied him in my sights and answered his baiting question.

"Sir, there appears to be some gray areas like the one you

described that aren't as well defined in the rule manual," I said without breaking a sweat. *Douche.*

"Bottom line it, McHenry. Will a deputy lose his job if he drives someone home and then accepts a drink of any kind?"

I met Stanley's challenge with my own. "Bottom line is that if a deputy is ever in doubt—don't. For instance, if you see a fellow deputy *loitering* at an apartment complex that isn't their home, and something seems off—approach him. If this fellow deputy is knowingly violating the ethics rules of the department but shrugs off your presence at the apartment complex, then the next course of action is to walk away and not get pulled in further. Of course, now the ethical question becomes does a deputy report another deputy?" *Screw me once, fuck you twice.* I may have just jeopardized my standing in the candidate process, but I wasn't about to let Stanley plow me over. Besides, I was sure he was just one of many senior department assholes who'd test me.

I gave him my best disinterested face and he barely acknowledged me.

"Folks, the bottom line is that regardless of the situation, without the expressed permission of the department do not accept any gift, special offer, free admission, or meal. These actions could lead to your dismissal from the department." He stood beside the podium. "Again, an entire week will be devoted to corruption during the academy."

Then why the fuck bring it up now? My dislike of Stanley was growing daily. I knew it was all part of the training, but Stanley seemed to relish psychologically testing us with real-world situations we'd encounter just to let us know he was monitoring us. *Creepy fucker.*

"Moving on to school safety, after the tragedy at Sandy Hook elementary, Los Angeles County approved nine million in school safety funds. That was *after* assessing school safety and realizing that most of the expense was in lock systems and hardware. At one point, a high school in Long Beach had twenty-nine outside entrances," he said.

"Long Beach?" The tension in class was too high for Milford Sims's perky, squeaky, little girl voice. "Sir, that's not part of our jurisdiction," she said.

"Sims, for Christ's sake, it was an example. We just lost a veteran deputy in Long Beach. So, by your logic we shouldn't care—is that it?" Stanley, who usually favored Sims, treated her with the same disdain he saved for the rest of us.

But Sims didn't cower. "Of course, not, sir. I just wanted to note that while Sandy Hook is a prime example of underestimating what a troubled individual will do, I was curious why a school in Long Beach was your reference point for safety violations when Los Angeles County is rife with school safety issues."

"I don't need to give you an explanation for anything. If I

chose to reference Long Beach, Lakewood or Lamont, I will. And what does it matter what city I chose when you clearly missed the obvious? Long Beach is where we lost a deputy and I lost a friend." The tension in his voice suddenly dropped and the hardened stare on his face softened, a bit.

Oh, fuck. Bernie was his friend.

"Sure, that makes sense." Sims just didn't know when to stop.

"Out." Stanley pointed toward the door and hiked his finger.

"Sir?"

It was the first time I heard Milford's voice quake.

"That makes sense? Sims, I don't have time to indulge you today, tomorrow, or next week and neither will your training officer. So until you can return to this classroom with the mindset to shut up, sit down, and respect senior officers to realize you don't know shit, but until that time, get out." Stanley's eyebrows furrowed until they met in the middle.

When she didn't answer or move, Stanley walked to where Milford sat and tapped his finger so hard on the edge of her desk that she flinched.

"Did I stutter, Sims?"

Her blonde ponytail barely moved.

"Good. Then. Get. Out." He grabbed her purse off the floor beside her feet and extended it like a bag of trash.

There was no doubt that Milford was an annoying, question-asking, squeaking pain in the ass, but she didn't deserve Stanley's misdirected anger. Shit, he wasn't mad at Sims. She stood and her normally confident demeanor shrank beside Stanley, who simply smiled. Milford reached for her purse just as Stanley released it. The purse and all its contents fell to the floor, and Milford scrambled at his feet to retrieve it. There wasn't anything good about that. My gut tightened and my jaw clenched.

Without thinking, I stood and squared off with Stanley, who was less than three feet away. "Sir, I realize a lot's happened in the department recently. But what happened to fostering good community relations?"

"McHenry." He slowly walked toward me. Each step was measured with precision and carefully timed. I knew Stanley's reputation for weeding the applicant pool down, but there were less than a dozen of us left, and Sims was one of the strongest candidates in our class. When she gathered her things, she practically fled the classroom. Besides, there was a difference between weeding out weak candidates and breaking the good ones.

"If you don't agree with my tactics, there's the door," he said.

I could practically taste Stanley's breath, but I didn't back down.

"Sir, if becoming a deputy means adopting tactics that are nothing short of bullying, then the department has more issues than public safety, school security, and improving community relations." I didn't break eye contact with him even when he postured toward me.

"Bullying?" Stanley narrowed his eyes until all I could see was the black slits of his pupils.

"Sir, what happened in Long Beach is…" I searched for the word and I thought of my uncle. "Tragic. But treating Sims the way you did isn't the answer, nor will it solve the question of who murdered a veteran deputy." I tried to bridge the distance with compassion.

"McHenry, you'll know when I'm bullying someone. Bullying." He shook his hands as if he was clearing the air of the verbal olive branch I extended. "Shit, I'd like you to try that sissy tactic out on the unincorporated streets we patrol. 'Excuse me, but stop bullying me.' *Jesus fucking Christ, McHenry.* You're right, the department *does* have bigger issues to deal with, like finding candidates who aren't afraid to protect and serve regardless of the conditions around them."

Which is exactly what I'm doing, you miserable fuck.

I was about to ruin what was left of my chance at becoming a deputy when Deputy Sergeant Fields appeared in the doorframe beside a frightened Sims. "Stanley, a moment please."

Stanley turned on the heels of his boots, but not before glaring at me one last time.

CHAPTER 29
REBEL

"*I did some digging.*" *In a* burgundy jumpsuit with a gathered waist, bell-shaped sleeves, and flared legs, Kathy looked like she'd stepped back in time. I half expected a glittery disco ball to hang from the ceiling in the administrative office. Kathy must have noticed me staring at her groovy getup.

"Hey, if you ever need something retro, I'm your girl."

I stopped gawking. "Girl, I *dig* your style," I said, to her amusement. "So, what'd you unearth?"

"I've got a realtor friend, Jeff, who ran title searches on the bank's parking lot and the bank because they're separate properties, and the results were pretty interesting." Kathy leaned against the blonde-colored countertop where the backup switchboard ate most of the space. Da Nise usually manned the monster, but she'd volunteered to rummage through the storage room for the last year of secretarial service orders while Kathy updated me.

"So, what'd you unearth?" I asked.

"Well, first, have you seen the newspaper today?"

I shook my head, thinking of my shower with McCutie, and I was pretty sure my cheeks turned red. I cleared my throat before I answered. "Nope, missed it."

She handed me the daily Long Beach paper. The headline above the fold would get people talking. "Deputy Sheriff Identified."

I quickly read the front page feature.

Long Beach, CA—Authorities have identified the African-American man found dead in a Long Beach alley over the weekend as a Los Angeles sheriff's deputy, according to the Los Angeles County Coroner's office.

The slain deputy was identified as 68-year-old Bernard "Bernie" Thomas, a thirty-year veteran at the sheriff's department and four-year veteran of the Long Beach Police Department. Thomas was discovered by a deputy trainee.

"I can't tell you how difficult it is for our department to lose an officer who had contributed so much to our department," Deputy Sheriff William Stanley said.

Thomas is survived by his two children.

"I wonder why they waited a week to identify him?" I said.

"They probably had to contact his kids. Bernie spoke about them a lot. They're both married and live in Colorado where his ex-wife is," Kathy said.

"Oh, sure, that makes sense." The picture that accompanied the article showed a much-younger Bernie in uniform. I wondered what Ryan would look like in an officer's uniform and my stomach responded with equal measures of excitement and dread. I never wanted to see his picture on the front page for anything other than a promotion. *Shit, Rebel, get a grip.* I slept with a guy and I was already planning our future. *What the fuck?*

I rolled my shoulders as if that would get my mind back to the task at hand. "So what'd you find?"

"Okay, well, Jeff said the bank property checked out, but that didn't surprise us. But then Jeff looked at the parking lot property and at first he thought it was standard title document—just like the bank." Kathy reached toward the fax machine, which I was surprised guests still utilized, and handed me a stack of legal papers.

"What am I looking for?" I asked, skimming the documents.

"Jeff said the first sign was that the title company was asked by someone other than the bank to insure title to a vacant lot in downtown Long Beach, which is the bank's parking lot and again separate from the bank."

"Is that normal?" I asked.

She shrugged. "Jeff claims that older real estate was often subdivided like that, so it wasn't *abnormal* to find two titles on the same plot in Long Beach."

I was browsing the documents for a name and date when Kathy pulled my attention away from the stack.

"So, the most recent title request for the parking lot involved a loan application for $85,000 through a private loan broker. The lot was valued at about $145,000 and records show that at one time there had been a house on the lot that had been purchased in the late twenties by a couple who ran a bakery. Apparently, the couple used the smaller house on their property and lived in a larger home on the upper parcel of land, which became the property the bank bought, tore down, and rebuilt into the bank," Kathy said.

"So wait, the bank bought the parcel of land that had the bigger house on it, but they didn't purchase the second half? Where did they think their customers were going to park?"

"I asked the same question and Jeff said the bank factored a dozen parking spaces into the planning and development phase and since it's primarily used for its drive-through services, the bank's never had an issue with parking," Kathy said.

"Nope." I shook my head. "No way. In the limited time I've been in Long Beach, the one takeaway I'm certain of—besides the fact that Club Roar is my one and only favorite watering hole," I said, and Kathy high-fived me. "—is that there's no parking in Long Beach. And what parking the city does have is coveted. So it's *really* hard for me to believe that the bank didn't want that extra space. Besides, someone already went to the effort to tear down the bakery and pave it. All that space is missing are fluorescent yellow parking stripes," I said.

"Agreed. But Jeff knows someone at the bank who said they couldn't expand until the bank could justify the initial return on their investment, which apparently they haven't been able to do in the last decade," she said.

"That's what Phil said in our first meeting. He mentioned that the bank wouldn't be able to keep up with the new lease payment at the current market rate, which is why he was looking into the space for overflow convention and parking space. But he said they were met with some resistance from a restoration committee that was focused on the property, and Bernie was on that committee," I said. "Apparently they were trying to conserve the land. But why would the land be so important?"

"Who knows? Over the years, parks have changed names, trees have been chopped down, and property lots have shrunk," Kathy said. "For all I know, the land could have been a burial plot."

I shuddered. "Nuh-uh, don't even joke about that. The Point has a property in Cheyenne, Wyoming, that's supposedly haunted.

I've only heard stories, but you don't mess with the dead."

"Oh, but wouldn't it be fun to get spirited away?" Kathy said, and I laughed. "But not to worry, the only unburying my buddy and I did was through title searches."

"And...."

"Jeff told me that since a title search requires a thorough examination of public records, to...." Kathy glanced at her notebook on the counter beside her and flipped to the next page. "Okay, here it is, he said that a public records search is to ensure that all facts regarding ownership, current and past, are disclosed, and that's when he noticed another small detail."

I stared at the accompanying loan documents until the text blurred. "I still don't know what I'm looking for."

"Neither do I. But what Jeff discovered is that there's an eleven-month gap between the date of the deed and the recording date, with taxes on the deed indicating a sale price of forty thousand, not a hundred and forty-five thousand, which is considerably lower than the original sale price and well below the market value of comparable vacant lots in the surrounding area," Kathy said.

"So maybe the new owners waited for another upswing on the market, but they waited too long, and had a fire sale," I said. "I mean, dumping property at a loss isn't illegal."

"You're right, but it is pretty sketchy, even borderline unethical, to own property connected to the property you're supposedly trying to protect," Kathy said.

I flipped to the back sheet, which was often the signature page of most documents, and noticed one signature. A notary's seal was stamped to the left of the signature. "Oh my God. Is that Bernie Thomas? As in *the Bernie Thomas* I found dead in the alley?"

"Same one." Kathy thumbed through the stack I held in my hand and the papers fanned out. "And it gets even better. Bernie was on past titles for hundreds of properties throughout Long Beach."

"What?" I stopped staring at his signature and made eye contact with Kathy.

"Yeah, it looks like Bernie liked to buy cheap land."

"Can we get a list of all the properties he was ever on title for? And then what they sold for?" I asked.

"Already did." Kathy grabbed a stapled set of spreadsheets off the countertop and handed them to me. A detailed analysis of properties and Bernie's subsequent ownership in them that dated to the seventies was in black and white.

"What the hell? Does a deputy sheriff make that much money to own so much?"

"Not even close," Kathy said. "But it looks like the preacher was preying on other people's property."

"Uh, you think? Some of these real estate purchases were all-cash offers, which would preclude the need for a loan," I said, glancing at the payment details. "But even buying the land dirt cheap, it would still be *really* expensive. So how did Bernie make his money?"

"And why was he buying and selling property?" Kathy said.

I smiled. "*That* one I can answer. Jealousy, love, and money are the most common reasons someone commits a crime. Or at least, that's been my experience. And in this case, I think Bernie hit the motive trifecta—he *loved money* and was probably *jealous* of those who had it. And based on this report, he was clearly buying cheap and selling high." I pointed toward the purchase price and sales price columns on the spreadsheet. "There's more than four decades worth of real estate transactions." I skimmed the spreadsheet to the listing agent. "Holy hell."

"What?" Kathy leaned into me.

"Steve Mendel is the listing agent on every transaction from 1974 to the late nineties, and then…" I followed my fingertip down the column, expecting to find what I did, but it still made my chest feel heavy. I wasn't a big fan of Phil's, but it seemed like the guy never had a chance. "In the late nineties, the realtor on record changed from Steve Mendel to Sheila Mendel."

"Okay? Who's Steve and Sheila Mendel?"

"Steve Mendel is Phil's father-in-law, Sheila Mendel is his wife, and Bernie was his wife's lover until he was killed."

"Just so I'm clear, after everything you and Kathy *just* told Ria and me, *you* still don't think Phil is the doer." Da Nise rapped her French tip manicured nails on the countertop in the administrative office.

I raised my shoulders. "I don't. Phil's a lot of things, but I've met evil, I've looked it straight in the eye." I thought of the Robertson brothers and shuddered. "Phil has a conscience. Hell, he backed down when Sheila raised her voice. I think Phil was probably mismanaging hotel funds, but murder?" I glanced at the newspaper headline. "Don't see it."

"Then why did you have me pull all these work orders?" She tapped her foot against the plastic carpet protector where the box of files was parked.

"Thank you. I would have done it," I said by way of apology, which Da Nise waved away.

"Ah, I'm not mad. I just don't understand your logic," she said.

Ria leaned against the doorframe with an ear toward her switchboard and Kathy sat with her legs crossed and her arms behind her head. All eyes were on me.

"Listen, I'm still going to pore through these invoices to see if I can figure out why Phil charged secretarial services to Bernie, but I think whoever killed Bernie was someone who had more to gain by his death," I said.

"Uh, and you don't think Phil did? Bernie's murder literally meant death to his wife's affair," Da Nise said. "Shit, if I was messing around behind Steve's back, he'd get all street on someone's ass."

"I never met Bernie in person, but he was pretty sizeable," I said.

Kathy wagged her finger. "Size don't mean a thing when a man's protecting his woman."

"Good point," I said, and glanced at the clock on the wall. It was nearing four. "Listen, you guys have been great. Why don't you take off? I'll cover the phones and log you out at five. I've got a year's worth of invoices to sort through and possibly compare to this spreadsheet of property transactions. I'm going to be here a while. No reason for you guys to miss out on a beautiful sunny day."

"I don't mind staying," Kathy said, which was a sentiment shared by Ria and Da Nise.

"Nah."

"Oh, don't forget the internal memo that if your car is going to stay overnight, you have to let security know or it could be towed," Ria said.

"When did that become a thing?" I asked.

"Hmm, I wonder?" Da Nise said. "When people leave their car overnight, it leaves less parking for the hotel guests and then we all get hammered for it."

I cringed. "Yeah, I may have stayed at Ryan's last night."

All three of them smiled. My phone dinged, and I glanced at it hoping for a distraction—it was a text from Ryan. "Yes, and it looks like shit happened during his preliminary training so he's going to stick around the department a little longer so...."

"Ryan, huh?" Ria's ruby-colored lips curved into a smile.

Again, I felt my cheeks flush. "He's a good guy."

"Yeah, he is," Da Nise said. "And it doesn't hurt that he's such a McCutie."

I rolled my eyes. "Okay, time for you guys to go home." We all laughed while I grabbed my stack of papers and headed toward Ria's desk. "Go have fun. I've got the front covered."

CHAPTER 30
REBEL

My eyes glazed across the numbers while I yawned. It was near eight, the switchboard was forwarded to the hotel operator, and I had moved to the administrative office and shut the door so no one would bother me. Not that there was anyone. The hotel wasn't hopping with conference guests in need of secretarial services. The files Da Nise had gathered were stacked beside me. I was halfway through them when I noticed I was reading the same invoice twice. I stood, stretched, and was headed toward the door to grab a soda from the vending machines on the second floor when voices startled me.

"There'll be ramifications for what you did."

"So now you're threatening me?" Her voice rose and I didn't move.

I recognized her voice, but I couldn't place it.

"*You* blackmailed me into working with you," she said.

"No." His tone was taut with anger. "*You* said it wouldn't work without you. That's not blackmail, *that* was following *your* suggestion. You put this all into action and now you're trying to walk away? Not going to happen."

"You're *loathsome* and I'm not going to deal with this."

Loathsome? There was only one Point employee who used that word for a put-down. *Lisa.*

No one spoke. I closed my eyes and listened. It sounded like Lisa was heading toward the direction of the elevators when he called out after her.

"I have witnesses," he said, and I felt my heart rate spike.

In the distance, she spoke. "I don't think I'm totally comfortable with where this is headed."

The next thing I heard was the ding from the elevator announcing its arrival.

Who was she talking to? And what did they witness?

Whoever he was, he was heavy footed. I quietly tiptoed toward the door and flipped off the light switch. Instantly the room darkened. I was about to huddle in the corner when I realized the door was unlocked. *Fuck.*

I fumbled with the lock as his footsteps grew closer. I turned the lever toward lock, ducked beneath the countertop below the switchboard, and slid the box of files, which was almost empty, silently in front of me.

The male voice spoke. "Gimme a second. Staff keeps leaving shit on and unlocked." The squawk from a radio buzzed after he spoke.

I pressed myself against the wall, lowered my head, and slumped my shoulders forward, convinced I was about to pass out. I couldn't lower my heart rate.

"Nah, it's locked. At least that's one thing going my way tonight. Yeah, that *meet and greet* didn't go as planned. Copy that. Meet you on the first floor in ten."

There were only two staff offices on the first floor lobby level—security and the front desk. And the front desk wasn't responsible for checking locked doors. Nor did they use radios. Neither did the front office nor security handle meet and greets with guests—that happened through conference services. The only person I knew from security was Rafael, who I met when I was drunk. But I hadn't been too wasted to remember he told me he was engaged to Lisa, who did handle meet and greets. *Fuck. Fuck. Fuck.*

I waited until I heard the elevator in the distance. And even then I waited. *If* that was Rafael, why was he threatening his fiancée?

I quietly grabbed the files Da Nise pulled and stuffed them into my camo backpack along with the spreadsheet and title searches Kathy compiled. I texted Ryan and his response made my heart stop.

Ryan: Out w Milly. TLK 2 U l8r o 2moro

"Milly?" I squinted, but my screen glowed in the dark and there was no mistaking what his message. *Milly. He's out with Milly? What the fuck?*

I had to get to my car and out of this hotel in short order, but something stopped me. Maybe it was my past experience with the Robertson brothers, but something seemed off. It felt like I was being watched, but there weren't any security cameras in the admin office. Or were there? All I knew was the longer I stayed in the dark, the more afraid I became.

CHAPTER 31
RYAN

"**M**cHenry, you don't need to stay with me. I'm not going to do anything stupid."

"Sims, what kind of future deputy sheriff would I be if I didn't drink with my future partner?" It was the second smile I coaxed out of Milford after leaving the deputy training center. The first was when she told me she preferred "Milly" to Milford, which she said sounded like a stuck-up bitch. I agreed.

After Stanley disappeared into Deputy Sergeant Fields's office, the class was directed to the training center where Deputy Sheriff Gonzalez, Stanley's partner, handed each of us our official letter of acceptance into the academy. The timing and oddity of the presentation wasn't lost on me. But fuck it, those who remained were one step closer to working the streets.

Still, the look on Milly's face hadn't been one of triumph. That's when I suggested we celebrate.

I raised my pint toward hers. "To the future deputy class."

Her glass clinked against mine.

"Was that strange or was it just me?" she said, wiping the corners of her mouth with a napkin, which made her seem more like a Milford than Milly. "I don't know what happened. One minute Stanley seemed agreeable, even smiling at me," she continued, her eyes wide with disbelief, "and the next thing I knew, he grabbed my bag and kicked me out of class."

"No, it wasn't just you. The deputy who was found dead in Long Beach was Bernie Thomas. He was my uncle's partner and it looks like he was Stanley's friend. *That's* what I think was really bugging him. It just came out sideways."

"I recently read this study by an FBI agent who interviewed thousands of criminals, many of them psychopaths, and when this agent asked how a victim was chosen, one person told him, 'Silverbacks don't go after silverbacks, they go after everything else.' I've never forgotten that quote because Stanley never went after me before so I guess I considered myself a silverback."

"Milly, you *are* a silverback. Stanley was becoming unhinged today," I said. "Not that I helped...."

Milly placed her hand on mine. "I wouldn't say that. You stood up to him today."

I didn't like her hand on mine so I nodded while I slipped my hand away and grabbed my beer. Her sudden laughter caught me off guard and I was sure my face showed my embarrassment, which simply caused her to laugh harder.

I rubbed my neck. "What's so funny?"

"Oh, that was golden." She wiped a tear from her eye.

"What?"

"The way you removed your hand."

"Oh," I said as casually as I could, "I was just thirsty."

Her blonde ponytail swayed from side to side. "McHenry, leave the lying to me."

I grinned. "That obvious?"

"Uh, yeah." She waved her empty pint toward the female bartender, who winked her way. I'd seen female bartenders do the same thing with Georgie.

"No way." I removed my baseball cap, brushed back my hair, and put it back on. "You're gay."

"Wow. *Great* detective skills, McHenry." Milly's laughter still wasn't helping.

"Yeah, yeah. Does everyone in the academy know?"

Her eyes flashed. "I don't know, does everyone know *your* sexual preference?"

Her feistiness reminded me of Georgie and I held up my hand. "My bad, I just thought by your comment that I was the last to know."

"You're probably the *first* to know," she said, which made more sense.

"I feel privileged," I said, and I meant it. "One of my closest friends, Georgie, goes through hell on a pretty regular basis because, like you, she's beautiful. Men either don't understand or refuse to understand when they're rejected. I can't imagine what it'd be like in the academy."

"While my sexual orientation can't legally preclude me from being hired, let's be honest, the days of 'don't ask, don't tell,' never really left. So I choose not to tell."

"I'm sorry. You shouldn't have to hide who you are in order to serve in the sheriff's department, but I do understand."

"Thanks, McHenry," she said as the bartender brought two pints our way.

Milly reached for her wallet, but the bartender waved her off. "Doll, we can settle up later."

"Thank you." Milly flashed a smile in her direction. "McHenry and I are celebrating a big win today."

"Then I'll make sure to keep your mugs full," she said, which brought the first real smile all night to Milly's face.

My thoughts turned to Rebel. I couldn't wait to see her again, hold her and tell her that I was officially in the sheriff's department.

CHAPTER 32
REBEL

"*Line 'em up and keep* 'em coming." I whirled my finger toward the bartender at Club Roar. It wasn't Milo, who served us the first time I was in the bar. Instead, a tall, very dark, extremely bald, well-built thirtysomething approached me. "Whatcha drinking?"

I pressed against the bar. "Do you know what a jackalope is?"

His eyebrow arched and piercing blue eyes stared back. *Damn.*

"I know some old timers around these parts believe that in the wild west a jackrabbit with antelope horns exists, but…" He grimaced. "I've never quite believed the stories. Sounds a bit too much like a Big Foot myth."

I flashed one of my best smiles. "Are you willing to believe?"

He grinned. "I'm willing to try anything once."

"Nice answer." I cocked my head to the glass display behind him. "You're gonna need the black cherry vodka."

He grabbed a silver-tinted bottle that had a crimson-colored neck.

When I finally mustered the courage to leave the office, no one was on our floor. Still, I got to my car as fast as I could knowing my next stop was the bar. I slid onto a barstool and the fine bartender unscrewed the cap on the vodka.

I inhaled. "Oh… do you smell that?"

He sniffed.

"Vodka-infused cherries," I said. "There's *nothing* better." I lightly rubbed my hands together. "Okay, next up you'll need grenadine, cola, and maraschino cherries."

I watched him stretch beneath the bar. His biceps actually bulged beneath his black and gold compression shirt. *Mercy.* He moved with the natural range and motion of an athlete and had the body to back it up. *Oh, that's all sorts of wrong.* I gritted my teeth to ensure my mouth didn't gape in amazement.

He gripped the edge of the bar and I imagined his grip on my waist. *This guy is fine.*

Mr. Hottie-With-A-Naughty-Body placed a tall glass on the bar and lined up the cocktail ingredients before me.

"So how do I make this mythical drink?" he asked.

I held up two of my fingers like a peace sign. "It's a layered concoction. First." I let one finger drop. "You coat the bottom of the glass with grenadine."

The red syrup clung to the sides of the large tumbler.

"Next," my index finger remained posed in the air, "add crushed ice and a heavy dose of vodka."

He looked up from mixing the drink and smiled. "Heavy dose, huh?"

I shrugged. "If you've heard the stories, then you know the jackalope is one of the smoothest, deadliest creatures... *ever*. If you skimp on the cherry vodka, you insult the legend."

Mr. Naughty Body chuckled. "Fair enough. We're having a slow start tonight, why not have some fun." He poured a double shot of vodka into the glass.

I clenched my fists in the air. "That's the spirit."

"And let me guess, I finish it off with cola and maraschino cherries?" he asked.

I clapped. "Yeah, you do!"

When he slid the drink before me, the glass had a haunting look. The bottom layer bled red and the top layer was a darkened black. It reminded me of my burning desire for Ryan, but he was with Millie. *Who the fuck is Milly?*

Suddenly I didn't want the drink.

"Did I do something wrong?" The bartender's spellbinding eyes carried concern. "Because I can remake it."

I shook my head. "Nope. You did everything right." I massaged my forehead. "You're having a slow start to your night and"—I glanced up at him—"my day kick-started with…." Shower sex? *Nope, TMI.* "Suffice to say, my day started *so well*, but it's not ending so great."

The bartender slowly reached for my drink. "*Maybe* this isn't such a good idea."

I weaved my hand in between his and retrieved my cocktail. "No, I'm good."

His shoulders rose slightly and I sensed a story was forthcoming. "There are only two reasons why an attractive woman comes into a bar alone."

I tilted my head. *Ahh. He said I was attractive. He's both hot and sweet.*

"They're either meeting someone or…."

"They got dumped?" I picked up the glass and let the sweet, tangy cherry cocktail rush down my throat.

His laughter made my dumpee status almost worth it. "Dump? I didn't say that," he said.

"You didn't need to." The vodka had a subtle sting that made me shiver. I stared at his athletic shirt that clung to his pecs and made the gold letters pop off the black. "I've never seen that logo for Long Beach with just the initials."

He laughed. "It's the logo for the 49ers."

I slowly shook my head. "No clue who they are."

"Long Beach State?" His eyebrow arched and I felt like I could fall into the pool of blue in his eyes.

"Oh, sure, Cal State Long Beach." I faintly raised my fist in the air. "Go Dirtbags."

"Not a fan?"

Instead of answering, I reached for my glass. The sweetness of the jackalope pulled me toward it and its aggressive bite made it less of a Wyoming myth and more of a legend.

He chuckled. "I'm Bryan." His hand extended across the bar toward me.

I hesitated. This could be trouble. "I'm Rebel." Our hands connected. And neither of us pulled away.

"Bryan!" The late dinner crowd started pouring into the underground bar.

He gently released my hand. "I'll be back."

I looked into his eyes that were as mythical as the jackalope and gently smiled. *Maybe he's not real either.*

A group of women in varying styles, shapes, and ages filed into the bar and filled every stool. They collected around me.

I glanced to the woman at my right.

"Why aren't you breathing?" she asked with wide brown eyes and a hint of playfulness to her voice. "Oh...." She began to nod. "You met Bryan, didn't you?" She slapped the bar and chuckled.

Her elbow nudged mine. "He stops a lot of hearts around here."

I laughed despite myself.

"I'm Trudy." She raised herself off the stool and leaned into the bar. "Hey, baldie."

Bryan glanced at her from the other end of the bar. "Let me guess," he raised his voice to be heard in the now busy, female-packed pub. "Chocolate martini?"

Trudy raised her shoulders to her ears and grinned. "You got it, sugar." Her honey-blonde hair against her ebony skin was all the convincing I needed to experiment with a new hair color.

I looked at the women who had commandeered the bar. "Are all of you here together?"

"Yup. Once a month, we tell our husbands or significant others that we have"—she raised her hands in the air and made finger quotes—"book club."

She quickly scanned Club Roar as if she was looking for someone. "Only we've been reading the same book now for a year."

I shook with laughter.

Trudy straightened her white floral print top that billowed over black leggings that stretched across her muscular, thick calves. She mischievously smirked. "I couldn't find a blouse with one flower so I settled on a dozen. Daisies and dandelions. I'm bringing sexy back," she said.

My cheeks hurt from smiling. "I'm Rebel." I held out my hand.

She swung her hand into my palm with a good ole fashioned Wyoming-like handshake that started high and ended low.

"Aye-yi-yi!" she said when our hands collided. "You've gotta firm handshake for a little thing." She rapped her fingers on the bar. "Now let's get hottie tottie pants down our way. I didn't lane split all the way from Los Angeles to chat you up." She quickly eyed me. "Not that you aren't worth it."

"I understand." I siphoned the last of my drink and swiftly, though hopefully discreetly, pushed the empty glass in front of me. If tottie pants came our way, I was ready to be served.

"Los Angeles, isn't that a long commute?" I said.

"Only forty miles from our neighborhood, but…." She waved toward Bryan.

Bryan walked toward the center of the bar where we sat. "Hello, ladies."

I felt my cheeks flush and understood why a group of desperate housewives would caravan into Long Beach. Bryan was one bartender worth the trip. With his sheer head, smooth, umber skin, and build he looked like a Greek god.

"I'm just in time for a refill." He removed my glass and began duplicating another jackalope.

"Miss Trudy, how'd you like to mix things up tonight?" Bryan asked.

"Like me on top and you on the bottom?" The playfulness in

her voice returned.

Bryan's face reddened. "What would Harold say?"

Trudy tossed her hands up in the air. "Harold… Harold's got thirty sports channels split on our wide-screen TV. Harold doesn't even know I'm gone."

Bryan slowly shook his head. "You and I both know that's not true. He already called to make sure you have a ride home."

Trudy glanced at me and winked. "Harold didn't call here because he knows I'm at book club."

I laughed so hard I snorted.

Bryan stopped and stared at me. "There's this girl I know and she does that."

Now I raised my eyebrow. "Not every woman can stake claim to that little trick. It's truly an art form."

He grinned. "I think it's sexy as hell."

I shook my head and took a sip of my black cherry vodka fortified jackalope goodness. Bryan held a cocktail shaker in his massive hands and shook the contents of Trudy's martini. He strained the milky chocolate drink into a dingy martini glass, but it still looked delicious.

Bryan poured the remnants of the martini shaker into a shot glass and tossed it back. His face winced. "Damn, Trudy, that's just too rich for my taste."

Trudy slowly swirled her finger around the base of her martini glass. "I'm too much woman for you, Bryan."

His cheeks flushed. "Maybe… maybe not." A wide grin filled his face. "For certain, Harold would never forgive me." Bryan then shifted his attention toward me. "So how's your jackalope?"

The bottom of my second drink neared sooner than I expected and so did the effects of four shots of cherry vodka. I held my thumbs up because I couldn't trust what I might say to Mr. Hottie tottie Pants.

"May I make you another?" he asked.

My head shook no while my mouth answered with a "Yes."

His laughter made me blush.

"Okay, maybe just one more," I said.

I don't remember hiking up my sundress or climbing onto the bar, but when I caught a glimpse of myself in the bar's backsplash, my dress was tied in a knot low on my hips and showcased my better curves.

The music, three jackalopes, and a few sample sips of Trudy's chocolate martini later, I truly believed I could pull off a *Coyote Ugly*.

Trudy bumped her hip into me. I braced my feet into my boots to prevent myself from falling. I bumped her back, but it didn't even register with her.

"You're my new BFF," she hollered to me.

I let out a good old-fashioned cattle call that bellowed throughout the bar. I drunk danced my way down the bar beside my new BFF.

"Show it off!" The women cheered and threw dollars at us.

My body rocked to the beat. Cherries weren't the only thing infused with vodka. Unencumbered by life or thoughts of who Milly was, I danced like no one was watching—even though I sensed someone was. I could feel his steely stare on my every move, but every time I looked toward his corner booth, he turned away. Fuck it. I didn't need games. I threw my head back and let my hair dance on my shoulders.

I stomped my boots on the bar and kicked into a little western boot dance. I struck the heel and toe of my boot against the wood beneath me and kept perfect rhythm with the beat. My feet moved with the speed and precision of my western ancestors.

Trudy got into the grove and together we clicked the back of our heels against each other. Trudy kept her clothes on, but I seriously considered shedding more when Bryan handed me another jackalope.

"Last call," he said.

I raised my last call cocktail in the air. "Let 'er buck!" I step danced my way up and down the bar. "Drink!" I pumped my jackalope in the air. "Drink! Drink! Drink!"

The women hoisted their mugs toward me. Beer sloshed over the frosted rims and when they slammed their glasses into each other's, I was baptized with beer.

I turned my head and smiled. Baptisms were meant to be a fresh start. *That's what I need—a do-over.*

I want a fresh start—no dead bodies, no hushed voices outside my office, and no Milly. My hips swayed back and forth to the beat of the music. But what I really wanted was what I had last night and this morning.

I want Ryan. But he was with Milly.

The music began to fade and so did my energy.

"What time is it?" I yelled toward Trudy.

"Gotta be close to two if Bryan gave last call."

"Two? In the morning?" My adrenaline spiked with the surge of another vodka shot. "Oh, no, no, no." I reached into the back pocket of my jeans. Empty. And my camo backpack was nowhere to be seen. "Where's my phone? And my bag?" Panic seized me. Standing on the bar, I tried to focus, but my vision was blurred. "Crap. I never called the hotel to tell them my car was staying overnight."

Bryan held up my cell phone. "I hope you don't mind but I took the liberty of stashing your backpack and calling one of your contacts."

I tilted my head. "You did?" I took the phone and his hand. He helped me hop off the bar into his work station.

Sweat beaded along the scalloped edge of my sundress and I was sure I didn't smell like one of the flowers on the pattern, but I didn't care. Bryan wasn't Ryan. *Maybe this is my fresh start.* I stood in front of Bryan and barely reached his chest. This guy went on for days and so did the look in his eyes.

I smiled up at him and took a step back. "Thank you for calling… um… who did you call?"

"Ryan McHenry. You didn't tell me you knew a Dirtbag. McHenry's a good guy."

My mouth formed a perfect O. "Oh. Wow. That must have been something."

He chuckled. "He was concerned. I told him where you were at and that it seemed like you had a bad day."

I hung my head. My hair fell off my neck and cooled me down. "Well, I'm sure *that* went over well."

Bryan placed his hand on my shoulder. "He gave me his credit card number and told me to take care of his Rebel rouser."

I glanced up at him. A knot settled in my throat. "Really?"

He nodded. "He said that since you arrived in Long Beach, things have been a little crazy."

I laughed. "Well, that's true." I glanced toward Trudy, who patiently waited to get off the bar. I held my hand toward her, which she swatted away.

"You got him, I want him too."

I laughed so hard my stomach hurt. Bryan helped Trudy from the bar, and she lightly kissed his cheek. "Remember," she stuffed a crisp hundred dollar bill in his front jeans pocket, "what happens at book club stays at book club."

He nodded. "Yes, ma'am."

Trudy tossed her head back and hollered, "Where's my crew?"

"We're waiting for your sorry ass." A collective call came from the front door.

Trudy smiled. "I'm off." She paused and gently touched my arm. "You didn't throw up, hook up, or criticize." She squeezed my wrist. "You're welcome to book club. First Tuesday of every month. Same bar. Same time."

I placed my free hand on top of hers. "Thank you. I haven't…."

"You're welcome." Trudy reached into her bra and withdrew a business card. She handed it to me.

It was warm and I chuckled.

"Listen," she said in a tone that suddenly seemed sober. "If you ever need anything, call. I know what it's like to be targeted for something I didn't create."

I looked at her and I was sure my face showed my puzzlement.

"Despite its size, Long Beach isn't a big town. And you've had a cop watching you all night."

I almost whipped my head toward the man in the corner, but she grabbed my wrist. "Los Angeles isn't that far away. If you're in trouble, you can lie low for a while."

I glanced at the ground. It was littered with bar napkins and peanut shells.

She tilted my chin toward her. "Hey, shit happens. If you need somewhere to crash, give me a call."

"I will." I placed the card in the pocket wallet on the back of my phone.

Trudy sashayed out of the bar and called over her shoulder. "Stop staring at my ass."

Bryan and I laughed. Bryan waited until the women of book club had exited to lock the door.

I snuck a peek toward the corner booth. The man was gone. Bryan began picking up glasses. "I promised Ryan I'd have you wait here until he arrived. He had someone else to drive home and then he was on his way." He grabbed a napkin and brushed peanut shells into the cup of his hand.

"Sure, of course, he's with Milly." I wasn't sure I wanted to see Ryan, but I knew I didn't want to be alone tonight.

Bryan pulled a black tub from beneath the bar and filled it with dirty glasses, which I wasn't sure were ever cleaned. When he placed the tub on the counter, he handed me a bottled water.

"Thanks. Trudy and her group drove pretty far to see *you*."

Bryan flashed his blue eyes. "It's a big crowd and despite what Trudy thinks, I usually can't handle that many women all by myself." He shot me a playful grin.

"Nice," I said and uncapped the water. I took a long drink.

"I can be nice." He raised his shoulders, which only pronounced his muscular build. "But according to my last girlfriend, I can also be a real douchebag."

I almost spat out my water.

"Easy there." He placed his hand again on my shoulder.

I swallowed and smiled. "You're not a *d-bag*. I know a d-bag and you're *not* one."

But he didn't seem convinced.

"Listen," I said. "I usually date or work for d-bags and I'm not even remotely attracted to or interested in working for you. So that alone rules you out from being one."

"Yeah?" His eyes questioned me.

"Oh, yeah," I said. "You're way too ugly and nice to be my type."

His face softened. "Thanks."

"I've had one too many jackalopes to lie to you." I patted his shoulder. "So, if you like someone, don't second-guess yourself because of one person's opinion of you."

A light rapping at the front door startled me and I jumped.

Bryan reached beneath the bar for the keys and a baseball bat. "It's probably McHenry, but…" He headed for the door. "Just in case.'"

I untied my sundress and let it fall to my knees. When Bryan opened the door, instead of Ryan walking through, the man with the spiky hair did. He flashed something to Bryan and barged into the bar.

My body drained of emotion. "You're not Ryan." When he approached me, I suddenly realized I knew him. "You're that guy who was at my apartment." It was the last thing I said before I fainted.

CHAPTER 33
REBEL

"*Rebel?*"

I couldn't seem to open my eyes. *Sleep coma.* That's what I called it when no matter how hard I tried, my eyelids refused to open. Only I didn't remember falling asleep. The voices around me got louder and more frantic.

"We've gotta get her up. She hit her head pretty good. She's been unresponsive for a minute. She could have a concussion. And with all that alcohol she drank…."

Who are they talking about?

"Rebel?" His voice again. "You've got to wake up."

"Rebel." My shoulder jostled back and forth. "Rebel, it's

Bryan… the bartender. I need you to wake up."

I turned on my side. The smell of stale beer brought me to my knees.

"Easy." Bryan placed his hand on my back. "Don't get up too fast. You fainted and fell pretty hard."

"Fainted?" I shook my head and wished I hadn't. "Ouch." I touched the back of my head and felt the start of a lump.

The man with the spiky hair knelt beside me. "Are you okay?"

I looked into his dark eyes and got no read. He threw my people meter off. I didn't know if he was a good guy or a bad one. Emotions pulled at me, but logic reminded me that just because Trudy thought he was a cop, didn't mean he was. But what did he show Bryan? *Was it a badge?*

"Rebel?"

He didn't sound like a cop. *Wouldn't he sound like a cop?*

"Are you okay?" He held eye contact with me.

I shrugged.

"I can drive you home," he said.

"I don't know you," I said, and began to inch away from him. *Hell, I didn't even know Bryan.* I was more drunk than I was sober and suddenly I realized how incredibly stupid I had been.

"Ryan knows me," he said.

"But Ryan isn't here to confirm that, is he?" I glanced at Bryan. "I thought you called Ryan. I thought he was on his way."

Bryan gently helped me stand. "He's probably still taking that other person home."

"Where's my phone?" I searched the floor and Bryan handed it to me.

"It fell when you did."

I quickly hit the last number called on my phone, and Ryan answered. "Is Rebel okay?"

"It's me." Every emotion lodged in my throat. I bit the inside of my cheek so I wouldn't cry. *"Can you come get me?"*

When Bryan unlocked the door for Ryan, Stanley or whoever he was shook hands with him.

"Keep her awake, she hit her head pretty hard," he said, handing Ryan my backpack and phone.

Sobriety began to work through my clouded senses. I glanced at Ryan as he drove and heaviness settled in my chest.

"Who's Milly?"

Ryan looked at me from beneath his Dirtbags cap and sea green eyes shone in the moonlight. *I thought you liked me.*

"She's a deputy trainee," he said.

I stared out the windshield as houses blurred past me. "Is that all she is?"

"Yeah, she's just a friend and today she was hit pretty hard by Stanley, who was acting like a dick in class."

"That guy you shook hands with?"

He chuckled. "Yeah, same one. He's a good guy. He just took out his frustration about Bernie's death on the wrong person."

I pressed the button on the door panel and cracked the window. The late evening/early morning air seeped into the car. I leaned my head against the door. "Why was he at the bar all night watching me?"

"He was watching you?"

I nodded.

"Uh, I'm not sure why he would do that," Ryan said, and leaned toward me. "You're okay, right?"

I barely nodded and Ryan didn't buy it. He grabbed my hand and kissed it. "Milly's just a friend. Her name's actually Milford Sims. Rebel, I'm so sorry if I made you think she was anything else."

"Nothing seems right. Stanley was the same guy at my apartment and he's at the bar tonight? And then you tell me he treated Milly like a dick, so you take her out?"

Ryan slowly exhaled. "Okay, when you put it that way, it's all fucked-up. If it helps any, Milly's gay."

I wanted to slap him. "Her sexual orientation isn't the issue."

"I know. I just thought it might help if you knew that."

"Asshat."

"That's what you called me the first night you met me."

I shook my head and it felt like the car spun. "Just to be clear, asshat isn't a term of endearment."

Ryan's laughter never failed to make me smile. "Got it."

"So why the fuck is this Stanley following me? Do you think he knows I'm in federal protection?"

"No." The tone of Ryan's voice was sincere. "I think he's still working Bernie's case and checking into everyone involved—even though he's probably been told not to. I think he knows more about why Bernie died."

"Yeah, like the fact that Bernie was making money hand over fist in a little investment scheme where he flipped property," I said.

"Is flipping a flop illegal?" he asked.

"No. It's legal and ethical when all parties involved with the property have accurate facts about the condition and value of the property," I said, slurring my words. "But flipping can also be a fraud-for-profit when a home is purchased and resold in a short time frame at an inflated value."

"But doesn't everyone want to inflate the value of their home to make more money?" Ryan said.

"There's trying to get a return on your investment and then flips when a fraudulent appraisal is given."

"And Bernie was doing this? He was buying up homes to flip at a higher cost?"

"I haven't gone through all the real estate transactions, but the majority look like land," I said.

"How do you flip land?" Ryan laughed. "Is that even a thing?"

"It was for Bernie because it looks like he focused on found land that was in the middle of a renovation process—like a historic home was being relocated or torn down. Then he bought the existing land cheap and waited until a bidding war ensued between the city and a corporation who wanted the land for something else," I said.

"How is that fraudulent and not just smart business?" Ryan said.

"Because from what I gleaned from the transactions, Bernie always bought land well below market value and then had it appraised six months later for a hundred times its amount," I said. "And fraudulent appraisals had to be how he flipped property for a profit. What I've researched is noted in my bag."

I glanced around the car for my backpack and the sudden movement made me sick.

"I've got your bag and phone in the back," Ryan said. "Let's just get home and get you to bed."

"Take me to my apartment," I said, looking out the side window and realizing we were headed toward his house.

"Okay." He checked for oncoming traffic before he pulled a U-turn. "I'll stay with you."

I shook my head. "No, that's okay. I think I want to be alone."

CHAPTER 34
REBEL

waited until the taillights on Ryan's car blurred in the distance. I stood at the base of the steps leading to the apartment entrance. I placed my boot on the bottom step. The motion sensor lights activated. *Shit.* I pivoted on my heel. I wasn't in the mood for a drunk conversation with the security guard. I'd enter through the garage.

I walked briskly into the night and I heard him call my name.

"Rebel?"

I closed my eyes. *Ryan. Why did you come back?*

"Rebel." His footsteps came up behind me.

I couldn't turn around. I didn't belong to him. We'd only had a night together. I reached up and wiped my eyes. I felt his hand on my shoulder.

"Hey, what's going on?"

I shook my head.

"Let's get you inside." He let go of my shoulder and grabbed my hand.

I held it closely and turned toward him. Tears streamed down my face. "I'm tired of running." I lowered my head. "I miss Wyoming, but there's nothing waiting for me there anymore." I buckled into the pain of the past and let go of his hand. My stomach shook and my back rattled with grief. "I thought I was okay, but I'm not. I don't know where I belong." I held my stomach, but I couldn't stop the quake that started in the pit of my gut and rose out of my mouth. I sounded like a wounded animal who just needed to be released from its misery. "I'm lost."

Ryan crouched before me. His hazel eyes locked on me.

"Rebel, don't ever say that. You're not lost."

"But I am. I go wherever Jude sends me. I feel like I'm between two worlds and I don't want to run anymore. And I don't think Wyoming is home anymore. But if it isn't, then where is?"

"Rebel." He rubbed his hand across his bearded growth. "I'm so sorry."

I stood and rubbed my runny nose on the hem of my dress. "My family's… not something I talk about." A hollow, emptiness engulfed me. "My biggest regret is leaving them. I live with that choice *every single day*." My hands instinctively balled into fists and sparked a flame that I rarely heard rise out of my mouth. "So just to be clear, what I did to the Robertson brothers is not something my family's proud of. In Wyoming, it's the code of the west where you keep to yourself and don't nose into other people's business. And don't tell me going to the Feds is something I should be proud of, because it cost everyone I love something."

"But you don't have to carry this alone."

"Until I met you, I would have called bullshit on that because *no one* has carried this with me or even offered to. And yeah, part of that is on me because what I did landed on my shoulders, but it's also...." I shook my head, but the emotions pulled on me to surrender the fight. "It's also how my family deals or rather *doesn't* deal with shit. What I uncovered with the Robertson brothers became one more Rebel move the Brandt family brushed under the carpet, hoping it'd go away. Instead, I did." I slightly shrugged. "Still, I couldn't let those men's lives who trusted me to report the Robertson brothers' abuse be for nothing." My hands unclenched and clung to my chest. "Those truckers never deserved to be swept away or forgotten."

Tears rolled down my cheeks and the night air bit at them with a sharp hunger for more. "I'm not making an excuse for the choices I made. But I'm realizing, probably too late, that wanting to do right cost more than I ever imagined."

The words escaped my lips and shook my soul to its very core. I couldn't stop the deluge of tears and I didn't want to. I lowered my head and released the sorrow.

Ryan reached for my hand. I closed my eyes and felt his pulse against mine. I slowly looked up at him before I spoke.

"I didn't know how to share this piece of my past with you because I hadn't fully accepted it. How do you tell a man you really like that you've already imagined a future with him, but you may be moved at a moment's notice? How do you even frame that so it makes sense? When it's made no sense to me?" I held his hand so tightly because I was afraid if I let go I'd sink. "So I did the one thing I'm good at doing—the one Brandt quality I seem to have mastered. I pushed down my past and denied how I felt."

Ryan pulled me toward him. "Come home with me."

"Why? I'm a mess."

"Because I like you too."

The awareness seeped into my skin. "I thought maybe what I told you last night about the whole Robertson thing pushed you away." I paused. "And then when you texted you were with Milly, I thought I lost you, which is stupid, because it's not like you're mine."

"You didn't lose me."

Hurt rolled down my cheeks. "I'm just lost."

The compassion in Ryan's hazel eyes broke down the last

barrier I had in place to keep me protected from hurt. In his eyes, I saw the future I wanted.

And when he pulled me into him, I felt sheltered from the storm that constantly brewed inside me.

"When are you going to get it?" He spoke in my ear. His was the voice of reason that cut through the clutter that crowded my heart and my head. "I *really* like you," he whispered.

If I hadn't been in his arms, I was sure my knees would have buckled beneath me. Instead, he kept me afloat.

"Why?" I asked.

"Because when I'm with you, I know where I belong."

I nodded into his chest. "Me too." I wrapped my arms around his neck. "Take me home."

Ryan slightly bent down and scooped my legs up in his arms.

"Oh!" His sudden move made me catch my breath and tighten my hold around his neck. "You literally swept me off my feet." Amazement clung to my voice.

He smiled. "Someone had to."

CHAPTER 35
REBEL

woke up with the start of a headache from all the jackalopes, but with Ryan's arm wrapped around me, I didn't even mind the rising, blinding sun. The city outside my apartment hummed awake. Ryan's scruffy beard rubbed against my bare skin. Heat radiated off his chest against me. I tucked into him and his hold on me tightened.

"I like you," I said with my back to him.

"I like you too," he said.

He gently pushed away my hair and seductively kissed my neck. My shoulders instinctively came up to my ears. "Oh, I love that but…." I started giggling. "It tickles. Kind of a pleasure-pain thing."

"Shh," he whispered in my ear.

It only made me giggle more.

He rolled me toward him and covered my mouth with his. I closed my eyes and inhaled his taste, touch, and scent.

I grabbed his ass and pulled him into me. I reached for the waistband of his boxer briefs and slid them down as far as my arm would allow. He stopped kissing me and grinned.

"Problems?" he asked.

I squirmed beneath him. "No problem. I just need to get to that beautiful… um… package of yours. I don't care if your boxers hang at your ankles or knees, I just want the goods."

Ryan laughed. "No woman has ever made me feel this desired."

I rolled my eyes. "You've been preparing to become a deputy sheriff, it's not like you had a lot of time to get busy before that."

Ryan looked away.

I whacked him on the arm. "Are you kidding me?"

"We've never really had this talk, have we?"

"Oh my gosh." I wrapped my legs around him and pulled him into me. "How slutty were you?"

Ryan grimaced. "Slutty is such a label."

I laughed. "Unreal. How many? How many women have you been with?"

Ryan's cheeks reddened. He leaned up on his elbows and stared into my eyes. "Twelve."

"Twelve total? Or twelve this year?" I asked.

His eyes moved up and to the right like he was visually remembering each lover.

"Okay," I said. "I just need a number, not a replay."

His eyes twinkled. "Twelve total… but *one* of those dozen was a repeat from the first go around. So really only twelve. You're lucky thirteen."

"Holy shit!" Again I smacked his arm. "You *are* a slut."

Ryan looked down at me and shook his head. "Really? How many men have you been with?"

"You're right, what's in a number? Thirteen, huh? That's lucky. I'm lucky number thirteen."

"Nice redirect, but not gonna work on me, Rebel. How many?"

I exhaled. "Well, there was Rob from the rodeo." I rolled my eyes. "That was my first and only rodeo rider. Then Mike, who shooed our horses. And Todd. So…." I mentally tallied them up. "You're my fourth."

"Honest?"

"No, I'm lying to you. I've actually screwed all the men in Wyoming and now I'm working my way through California. What do you think? Yes, I'm honest."

Ryan chuckled. "Okay. So no regrets. Our past is our past and we just move forward."

I nodded and then slowly smiled. "Then move off those boxers."

Ryan rose up and when he did the spicy scent of his chest infused every molecule that hung between us.

"God, I love how you smell." I leaned up and buried my nose in his muscular chest.

"If you like that hair…." He playfully looked at me.

I scooted down beneath him. He slid to the side and pulled the blankets around me. I kissed my way down his body. When I reached his hip and the long sensuous curve that dipped into his waiting cock, I cupped him in my hand. My mouth engulfed him. His body arched and a low moan rose from his throat.

I closed my eyes and listened to the pleasure I evoked. The way his body responded to me made me hunger for more. *God, I like this guy.*

I teased and taunted him. I wanted it to last forever. I took my time and explored his body with my tongue. I wanted to know every inch of his body as well as I knew my own, so I licked until I found my favorite spots. He rose to meet my lips that his cock parted, and he moved in and out of my mouth with the promise of a very happy ending.

Ryan reached down and pulled me toward him. "I have to have you." He flipped me gently onto my back.

My mind filled with the sexy picture in front of me. His chest. His lips. His need for me. My heart beat with his—it would always belong to him. It was something I just knew.

Ryan's passion ignited. He drove in me with the sexy force of a man claiming his woman, and I responded.

My body arched beneath him to match his want. Our bodies collided as we found the rhythm between us. It wasn't a fevered pitch, but a slow claiming of each other. A shared climax with our eyes locked on each other and our breath in perfect unison.

Ryan gently collapsed on me. Sweat beaded off his head and onto my cheek.

"McCutie, where have you been hiding yourself?" I whispered in his ear.

"In Long Beach. Waiting for you."

CHAPTER 36
RYAN

"*think your kitchen is my* favorite place," I said while Rebel curled up in a tall chair in front of the bar that extended from the kitchen.

"I thought my bedroom was your all-time fav." Her wink was as adorable as her messy curls.

Antique beams crisscrossed the kitchen's ceiling with a drop-down light as the centerpiece. The contrast of rustic and modern blended nicely.

"Tell me again how a conference services manager can afford this?" I asked while I washed my hands in the stainless steel sink.

Rebel's voice was soft. "Jude paid for the first six months."

"That's right." I grabbed a paper towel. "I suppose when you've lost everything, there's nowhere else to go but up." I finished drying my hands and tossed the crumpled towel into the corner trash. I hit the mark and smiled at her. "Nothing but net."

Copper cookware hung from the walls. I grabbed a large skillet.

"From where I'm sitting things definitely went up," she said.

I lit a burner on the hooded stainless steel stovetop. The stove sparkled with a backsplash of Spanish tile that added yet another accent of country-infused charm. *I could live here and play house with her—easily.*

I opened the oak spice rack and grabbed the only glass jar that wasn't empty. The spices fell like confetti into the skillet.

"You hungry?" he asked.

"Are you cooking?" she said. "You *never* need to ask if I'm hungry."

I grabbed eggs from the refrigerator and cracked them into the skillet. They sizzled and blended with the heated spices. A zesty aroma infused the air and awakened my appetite.

While the eggs cooked, I placed bread in the toaster. Rebel reached for a slice and I smacked her hand with the spatula.

"Good hell!" She quickly recoiled her hand.

"Wait for it." I folded the omelet in half and drizzled shredded cheese on top.

I slid half an omelet on her plate and wiped the edges carefully with a dishtowel. Pride flashed across my face when I presented her with breakfast.

"Thank you," she said, and picked up her fork.

I grinned, carefully folded the dishtowel, and placed it on the counter.

Her fork was midway to her mouth as cheese oozed from the silver tongs. She bit into the mouthful of cheese and fluffy egg and her eyes instantly closed. "Heavenly. This has got to be what the angels serve for breakfast."

When she opened her eyes, I was staring at her. "Not many women make eating a sensual experience."

A sly grin swept across her face. "It's a skill." She reached for the butter dish I'd placed on the bar and cut a square with her knife. The butter glided across the bread. "I'm going to be two-ton Tilly if we ever get married."

The knife slipped out of her hand and clanged against the bar. She fumbled to retrieve it. "I *so* didn't mean that." She rolled her eyes. "Hunger. I talk crazy shit when I'm hungry." She nervously laughed.

I reached across the bar and held her hand. "It's not crazy talk."

The thing about Rebel's smile was its impact on me. Her face lit up, her brown eyes sparkled, and it made me happy. It was that simple. When I was around her, I was happy.

I walked over to her and wrapped my arms around her. She felt warm against me. "I don't know about the other guys and I don't care, because when I met you, I thought, 'Move over, fellas,

I'll love her.'"

She leaned her head against my chest. "Cupid struck me hard when I met you."

I kissed her cheek and then sat in the chair beside her, pulling my breakfast toward me. "So, in order for us to live our happily ever after," I said with a grin, "we have to solve this thing that's hanging over our heads."

"Jude and Wyoming?"

"No, that'll work itself out, especially now that my dad's representing you. The albatross around our necks is Bernie and whoever killed him." I squeezed her hand. "I think that finding Bernie's murderer will put to rest a lot of unnecessary suspicion. And let us get on with our lives."

"For our happily ever after?" She chuckled like my intention was a joke.

So I leaned over and gently kissed her. "Rebel, once in a while, despite heartache and loss, life gives you a fairy tale. And I'm not about to let ours slip away."

CHAPTER 37
REBEL

ONE MONTH LATER

Kathy, **Da Nise, Ria, and** I stared at Ryan.

"It'll work," he said.

I scratched my forehead. "A month ago the only thing you were convinced of was that we had to find out who killed Bernie, but now you're convinced there was some *conspiracy* happening in the hotel to expose Bernie for his land fraud practices?"

Ryan raised his arms and interlaced his hands behind his head. He looked like a man surrendering or being held hostage, I wasn't sure which.

"Listen, a month ago, I was just accepted into the sheriff's office. Now I have more than thirty days of training in how to look at murder. And more importantly, a month ago, security footage of Bernie being killed hadn't been leaked to the press. That was… brutal." He stared off into the distance. "All I know is what I'm trained to know. And as a deputy sheriff, I look at the facts. Not *always* objectively." Ryan paused, glanced at me, and raised an eyebrow. "But 99 percent of the time, I'm reasonably objective. I'm able to look at facts and then piece the crime together. And the facts are on this board." He pointed his left elbow toward the bulletin board Kathy had in her office. It had been our ongoing project.

The board was full of colored push pins. A red pin held the property spreadsheet Kathy's realtor friend had provided. A blue pin was stuck in the list of Long Beach company stakeholders that Bernie screwed when he bought the parcel of land they needed to expand and then sold to the city or larger corporations with higher bids. A green pin held the secretarial service spreadsheet that detailed Phil's involvement in mismanaging hotel funds, which took me weeks to compile. And a yellow pin held a copy of the title deed for the last property scheme, the parking lot adjacent to the bank, that Bernie ran.

"The facts are that hotel security and the police were the only two entities that we *know of* that had access to key pieces of evidence," Ryan said. He lowered his arms. "My gut tells me that whoever leaked the security CD to the press was also *somehow* responsible in his death."

The newspaper outlets and television stations repeatedly ran pieces of the footage that showed someone in the shadows strangling Bernie. It was, in a word, gruesome. But thankfully it didn't show me moving his body. Ryan had convinced me we probably weren't on tape for a reason. He believed that whoever leaked the tape, cut the feed after the murder. Anything that happened after the murder wasn't recorded. It's why the cops came up short when they looked through the security footage. Big chunks of time were missing. It's probably also why Stanley showed up at my apartment and Club Roar. As Ryan reminded me, I found the body and perhaps a little too conveniently in Stanley's opinion. He had to rule me out as a suspect and he must have because I no longer felt his shadow looming over me. But if the security tape ever surfaced of me moving Bernie's body, Stanley's interest in me may resume. For now, events before Bernie's death were captured, but there wasn't much afterward. I knew it was selfish to be relieved that my involvement was probably never revealed on the security feed, but the last month had been the calmest since I left Wyoming. And I was beginning to appreciate the simplicity of a quiet life with Ryan.

"But this plan?" Kathy slowly shook her head. "*Not* seeing how this is going to work out."

"Yeah, I'm a little skeptical, too," Da Nise said.

I caught Ria and Ryan exchange a knowing glance.

"What?" I asked.

"Rebel, I'm sure this won't be easy for you," Ria said. "But if it'll finally resolve Bernie's murder and possibly lead us to why it happened, what do we have to lose?"

I felt my blood pressure spike. "Lose? Are you kidding me? There's a lot to lose." I walked toward Ryan and placed my hand on his chest. "This man for starters."

Kathy grimaced. "Ryan's not the one in danger."

I dropped my hand off Ryan.

"Kathy's right," Da Nise said. "Rebel, if this doesn't work, it's not Ryan the murderer will come gunning for, it's you."

Ryan stood behind me and placed his hands on my shoulders. "Rebel, they're right. You're one of the last people to see Bernie alive. You're also the one who will be placing a target on yourself by revealing to the hotel board that Phil was mismanaging hotel funds by using Bernie's account. If this doesn't work out, the killer could come after you."

The finality of what he said was sobering.

"You're still assuming Phil's the killer," I said.

"Not necessarily, but I think he's involved. Which is why my plan has to work," Ryan said. "It's important we follow my plan and keep Rebel's involvement to a minimum and focus the attention toward me."

I knew Ryan's motives were pure, but I didn't like it. Still, he wanted and needed my approval… "Okay… I'm in. I don't like it, but I'm in."

"Excellent," Ryan said. "For this to work we all have to act like Bernie's death isn't our focus, but the financial improprieties with hotel funds is."

"Yup, Bernie's death was nothing to us. Mismanaging hotel funds is. We've got to sell that narrative," Ria said.

Ryan's majestic hazel eyes honed in on me.

"There had to only be a handful of people who knew that Bernie was running a property game," Ryan said. "And even fewer who knew about Phil."

"Let's not forget Lisa," I said, and the girls shook their heads. "What?"

"I get that what you heard between Raphael and Phil's blonde troll didn't line up for you, but honestly, if I was Raphael, I'd lose my shit with her all the time," Da Nise said.

I thought about Lisa and she was a pain in the ass.

"Besides, the sooner we flush out whoever *was* involved in this, the sooner we'll narrow the suspects."

"If it can bring an end to this, then the sooner we start the better," I said.

"The hotel board meets tomorrow," Kathy said. "I called Lisa and made sure you were put on the agenda."

With all eyes on me, I smiled and sounded as reassuring as I could, knowing my accounting skills would mean the end to another man's career. "I've got this."

CHAPTER 38
REBEL

arrived early to the hotel the next morning in a suit I managed to pull together from what I had in my closet. The skirt and blouse matched, but I wasn't sure about the dress jacket. And I definitely knew my black cowboy boots pushed the limit on professional, but I had to wear something familiar. *Where the hell was Georgie when I needed her?*

The conference services administrative office was quiet without the girls' stories and laughter. I started the coffee and headed to open Kathy's office, and noticed the light beneath the door.

Kathy was my reuse, recycle, refurbish queen—there's no way she'd leave a light on and waste electricity.

I tentatively approached the door and quietly turned the door handle. Locked. *Well, there's a first for everything. Kathy left the lights on.* I unlocked her office, which was empty. The bulletin board with our growing body of evidence of Phil's mismanaging of hotel's funds was front and center. He wasn't creating fake vendor accounts as I thought. He was actually double billing. I flipped through the spreadsheets that showed that Kathy's hourly rate had been billed to Phil and another client for the same time spent working, which was tantamount to overcharging. Kathy's time was actually spent working on Phil's secretarial services, which he then billed to one of a myriad of conference center clients. Kathy reminded me that clients who utilized our secretarial services rarely read their bill, which was pretty typical of a Point Resort guest. A hundred-dollar secretarial bill wasn't going to raise flags compared to room service, the spa, or a bottle of wine. But Phil's double billing might explain why we didn't have a lot of repeat business. *Asshat.*

The piece that I hadn't been able to account for was the decades-long list of property transactions that Bernie was involved in. There wasn't anything illegal about Steve or Sheila Mendel representing the real estate transaction.

I unpinned the stapled spreadsheets, grabbed a cup of extremely hot coffee, and returned to Kathy's office. The chair in front of her desk was probably the most comfortable in the hotel. I sank into the overstuffed goodness and reviewed the list of properties Bernie had bought low and sold high. I practically knew the property locations by heart and had even driven to a few of the them, but I couldn't shake that I'd missed something.

With fresh eyes and a cup of steaming black coffee, I skimmed each column. Date. Purchase Price. Location. Seller. Buyer. Sales Price. Variance.

I browsed the seller section. Most were banks who had repossessed the land through default of payment by the original owner, but there was also individual and corporate ownership. B. Jones, A. Hardey, N. Reich, E. Etna, B. Favorid, U.T. Best, C. Market.

I set my coffee on the edge of Kathy's desk and turned her computer toward me. I entered our password and clicked the Internet icon. I had googled the property lots, but I hadn't gone through the entire list of owners. I began to enter the names into the search bar, and each search was like an obituary for a business Bernie had closed due to his greed.

"Okay, U.T. Best, let's see who you are… or were." I hit Enter and was redirected to a website and vintage photo of a supercute shorefront shop with blue and white awnings. Undeniably the Best was written in navy-colored script on the white cottage-like door.

"Undeniably the best…." I leaned toward the monitor. "Why does that sound familiar?" In the picture, a good-looking guy stood beside a woman who held a toddler. Colorful kites were staged in the windows beside beachy items. "Huh."

I leaned into the chair and stared at the shorefront store that I knew no longer existed. I took a sip of coffee and placed it back on Kathy's desk beside her moonrock that served as her paperweight.

I flipped through the spreadsheets to U.T. Best and followed my finger across the stats.

Date: 1998

Purchase Price: 50,000

Location: Shoreline

Seller: B. Thomas

Buyer: LB City

Sales Price: 100,000

Variance: 50,000

Lot 1 – adjacent to CM

I glanced at the monitor. "If Bernie bought Undeniably the Best from the city, that meant the store had to have been in default?" I hit the zoom feature on the picture and noticed that the space next to the shoreline shop looked like a closed convenience store. I zoomed in further and noticed Corner Market on the marquee.

I hit a new tab and pulled a current picture of the shoreline. I zoomed and where the Corner Market convenience store and Undeniably the Best had been, a restaurant now consumed both spaces.

"So, Bernie bought Undeniably the Best, and let me guess, he already owned the Corner Market?" I glanced at the spreadsheet to the listings.

"Anyone that stood in Bernie's way was killed." Her voice startled me and I flinched.

"Fuck!" I turned and saw Lisa in the doorway. In a pink suit and matching heels, *holding a gun*, her Elle Woods look turned menacing.

"Well, figuratively speaking." She approached me with a terse smile on her face. "If a small business owner didn't want to sell, Bernie bought the properties around it, or sent the gangs to graffiti it until they were forced out." I was about to stand when her hand pressed into my shoulder. "Relax. You've been quite the busy bee."

She closed the door with the butt of her gun. Adrenaline kicked in and I was on high alert. My bag and cell phone were in the admin office. I glanced at the picture of Undeniably the Best and stared at the little girl. I looked at Lisa and back to the monitor. *Fuck.* The little girl in the photo was Lisa.

"Is that what happened to your parents' shop?" I asked in the most even tone I could muster. Revenge motivated her. And there was nothing more deadly than revenge.

"Bernie is what happened to my parents' store." She wouldn't look at the monitor. "He drove my family to ruin."

"I'm sorry. It's kind of hard to forget the person who ruined you and your family," I said, and there must have been something in my voice because the vacant look in her eyes shifted. "There was a company where I'm from that ruined a lot of lives, and in turn, I let them tear apart my family," I said.

"Don't try to relate to me," she said. "You don't know anything about me."

"You're right." I leaned away from the barrel of the Glock she pointed toward me. "I don't. But I know that Bernie was greedy and so was Phil."

Her laughter was chipped and edgy. "I wasn't tied up with Phil's petty bullshit. He was just trying to keep up with his slut of a wife's income so he could hold on to his portion of their computer component business. If he wanted to skim off the top, then I wasn't about to stop him. But Bernie?" Her blonde ponytail swung behind her. "He destroyed families."

"So you destroyed him?"

She waved the gun and I stopped breathing. "Bernie destroyed himself. When he bought the vacant bank lot and then tried to hold the hotel hostage to his asking price with his restoration committee, that's when I realized if he wasn't stopped he'd continue destroying people's lives. He had to be stopped."

"Of course." I swallowed, leaned on the edge of the seat, and pressed my weight against the side of Kathy's desk. If I could tip it over maybe it'd distract her.

No matter how hard I leaned into it, the desk didn't budge. But my coffee cup did. *That's it.*

"Is that why you arranged to meet him in the alley?" I asked, completely fishing.

"*Loathsome.*" Her shoulders shuddered. "He actually thought I was interested in him."

"What I don't understand," I said while I kept my eye on the gun, "is that Bernie was a good-sized guy. How'd you, uh…."

Her blue eyes zeroed in on mine. "Strangle him?"

I nodded and moved toward my coffee cup.

"Well, that's his fault. He was always wearing that long chain for his cross—like anyone believed he wanted to be a preacher," she said.

The red marks on his neck made sense.

"Still." I shook my head. "I'd have a hard time strangling him and I've roped cattle. But the size difference between you and Bernie was great." I reached for my cup when she hissed.

"Move and you're—"

Too late. I grabbed the handle and threw the hot coffee at her face. She dropped the gun as her hand instinctively went to protect her face. I ducked and when the gun didn't misfire, I scrambled out of my chair and reached for the door.

Lisa grabbed my wrist and I slammed my elbow hard into her pink-clad midsection. She doubled over and I grabbed the gun. "Don't think so."

She fell to her knees and I wanted to kick her, but instead, I firmly planted my cowboy boot on her back until she lay on the floor facedown. "Keep it up, bitch, and I swear to God I'll break your back."

I moved my boot until it pressed into her shoulder blades.

A wry grin filled her face. "You don't have any proof. All you have is my word against yours."

The night of Bernie's murder replayed in my mind. I'd run to my car, and Bernie's cross sparkled and caught my attention. He didn't have his glasses and his cross was in his hands. When I moved him, the sensor lights from the bank had gone on. I'd shielded my face because I didn't want to get caught on their security feed, but it wasn't the bank's security I should have worried about.

"The hotel's had the proof the entire time." I looked down at Lisa. "Security has footage. You may have convinced Rafael to kill him, but he has you on camera first."

Lisa said nothing, but her gaze shifted.

Bingo.

"He's the one who sent the footage of you to the news," I said.

"I wouldn't pat yourself on the back, sweetheart, Rafael has you on the security feed, too."

So much for Ryan's theory that the tape was stopped. I dug my boot into her back. "Listen, bitch. I may have moved Bernie, but I didn't kill him. That's *all* you."

Lisa arched beneath me and spoke with her head tilted up. "No one will ever believe that I could do anything like that. But you're trailer trash. God only knows what else you've lied about."

"Yeah, well." I leaned my weight onto my foot and pressed down on her until she winced. "Looks like this trailer trash just schooled your ass."

CHAPTER 39
REBEL

I *carefully stirred the pasta. **Don't** overcook this.* French bread was in the oven and a timer was set to prevent scorching the edges.

A homemade apple pie was cooling on the wire rack. And it actually looked like a pie. I smiled.

"McCutie, you've got to see my pie."

All I heard was his chuckle from the bathroom.

"*Asshat.* It's dessert for your dad. He's still coming for dinner, right?"

"Has he missed a Sunday since we began living together?" Ryan said from the closet.

"Well, it's only been two weeks," I said.

"Best two weeks of my life," he said, and I smiled.

The Sunday paper was on the counter beside the pie. The headline didn't make me smile, but it did bring closure.

TWO ARRESTED FOR HOMICIDE

by Zack Humphries, Staff Writer

A hotel security guard and conference services assistant director were arrested in connection with the homicide of Los Angeles Sheriff Deputy Bernard Thomas. Lisa Evans waived her first court appearance and entered into a plea agreement with the Los Angeles County District Attorney's office.

Evans and Rafael Penez were arrested early Thursday morning for their alleged parts in the strangulation death of 68-year-old Thomas, said Long Beach Department spokesman Sgt. Jeffery Littleton.

Evans and Penez have been charged with one count of murder and one count of evidence tampering, Littleton said.

Police were following leads in the Thomas case and asked for the public's help in his death. Late Friday, nearly two months since Thomas's murder, Deputy William Stanley, Internal Affairs Investigator with the Los Angeles Sheriff's Office identified the late Thomas as complicit in property fraud cases that date back to the late seventies.

"I don't think he ever thought how his fraudulent practices hurt the lives of many," said Stanley, who worked with deputy sheriff Ryan McHenry to trace the extent and history of Thomas's property fraud.

In a plea bargain for her cooperation and to avoid a public trial, Evans entered a guilty plea for evidence tampering. Evans identified Penez in the strangulation death of Thomas.

Evidence tampering? I drew a deep breath. I knew off the record that Evans had struck a deal with the devil to walk away from the murder charge. Despite the security tape evidence that showed Lisa led Thomas to his death, she stuck to a story of post-traumatic stress disorder from Thomas's victimization of her family's business. And there was no way to disprove her claim. The psych evaluation confirmed she had the signs of PTSD and wasn't in her right mind.

According to Ryan, Lisa insisted that Rafael made the decision to strangle Bernie and she tried to stop him. The final sentence in the story, though, made my heart stop.

"Evans was sentenced to ten years in prison. Due to her cooperation, she will be eligible for parole."

Ryan placed his hands on my tight shoulders and began to massage out the tension. "She won't make parole."

I leaned my head against his chest. "That's what your dad said about the Robertson brothers when he got the FBI to agree to my video testimony."

"Yes, and in both cases, the Robertson brothers and Lisa got the maximum sentences." Ryan kissed my forehead. "Listen, I'll go to every parole hearing that Lisa has and testify to the parole board that she's a danger to herself and others. And Stanley's agreed to do the same. He was worried about your safety before either of us realized Lisa was involved."

"Yeah, who knew Stanley had a heart?" I laughed.

"He does. And we'll both go to her parole hearings."

"You'd do that?"

His hazel eyes were unwavering. "I *will* do that."

"Ah, McCutie, you're the best." I turned around in his arms.

He leaned toward me and kissed me. Slowly. Tenderly. Passionately. It was the kind of kiss that led to promises of happily ever after.

THANK YOU

Thanks for reading *THE CHANGEUP*. I do hope you enjoyed Rebel and Ryan's story. I appreciate your help in spreading the word, including telling a friend. Before you go, it would mean so much to me if you would take a few minutes to write a review and share how you feel about my story so others may find my work. Reviews really do help readers find books. Please leave a review on your favorite book site.

Don't miss out on New Releases, Exclusive Giveaways and much more!

Join my newsletter: www.marybilliter.com

I'd love to hear from you directly, too. Please feel free to e-mail me at marybilliter@ymail.com or check out my website www.marybilliter.com for updates.

ACKNOWLEDGMENTS

I had two pre-edit beta readers for *The Changeup* – my brother, Stephen Billiter, and Ruthie Smith, an avid reader and friend. They each provided invaluable insight that allowed me to shape this work into the story I envisioned. Thank you so much for your patience with me and your quick turnaround with edits and suggestions. This story is stronger and richer because of what you both put into it and for that I am immensely grateful. Thank you.

To FBI Special Agent Judith M. Chilen, thank you for not hanging up when I called the Jackson, WY field office and asked if I could meet with an agent to collect research! You were so generous with your time, information, and field experience that it made writing this story a real treat. Thank you so much.

Now a bit about my cast of characters in this Long Beach-based story. Da Nise, Ria, and Kathy were based on three young women I had the pleasure to work with when I accepted a job in property management. I was in my midtwenties and my knowledge of buildings, maintenance, and providing office support was as limited as my income. But I needed a paycheck to pay for my new, red car and managing a high-rise building in Long Beach was the door that opened. La Nise Redmond, Maria Bell, and Kathy Roberts (now deceased) taught me that to be an effective manager all I had to do was stop talking, be present, and listen. And relax. The women were constantly reminding me to chill the heck out! I was young and stupid and they guided me through adulthood. Thank you, ladies.

What I remember from that time in Long Beach was how often we laughed. I was probably the worst manager to ever oversee that office building, but Da Nise, Maria, and Kathy were the best of the best. Clients loved them. Realtors adored them. And I would have been lost without them. So, ladies, thank you for shaping me into the assistant director I now am. The lessons you taught me have not been forgotten. Kathy, I think of your kindness, funky clothes, and good will toward all. I miss you more than you know.

I began my career in hotel and building management in Long Beach so having this story set in Long Beach seems serendipitous.

I have always wanted to grow a series and Hot Tree Publishing with Becky Johnson at the helm and book editor Olivia Ventura navigating the words, has allowed my resort romance series to become a reality. Thank you for wanting to see women succeed and for making every effort for that to happen.

So to my patient husband, Ron Gullberg, and my children,

Austin, Kyle, Ciara, and Super Cooper, who have lived with a wife and mom that has the door shut all the time to write—now we play. It's time to just *be* for a little bit. Thank you for getting as excited about my resort romances as I have and for cheering me on with each book.

Each book in my resort romance series has represented a part of my battle with breast cancer. As a breast cancer survivor, it's important to me to share with my readers my journey through this life-altering, deadly disease that affects not just the one afflicted but every life that person touches.

When I began writing *The Changeup*, I realized I had told every aspect of my journey through six storylines. So to my readers, thank you. You have been an integral part of this journey and your support has meant everything.

And finally, to the writer and reader in my life, who never got the chance to read any of my published works, but whose influence of me remains everlasting. Dad, there's not a day that goes by where I don't speak to you or ask for the word I'm searching for— and you always answer. And when I misplace my keys or glasses, you always lead me to them the way I led you to yours. You are now *my* finder. I miss your smile, your laughter, and your hearty pat on the back. Thank you for pushing me in my craft to learn from others, listen, and be the best journalist I could be.

Mom, you were my everything—you were my first call, my

biggest supporter, and my lifeline. There are many days where I feel lost without you. Then I hear your voice and I know that you have simply slipped into another place. Dad was the writer in the family, but Mom, I learned how to write from your love of reading that you passed onto me. When you taught me how to write a report for school, I learned the value of research. You taught me to talk to everyone, read everything, and to keep an open mind. Every book I write contains a level of research that makes the story fuller and better. Thank you. When I write, I try to create a book that *you* would lose a day reading. And, at times, I think I've come close!

I love you both and miss you more than is imaginable.

—MARY

ABOUT THE PUBLISHER

Hot Tree Publishing opened its doors in 2015 with an aspiration to bring quality fiction to the world of readers. With the initial focus on romance and a wide spread of romance subgenres, we envision opening up to alternative genres in the near future.

Firmly seated in the industry as a leading editing provider to independent authors and small publishing houses, Hot Tree Publishing is the sister company to Hot Tree Editing, founded in 2012. Having established in-house editing and promotions, plus having a well-respected market presence, Hot Tree Publishing endeavors to be a leader in bringing quality stories to the world of readers.

Interested in discovering more amazing reads brought to you by Hot Tree Publishing? Head over to the website for information:

WWW.HOTTREEPUBLISHING.COM